"Are you trying to seduce me?" Jillian asked him.

I'm trying to find a way to save you, he ached to tell her.

"Would it frighten you if I was?" he asked instead. Everything in him stilled, waiting for her answer.

"Yes," she said simply, then added, "And no."

"You're so vulnerable, Jillian," he said, and meant it from the best part of himself.

"And you are so very alone," she said softly, not having any idea how shockingly accurate she was.

"You don't know how alone," he told her.

"Should I be frightened?" she asked.

You should be terrified. You should run as far and as fast as you can.

Dear Reader,

We've got another top-notch month of eerily romantic reading for you, with a book you won't want to miss.

Something Beautiful is by Marilyn Tracy, one of your favorites. Single mother Jillian Stewart finds herself trembling in fear at the mention of her daughter's imaginary playmate—and trembling with passion in the presence of handsome handyman Steven Sayers. But is there more to their attraction than there seems to be—and could it lead to a deadly conclusion?

As always, I hope you'll enjoy this journey to the dark side of love, and that you'll return next month for Evelyn Vaughn's *Beneath the Surface,* the latest in her miniseries, The Circle.

Yours,

Leslie Wainger
Senior Editor and Editorial Coordinator

Please address questions and book requests to:
Silhouette Reader Service
U.S.: 3010 Walden Ave., P.O. Box 1325, Buffalo, NY 14269
Canadian: P.O. Box 609, Fort Erie, Ont. L2A 5X3

MARILYN TRACY

Something Beautiful

Published by Silhouette Books
America's Publisher of Contemporary Romance

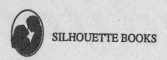 SILHOUETTE BOOKS

ISBN 0-373-27051-8

SOMETHING BEAUTIFUL

Books by Marilyn Tracy

Silhouette Shadows

Sharing the Darkness #34
Memory's Lamp #41
Something Beautiful #51

Silhouette Intimate Moments

Magic in the Air #311
Blue Ice #362
Echoes of the Garden #387
Too Good To Forget #399
No Place To Run #427
The Fundamental Things Apply #479
Extreme Justice #532

MARILYN TRACY

lives in Portales, New Mexico, in a ramshackle turn-of-the-century house with her son, two dogs, three cats and a poltergeist. Between remodeling the house to its original Victorian-cum-Deco state, writing full-time and finishing a forty-foot cement dragon in the back-yard, Marilyn composes full soundtracks to go with each of her novels.

After having lived in both Tel Aviv and Moscow in conjunction with the U.S. State Department, Marilyn enjoys writing about the cultures she's explored and the people she's grown to love. She likes to hear from people who enjoy her books and always has a pot of coffee on or a glass of wine ready for anyone dropping by, especially if they don't mind chaos and know how to wield a paintbrush.

To my beautiful nieces,
Penny, Sunday and Vicky

PROLOGUE

Steven Sayers turned his gaze from the lovely woman standing inside her sprawling adobe home to the waning afternoon sun. He closed his eyes against the red glow and held his palms outstretched. He felt the faint, delicate caress of ultraviolet light, took it inside his skin, letting it warm him, restore him.

He tried to remember what it had felt like to live in nothing but light, to be as insubstantial as the wind, as intangible as a dream. But ten thousand years of this body had stolen all but the dimmest of recollections.

Oh, to be one with the universe again, to stretch into infinity, a blaze of light, a burning star, pure reason and mathematics, blending with and sharing that searing core of energy.

Or to be here, once and for all—really, truly here—a mortal possessing all of a mortal's chaotic longings, lusts, that eagerness for laughter, for joy. To feel a mortal's simple acceptance of love, friendship, even pain.

But Steven Sayers was neither one nor the other. He was trapped somewhere in between. In many ways—in the sensations, the briefly intense moments of feeling— he felt he was more than he used to be. And then, when that brief moment passed, he always found himself less, aching for something he couldn't quite grasp, couldn't hold in his all too seemingly mortal hands.

For ten thousand years, longer than recorded human history, he'd roamed this earthly plane, forever searching for those few like him, those few whom he fought so fiercely. Ten thousand years of battles stretched out behind him, a harshly cut swath of destruction in a cosmic war started so long ago that habit had overtaken zealousness and painful memories of human contact made him shrink from what few offers of companionship had been given.

Those moments of contact, their shockingly swift intensity and their equally lightning-quick demise, had, over the years, made him reluctant to reach out, made him almost resentful of the very mortals he championed—if such as he could be called a champion.

So it was far easier to remain distant, to hold himself aloof from all forms of society. He'd tried entering it fully, and found it only brought pain and longing. And in ten thousand years, it was far simpler to disappear for decades at a stretch, waiting for the next portal carrier's birth, spending solitary years reading, contemplating the secrets of humanity, pondering the questions of what comprised the soul, what separated the soul from the man.

Then, when he felt the portals born again, he would come forward, tracking their growth, following their development. And the battle would rage anew. And thus far, while he'd often failed to win, he'd never lost. Until now.

Now Steven knew with utter certainty that his ten-thousand-year hell was soon to end. The longings would end, the aching would fade away forever, no matter if he was victor or vanquished.

The autumnal equinox was only two weeks in the future, and the final battle would be waged on that night. With only two of them remaining, and so much hanging in the proverbial balance, no stalemates would occur this time. This one battle would end the war once and for all. Forever and, hopefully, for good. And only one could be deemed a victor.

In reviewing those ten thousand years, Steven decided he felt only two regrets. One was that he could never experience the single perfect moment he granted those unfortunate mortals who gave their lives for his war. He would never be able to snatch one day, one hour, from his ten thousand years and say, "Here it is, this is my finest hour." Because for him there were only endless days and nights, all stretching together, links in a hellish chain, moments spent waiting for battle, fighting, only to wait again.

His only other regret focused on the woman inside the house, the carrier of the portals. In two weeks' time, she would have to die—and with her final gasp, he would give her back her finest hour, her perfect moment. It was his one magic, his one gift. A cosmic consolation prize.

But Steven didn't want to grant that moment to Jillian Stewart. She didn't deserve it.

CHAPTER ONE

Jillian Stewart leaned her forehead against the cool glass panes of the French doors leading to the side courtyard. She felt grateful for the support and irritated at the aching need for it.

She could hear the slightly rasped voice of her friend, but wasn't really listening to what Elise was saying. She heard the soft clink of the china coffee cup more clearly than any words.

Would the hurt of losing Dave ever go away? she wondered. Would the pain ever become just another of life's more uncomfortable memories? A full year had slipped by in a time-warped blur, and grief still crawled into bed with her at night. Pain still taunted her in the early morning when she stretched her hand to feel her husband's warmth and found a cold, empty pillow instead.

Too often she'd found herself standing beside the empty hammock, a soft drink in her hand, staring vacantly at the leaves caught in the now-frayed webbing. She couldn't count the times she'd passed the den sofa on a Saturday afternoon and reached out to pat feet that would never again scuff the hand-carved armrests. And the silence from his studio still seemed deafening, Dave's unplayed Steinway a constant reminder that more than her husband had been buried with him that stormy autumn morning.

Even the world outside their rambling adobe home seemed to tease her, mocking her efforts to maintain a semblance of normality. Everything about Santa Fe seemed to whisper Dave's name, conjure his image. He had loved the city so, delighting in the sharp seasonal changes, the deep snows—*Jillian, Allie, find your skis, grab your mittens, there's a slope with our names on it*—the lazy summer afternoons—*Let's skip your gallery opening and open a bottle of champagne instead*—the biting chill of a spring evening—*Do you need a jacket, hon? Or are my arms enough?*—and the long, golden Indian summers, brisk and beautiful autumn days...days like today.

How many times in the past, when Dave was still alive, had she chastised herself for feeling that his love was tempered somehow, that he couldn't reach the inner part of her, touch that well of love she had to give? How many times had she felt empty, longing for some undefined magic that he'd never touched?

Until he was gone.

Until days like today, when the sun would have beckoned him, would have made him call her name.

But now, this afternoon, another man held her attention. The man raking leaves outside had green eyes, not honeyed brown, and his chiseled face carried none of Dave's softness, nor a hint of Dave's tenderness. Somehow that made her feel easier about him, as though the sheer magnitude of the contrast to Dave distanced him, made him safe.

"Jillian—"

She didn't answer, didn't turn to look at Elise Jacobson. She scarcely even heard the question inherent in the inflection of her name.

"Jillian? Hey, do you hear me?" Elise asked. Her voice seemed to come from a thousand miles away.

Several times during the past year, she had forced herself to meet Elise at one of the sidewalk cafés that Dave had frequented, and had been unable to meet her friend's sympathetic gaze, and her hands had trembled too much to lift the cappuccino to her lips. And how much of that trembling had come from guilt, from knowing that, like him, she'd kept some vital part of herself blocked from him?

Elise said now, "I was thinking we might go to Hyde Park this weekend, let Allie get dirty in the woods... You know, all that sort of females-communing-with-nature stuff. We could even play out some kind of welcome-to-autumn ceremony, kind of an equinox ritual."

Jillian still didn't turn around. She continued to watch the green-eyed stranger working with such intimate knowledge of her property, her land. Not for the first time, she found herself lulled by his steady progress, even as she tensed at some scarcely recognized power that seemed to emanate from him.

"Just think about Hyde Park... the sound of Stellar's jays in the pines, the mushrooms and toadstools hiding underneath the brown needles..." Elise said. "Don't you want to go?"

She didn't know how to answer Elise, because no matter how much time had passed, no matter how many times she might take her daughter to Hyde Park to stroll in the pines at the edge of the Santa Fe National Forest, once she found the narrow creek that meandered through the canyon, she would inevitably hear Dave's exuberant laughter, his lilting call, as she heard it for the entire span of their marriage. And she would turn to look for him through the pine branches, only to discover he wasn't there. Again. As usual. And she'd have to once more realize that now he would never be anywhere, anymore.

God, how she missed his laughter.

The muscled man carefully drawing the golden aspen leaves into a perfect circle never laughed. At least she had never seen him do so in the two weeks he'd been with her. She was glad of that, too. She didn't want to hear a man's

deep, rumbling mirth, no matter how she had once craved
Dave's, no matter how much she ached for it still.

In fact, she thought, Steven's very silence, his seemingly innate sadness, soothed her. It kept him distanced
from her, separate. And let her feel easier about his
presence, because she recognized in him that need for
solitude, a need almost as deep as her own.

Or would she be wiser to acknowledge the simple, undeniable fact that he intrigued her, and had from the first
moment he'd shown up on her doorstep two weeks ago,
telling her—not asking—that he would do odd jobs
around her property in exchange for a place to stay.

Two weeks later, she still recalled that feeling of holding her breath when he spoke, of her heart pounding too
furiously in her chest, not in fear of him, exactly, but
perhaps in acute, nearly painful awareness.

She hadn't been able to place his unusual accent, an
odd combination of old-world courtliness and a hint of
foreign parts, and while showing him the various court-
yards and niches on her grounds, she had asked him
where he was from.

His short "All over" hadn't allowed her any clues to
go on. Nor did his looks. His hair was a rich golden
blonde, almost Nordic in its wheaten, honeyed color, and
was longish in the back, shorter around his chiseled and
deeply tanned face, creating the effect of a mane and an
overall impression of lionlike tawniness. His lips were full
enough, but they so seldom curved in anything remotely
resembling a smile that they gave the impression of being thin.

Only his eyes gave anything away, and she was wholly
unable to interpret what she saw there. Mystery, perhaps, or a measure of having witnessed too much, of
having seen too many terrible things. And she often
caught the impression of a deep, abiding loneliness, a
separateness more complete than any she'd ever wit-

nessed before. And she had to question whether her curiosity about him stemmed from this last supposition, whether in both of them having encountered terrible things they had something in common. She, too, had been through too much in the past year.

But beyond his looks, his accent, even his silence, Jillian had felt a strange recognition of Steven. A connection of some kind. From the first moment, she'd had the feeling she'd seen him often, almost as though from a distance, like a barely glimpsed face in a crowd, a character half remembered from a movie. As a child? In a dream?

"I don't trust him," her friend Elise said now.

"Who?" Jillian asked absently, watching Steven as he paused and again turned his face to the waning sun, as seemingly unaware of her attention today as he'd been yesterday or the day before. And yet now, as she had all the other times she watched him working, she had the distinct feeling that he remained totally alert to her presence, to her gaze upon him.

As he'd done several times in the past two weeks, he closed his eyes against the sun, facing it almost as if it were much more than a mere source of energy, as if it were *his* source, his private supply. His already deeply tanned face seemed to draw in the light, to hold it somehow on those granitelike golden cheeks. His muscled body was as still as a statue and as finely crafted. His entire stance seemed ritualistic, somehow, and this, too, stirred a faint eddying of memory. She'd seen this somewhere, sometime. But when . . . where?

"*Him,* your handyman...gardener, whatever you want to call him," Elise said.

The man outside seemed far more than that. Somehow, when Elise gave a name to Steven's profession, something in her tone made him sound like a person seeking a handout. From the first moment, he had struck

Jillian far differently, almost as though he echoed some primordial chord deep within her, a musical note she scarcely understood.

Watching him absorb the sun now, Jillian realized that in very many real ways she'd been the needy one, not him. In an odd sense, by cleaning out a year's accumulation of leaves, trash and old branches, he seemed to be cleaning out some dark corner of her soul.

She'd apologized for the state of the haciendalike grounds when she showed him around. He hadn't smiled or tried to make her feel at ease.

He'd said, "Work is a fact of life. No task is ever quite finished."

The words were simplistic, almost banal, and yet Jillian had been struck by the comment, and by the sorrow inherent in his voice as he'd spoken. And the almost supreme ennui—a stark boredom, or perhaps indifference. How could she not trust a man who had so effortlessly lifted the burden of guilt from her shoulders?

She said to Elise now, "His name's Steven Sayers."

Her words etched the cold glass with clouded breath, and she realized Steven's absorption of the sun's warmth had to be illusion only; the dimming afternoon was frigid. She thought of her daughter walking home from the bus stop. Should she go get Allie, cart her those last few blocks in the warmed Volvo?

"It might as well be Jack the Ripper, for all you've found out about him," Elise said.

Jillian smiled, and looked at Steven even more closely, trying to see what triggered Elise's doubts. He remained perfectly still, eyes closed, one hand holding the rake out to his left, the other open-palmed, stretched wide, conical fingers splayed. He appeared to be doing far more than simply drawing the warmth of the late-afternoon sun; he looked as though he were truly pulling it into him, collecting it for later use, storing it deep within him.

What would it be like to touch him now, to feel that heat against him?

Jillian shivered.

Elise didn't seem to notice and continued speaking. "No references, no background check. Get real, Jillian. You're a rich woman. He could be *any*body."

He *was* anybody. And there was no way she could explain to Elise that she did know things about him, little things, bits and pieces of information that allowed her to form a tentative bridge of trust.

She'd taken over some linens for him that first night, and she'd seen the books he had neatly arranged in the small guesthouse bookcase. They were all hardbound, making her wonder what manner of man carted a trunkload of heavy books with him in his apparent vagabond-like lifestyle.

All the books appeared to be old and well read, and the authors ranged from Ovid to Malory to Anne Rice. Some of the texts were in what appeared to be Greek or Russian, while others were in German and Latin.

But she hadn't told any of this to Elise, and didn't now. The fact that the man could apparently speak several languages and yet sought a job as a handyman-gardener would hardly jibe for her friend.

"He's a good worker," Jillian said, trying not to sound defensive.

Aware of how long she'd been staring at him, and unwilling to give Elise even more food for thought, she dragged her eyes from the unusual man communing with the sun, turned finally and sat down at the table again. She deliberately sat with her back to the courtyard and the man.

Steven.

She smiled at Elise, and her friend smiled back, but said, "Admit it, honey, he's as different as they come."

Jillian couldn't argue that, and didn't even try. Steven Sayers epitomized "different." His direct gaze gave nothing away, no hint of desperation for a job, no subservience, either. His broad shoulders remained squared and set and yet, oddly, presented no confrontational attitude, either. He projected a profoundly stark take-me-or-leave-me acceptance of the odd vagaries of life.

He responded to any of her questions—and, contrary to what Elise thought, she had asked a few—with simple one- or two-word answers. And he tackled the various projects around her house with a quiet and steady determination that was reflected in his progress, not his demeanor. But these "differences" were what made her welcome his presence.

"You slay me, Jillian," Elise said now, shaking her head and, inadvertently, her coffee.

Jillian was truly and openly grateful for this friendship, thankful that at least one person around her remembered Dave, had known him before his death, and yet still included her, as well. All her other friends had slowly, almost deliberately, faded out of her life. Perhaps they had been as tormented as she by Dave's death, as guilty as she, maybe, but instead of little things reminding them, *she* was the reminder, the constant harbinger of doom, the widow who underscored their vulnerability, who told them death waited like a hungry lion, just out of sight, eager to take, desperate to consume.

Those friends, those who had retreated from her, were the same ones who had urged her to move, start a new life, get out of Santa Fe, find an ocean somewhere, a deserted island, perhaps, and paint again, to go anywhere, do anything but be too near them. And when she hadn't gone, they had deserted her instead, almost too easily and readily finding their own Santa Fe islands, safe harbors against the pain of knowing that all does not always end well.

This was true for everyone but Elise, who mothered her, hectored her and chided her for not checking Steven-the-handyman's references, clucked at her over forgetting Allie's therapy appointments, and loved her at least as much *for* her faults as despite them.

So she had let all but Elise disappear, but she hadn't moved. She couldn't have done so a year ago, and she still couldn't. It would be like closing the door on her marriage, on her and Dave's life together, their happiness, the richness of that joy. Even their grief therapist, still working once a month with both her and Allie, frequently suggested putting the rambling adobe up for rent and trying a different locale for a time, letting the traumas of the past heal before returning.

But Jillian knew those traumas would only be waiting for them when and if they came back. Besides, this creamy-walled, sprawling hacienda represented *home*, even if the great warm heart had gone out of it.

Elise glanced outside and back at Jillian before lowering her voice to ask, "What if this Steven guy is a murderer? What if he's a child molester? I tell you, Allie acts oddly around him. Now, doesn't that mean something?"

"These days Allie acts oddly around practically everyone," Jillian said, but with no bitterness or shame.

What had happened to her daughter, to them, had changed their lives at the fundamental core; any altered behavior was only to be expected, tolerated, then slowly, slowly modified.

"Kids know things. You can always trust a child's instincts when it comes to...well, *bad* people," Elise said in an even more hushed tone, as if Steven were capable of hearing her through the double-paned French doors and three-foot-thick walls and despite the reality of his standing a good fifty feet away.

Jillian didn't bother to answer. The truth was, kids didn't know things; they learned them. In Allie's case, it had been the hard way. And thanks to that year-ago horrible morning on the way to school, this particular eight-year-old didn't have a clue about what was good or bad and her mother certainly couldn't tell her anymore. When it came right down to it, Jillian suspected that no human being, unless psychic, had an instant recognition of either good or bad.

"Have you checked to see if he has a gun?" Elise whispered.

Jillian couldn't help it, she chuckled aloud. It felt good. "By doing what, Elise? Sneaking into his house and searching his things?"

Elise looked thoughtful. "It's *your* house. Guest-house, anyway," she said, but she shrugged, as though acknowledging Jillian's question and her own amended answer. "Well, you could ask him, couldn't you?"

"I can just picture that. 'Excuse me, Steven, but do you have a weapon you plan on using on my daughter or me?' "

Even Elise had to choke back a laugh. That choked sound was one of the things Jillian most dearly liked about Elise.

"Well, anyway, you have to learn to be more careful."

Jillian's smile felt frozen now. Being careful had nothing to do with survival. She'd been cautious and careful all her life. Dave had been *careful*. Even on his last awful morning, his seat belt had been fastened, the insurance current, Allie strapped in, the door locked on the passenger side and Allie's school lunch neatly folded into her hand-painted lunch pail. But none of Dave's anxiety, concern or even occasionally scattered solicitude had stopped the random bullet from that drive-by shooting. And not a single element of the loving regard that Jillian had poured into their marriage had prevented that .38 caliber thief from stealing Dave, or his music, his passion, his fathering, his soul, and so very much more.

Something in her rigid smile, or perhaps something lurking in her eyes, let Elise catch a glimpse of her thoughts, for her friend said quickly, "Oh, honey, I'm sorry. I know there are things you can't foresee."

Her voice dropped nearly an octave, and she nearly spit out an epithet before continuing, "Forget I said anything. I'm just a worrywart." She patted the table, as if touching Jillian's hand.

Jillian shook her head, trying to shake away the memory of that agonizing day, the worse-than-despairing year of days since.

"I'm fine," she said.

Elise, ever the cheerleader, leaned forward slightly, her ruddy face free of any smile now, her mouth drawn into a serious line, her eyes urgent. "At least you're painting again," she said.

Jillian nodded. It was a true statement, but it made her feel guilty nonetheless. She *was* painting again, not the light, airy abstracts that had so delighted Dave. Instead, she was creating dark, angry, real and surreal accounts of the fury and confusion that reigned in her. And most of all, these new and frightening paintings all too often depicted the helplessness she felt upon hearing her daughter's screams in the middle of the night. Surreal doorways, openings to terrible, evil places, horrific eyes darkly beckoning. Were these desperate paintings wholly representative of her life now?

Only yesterday she'd discovered that the pairs of haunted eyes in the roiling clouds beyond the jambs of the last three nowhere doors were the same exact color as Steven's. What did that foretell? What did it mean? His eyes were the doorways of her own soul? That was too heavy and too complex even for Jillian's present dark mood.

"So, that damned bullet didn't get everything, did it?" Elise asked almost harshly.

Jillian looked up in surprise. Was this the secret to their friendship, that Elise was able to tap into some underlying empathetic emanation, or was it that she was nearly telepathic?

Elise nodded, as if Jillian had voiced these questions aloud. "I *know,* Jillian. Don't you think I've been angry about it, too? It was bad enough to lose Dave, his gorgeous music. And to see what you and Allie were going through? But, my God, you stopped painting, too. It was like that murderer stole *you* also."

Jillian nodded slowly, fighting tears that threatened to spill, to blur her vision. She blinked rapidly, willing them away. Elise was right, and too terribly on target. She had felt that way, still felt that way to a large degree. That bullet had stolen her joy in *living.*

"It's okay, you know," Elise said. "It's just me here now. Not some shrink with nasty questions about your mother and your second cousin's older brother. I know what hell it was to live with Dave sometimes. I knew him before you did, remember?"

Jillian smiled weakly, and then, almost to her relief, found herself saying, "Sometimes at night, when I wake up and remember that he's not here, I've gone to sit at the drafting table, or maybe in front of the easel. And nothing would come. Not even a glimmer of an idea. All I could think about was, who would I show it to now that Dave was...gone. At least he kept me honest."

"You could always call me, you know. I want to see your work."

Jillian looked away from Elise, unable to continue while directly meeting her friend's blatant sympathy. She half turned in her chair, profiling both Elise and the outside doors. She thought of the way Steven had stood so still in the courtyard, and drew on that image for some semblance of strength.

How could she explain to Elise that the paintings weren't 'work'? They were agony, despair, rage. They were the darkest, angriest part of her. The guilt over the marriage, which had been broken long before Dave's death? The guilt over knowing that both of them, no matter how much they might have loved, had held some special ingredient back? Whatever they represented, whatever they displayed, Jillian knew they were the doorways to the ultimate torment in her soul.

"Anytime, Jill," Elise said.

Jillian didn't tell Elise that it wasn't—couldn't be—the same as showing Dave. She didn't have to; Elise knew. But just yesterday, hadn't she considered showing a recent piece to Steven? Somehow she'd thought he would understand it, perhaps even be able to explain it to her. Was it because he'd told her, only last week—when she'd said he didn't have to call her Mrs. Stewart, but could call her Jillian—that someone had once told him that even "the prince of darkness is a gentleman."

She couldn't remember the context, why he'd said it. She only remembered being teased by the odd phrase, feeling it fit him somehow. A browse through *Bartlett's Familiar Quotations* had revealed the quote as coming from Shakespeare's *King Lear*. A man who quoted Shakespeare while cleaning out gutters was a man who might understand the dark side of life, she'd thought then, and remembered now, smiling a little.

She'd thought it a remarkably apt remark from him. "Child Rowland to the dark tower came..." That was what Steven reminded her of, a haunted man in search of himself, in search of some dark and terrible truth.

Elise, perhaps encouraged by Jillian's smile but misunderstanding it, said, "Jill, you're actually drawing something. And, honey, they're *good*."

Jillian tried letting this sink in, attempted to feel the truth in Elise's words. The paintings were well drawn, well executed, but *good?* That was a judgment, not an absolute, an abstract instead of a truth. What was *good* about doorways that led nowhere, openings that only revealed glimmers of dark, terrible universes beyond?

For some inexplicable reason, the doorways reminded her of Steven. The dark tower? Was that why she'd thought he could explain them to her?

Elise said something else, something about the new "jeweled" effect in her recent work.

Jillian asked her, hearing the angry note in her voice come through, despite her attempts to quell it, "Do you know why my new paintings all have that jeweled effect, that brighter-than-bright sheen to them?"

Her friend murmured an uneasy negative.

Jillian felt her lips curve, but she knew it wasn't in a smile, unless this time it really was born of bitterness. "They're that way because the whole time I'm painting, I'm crying. And I paint what I see."

She heard Elise murmur a placating something, but her heart was pounding so loudly, the words didn't penetrate. She couldn't sit there any longer. The restlessness that had so thoroughly claimed her during the past year triggered, and forced her into action. She moved back to the window and stared out at the courtyard.

Steven was no longer absorbing the dying rays of the setting sun. He was standing facing the doors, just in front of the pile of leaves, looking as though he'd risen from them, a golden phoenix from unburned ashes. His hands hung loose at his sides, the rake abandoned against the trunk of the apricot tree at the far south end of the courtyard.

His eyes were open now, and filled with light, as if he truly had taken in the sun's rays and transformed them into a startling green. The color was oddly out of place in the late-afternoon desert Southwest, and was as luminous as the jeweled colors in her paintings. Blazing emeralds.

It was at least three seconds before she realized she was gazing directly into his eyes, staring at him, frozen, and when she did, she felt strangely linked with him, her heart pounding in a strange combination of fear and poignant recognition.

Had her swift rise from the table called his attention, or had he been watching her all along, as she all too often watched him?

She could read nothing in his closed expression, no understanding, no pity, yet she felt a powerful emotion emanating from him all the same. That emotion wasn't tenderness or concern, nor did it seem to carry any nuances of sexuality or even sensuality, though he certainly exuded all of those things on a physical plane. But whatever he was thinking or feeling seemed to radiate out from him like an aura taking flight, dark and filled with purpose, but its meaning obscured, hidden from her. She could have sworn she felt it race across the distance, and gasped at the raw intensity of it.

Shock rippled through her. He's like my paintings, she thought, and instinctively raised her hand between them, laying her palm against the cold glass. Was she reaching for him, or warding him off?

She could feel his power, and didn't understand it. He was dark and light at the same time. Extremes. Sharp contrasts and angles, hidden messages and sparkling truths.

Staring at him, linked with him, she felt words form in her mind. Were they coming from him? No, from within herself. Again, like her paintings.

"Jillian?"

"Dark with excessive bright."

She had murmured the words aloud, almost like a talisman. Or were they a plea?

Why hadn't she looked away from him? Why was she continuing to stand there…locked in his gaze? And what was it about the words *dark with excessive bright* that had so captured her thoughts, snagged her memory?

Then she remembered. Steven had said the words the other morning while clearing the overthick woodbine from the side of the house. What had he meant then, and why had the words seemed to hold so much more than mere statement in them?

"What's that from?" Elise asked.

"What?" she asked faintly, as though from far away. She couldn't break his gaze, felt she was drowning in it, dizzy, aching. What was happening to her? She felt as if one of her dark doorways were opening slightly, and if she stared at him much longer she would see the roiling clouds with the haunted, hungry eyes seeking her.

"Earth to Jillian. I said, 'What's that from?'"

Steven Sayers—the gardener, she reminded herself, half hysterically—looked away first, turning his head as though purposefully ending this unusual connection. He walked slowly back to the apricot tree and took the rake in his left hand. Without looking back toward the house, he resumed his careful tending of the pile of leaves.

Jillian fought nausea, found herself shaking and raised trembling hands to hug her suddenly cold shoulders. Her grandmother, had she still been alive, would have said a wolf had just passed over Jillian's grave. She knew it was far more serious than that, far more real. If she'd stayed linked with him a moment longer, she knew, she would have lost herself somehow.

"Sounds like something I've read," Elise said.

"What?"

"That 'dark with excessive bright' thing."

Jillian drew a deep breath before turning around. "I don't know. It sounded familiar to me, too, but I...don't remember where I...read...it."

"Shakespeare? Donne? Maybe Spenser? It doesn't sound like a standard biblical verse, but I could be wrong."

Jillian's chill fell away as swiftly as it had come upon her. She moved back to the table, but didn't sit down. Was she subconsciously signaling her need to be alone?

She leaned against one of the high-backed oak chairs and said, "I always forget you're a scholar."

Right now she wished Elise were really the white witch she professed to be, could really see into one of her myriad crystal balls and explain what Jillian had just experienced. Because it had been *something*. Or as Allie was fond of saying lately, something beautiful. Beautiful in the sense of "awesome," a concept with a dual-edged sheen, at one and the same time both exceedingly lovely and woefully dangerous.

Elise winced and waved her hand. "You're the scholar, sweetie, remember? You're the one who reads everything known to man. Before you started painting, anyway. Maybe that's the secret to your art, you bring it a little old-worldliness.

"Anyway, nowadays, scholars do research and get to read all the time. They're eligible for Nobel Prizes and a billion grants. I'm one of the publish-or-perish crew, remember?"

Elise stood up and shook her pleated wool skirt as though such an effort would remove the long-creased wrinkles in it. "Speaking of which, I have an abstract I have to finish by Thursday, and this being Monday and I haven't even begun reading the material, let alone writing the damned thing, I'd better set my sights on the computer—"

Allie burst through the front door at that moment, bringing a blast of chill air with her as she sprang into the dining room. She spun her bookbag onto the small desk reserved for just that purpose and skidded to a semihalt.

"Have you seen Lyle?" she called, then, apparently remembering some semblance of manners, muttered a breathless greeting to Elise and her mother.

"How was school?" Jillian asked.

"Fine. Have you seen Lyle?"

Jillian felt rather than saw Elise's ironic gaze and heard Elise murmur, "None of us ever have, hon."

Allie didn't seem to notice. She ran on through the kitchen and down the hallway to her bedroom.

Jillian heard the door slam open, and heard her daughter's cheerful voice recounting snippets of her day. To Lyle. She felt a momentary stab of unreasonable jealousy; Lyle received all of Allie's confidences, those little details once shared with her mother.

Jillian waited a moment before turning to meet Elise's eyes. As she had expected, Elise was studying her with a cross between amusement and commiseration.

Elise gestured toward Allie's unseen bedroom and said, "Now *that* really *does* give me the creeps."

"Gloria says—"

Elise held up her hand. "Spare me Gloria's immortal words. I know she's got a degree in realigning your head, but let's get real, Jillian. Allie is down the hall this very minute, talking to an invisible rainbow creature. And from what I can see—and hear—he talks back."

"You can hear him, can you?" Jillian asked, smiling faintly, but feeling a frisson of reaction nonetheless.

"Not him, I can't, but I can tell from the things Allie's been saying that *she* sure thinks she does."

"That's the whole point of having an imaginary friend," Jillian argued.

She hoped her light tone masked the doubts she held about the wisdom of maintaining the fiction that Lyle was something real. But the grief therapist thought Lyle's appearance was a breakthrough of sorts, that his presence signaled an attempt on Allie's part to rise above the trauma of her father's death.

Gloria claimed that Lyle would allow Allie to communicate many of the difficult aspects of dealing with the pain of having actually been in the car and having had to watch her father die in her presence. And Jillian had to admit that since Lyle had come on the scene, Allie had finally started acting out her anger, her completely understandable rage.

So Lyle had to be a good thing, no matter how little Jillian might appreciate the acting out, the breakage of an old vase, the temper tantrums resulting in books knocked from the shelves, the scattering of papers, art supplies, anything of value to Jillian, then the lies about it afterward. Perfectly normal, if wholly disliked.

Elise said now, "You know, I've resisted the idea of you guys taking off for the wild blue, but I've gotta tell you, between your Steven and Allie's Lyle, I'm changing my mind."

"He's not *my* Steven," Jillian protested, but even to her, the words lacked conviction.

Luckily, Allie came running back into the dining room; her appearance blocked Elise's quick rejoinder.

"Can we watch TV?" her little girl asked, making it clear by her actions ₍nat Lyle was with them in the room.

If she was entirely honest about Lyle, Jillian thought, she would simply tell her daughter that she hated the invisible creature, that he frightened her a little. A lot.

But she said instead, "There's still a few minutes of daylight left. Why don't you—and Lyle—run off some energy? I'll bet if you ask, Steven will let you jump into that pile of leaves he's just raked."

Allie looked willing enough, and transferred her gaze to an empty spot some three feet away from her, and apparently at eye level. The question was obvious on her face. She nodded once, and then, her face stiffening, turned back to Jillian. The honey-brown eyes so like Dave's met Jillian's pleadingly, as if asking for understanding. As they did the times she lied to her mother.

"Lyle says he doesn't want to go outside."

Jillian could have sworn that Allie *did* want to go. She withheld a shudder. How could Allie have created an imaginary friend with such a fierce hold over her? Was Gloria right in believing order was the whole point of Lyle, a search for some kind of control in a world gone to chaos? Or was there something else going on here?

"Why doesn't he want to go outside?" Elise asked, with a degree of probing Jillian didn't care for—not because Elise was too curious, but because, as Jillian had come to realize lately, she wasn't any too sure she wanted to hear the answers.

Allie cocked her head again, as if listening, her eyes taking on that intent focus on absolutely nothing. Jillian knew some actors would have paid a fortune for the secret of that particular trick.

As was usual while watching Allie listen to "Lyle," Jillian fought the feeling that Allie really was seeing something, something that *wasn't* her imagination, something all too real.

Allie turned her gaze to Elise, and said, "Lyle says Steven's out there. He says he doesn't want to run into Steven yet."

Elise shot Jillian a sharp look, her round face filled with What-did-I-tell-you?

"What do you mean, *yet?*" Jillian asked.

Allie shrugged. "I dunno. That's just what Lyle says. Can we watch TV now? I don't have any homework."

Jillian absently consented and carefully avoided Elise's gaze as Allie left the room. Allie elaborately stepped aside, allowing her invisible friend to precede her through the archway leading to the den. Her slender young body arched against the doorjamb, precisely the way a person would do to allow someone—or some*thing*—with considerable girth to pass through.

Elise cleared her throat, then slowly said, "I'd say an extra little chat with Gloria Sanchez is in order here."

"Based on Allie's comments about Steven?"

"Based on everything, Jill. I'm not kidding when I say there's something scary about this whole picture—"

"Mommy?"

Jillian felt a jolt of adrenaline course through her, and couldn't hold back the slight start her daughter's sudden reappearance had caused.

Elise also seemed startled. She muttered a curse beneath her breath and dramatically held one hand over her full breasts. "Sweetie, if you don't want Aunt Elise to become invisible, too, don't, for the love of heaven, sneak up on us like that again!"

Allie smiled, but Jillian could see the abstraction on her daughter's face. "Lyle says not to ask Steven to come in the house, okay?"

Jillian felt a chill work down her arms. She couldn't help it, she looked over Allie's shoulder, as if expecting to see the invisible friend standing there, gauging her reaction. Allie had often referred to him as something beautiful. What was beautiful about this sort of control, these implications of danger?

She forced herself to speak. "Why would Lyle say something like that?" she asked. She hoped her voice didn't sound either accusatory or as nervous as she felt.

Allie shifted, as though allowing something to pass back through the archway, again politely offering room.

Jillian deliberately focused her gaze on Allie, refusing to let her eyes slide to the nothing beside her daughter.

Thinking of Elise standing there watching, warning undoubtedly lining her face, she asked, "Doesn't Lyle like Steven?"

Allie turned to stare into space again, and she nodded a second time.

"I'll tell her," she said before turning back to her mother. "Lyle just doesn't want Steven in the house. He says it's too soon."

There's no such thing as Lyle, Jillian told herself firmly.

But, much as she might want to do so, she couldn't say this to Allie. Because for Allie, Lyle was very, very real. Too real, maybe.

When Gloria had suggested that the imaginary Lyle might be a means of breaking through Allie's grief, Allie's way of attempting contact with the outside world, Jillian had agreed to go along with the myth that Lyle was a real being, that his presence in their home was a welcome one. But, if she was to be honest, she had to agree with Elise. The whole concept was vaguely disturbing, and made her feel deliberately distanced by her little girl.

Through Lyle, Allie had, in the past month, said the most unusual things, comments that seemed remarkably adult, phrases that sounded strange upon the lips of an eight-year-old child. The grief therapist claimed this was consistent with trauma survival.

Jillian wondered.

And now Lyle didn't want her asking Steven into the house. It wasn't as if she had, or had really even considered doing so. So why had Allie brought it up? Was this an important key to Allie's thoughts? She hadn't said she didn't like him, she'd said it was "too soon." What exactly did that mean to Allie?

Jillian wondered how Dave would have handled something like an invisible creature living within their safe walls, and knew with a sharp pang that the situation would never have arisen. It was due to Dave's death that the imaginary creature was there. And it was due to his loss that Allie clung to Lyle's company.

Jillian fought the rise of anger against Dave, that overwhelming sense that by dying, he'd abandoned her, left her to grapple with things he should have been there to share with her. *Forever,* he'd said, but he'd lied. Right from the start.

For Allie's sake, she now strove to find a light note. "Why would Lyle be worried about Steven coming into the house? Is he afraid he'll have to give up some space, that we'll ask him to move back to the lilac hedge?"

Apparently she'd hit the right tone, because for a split second Allie's face lightened, and she actually seemed on the verge of a giggle. But then she sobered and her eyes turned to that empty—but all-too-real—spot where she could perceive that which no one else could.

It was more than simply disconcerting to see her daughter's eyes unerringly return to the same exact height every time she turned to look at the ever-present Lyle. And it was even more unsettling at times to watch Allie's gaze follow an imaginary being's apparent progress around the room.

Jillian found herself tensing, waiting for Lyle's next pronouncement, not even able to correct herself, to remember that it was Allie doing the thinking, the translating, the speaking. Because it didn't seem like Allie at all.

Allie's eyes turned back to Jillian's, looking up, and she frowned a little, as if puzzling out Lyle's unheard comment. "Lyle says Steven isn't real."

"What?" Elise and Jillian said in unison.

Jillian couldn't begin to understand this latest twist of her daughter's mind.

"Whoa..." Elise murmured. "This, I don't like."

Allie cocked her head, listening, not to Elise, but to that invisible, inaudible voice, then said, inexplicably, "Lyle says, just whatever happens, don't let Steven inside."

Allie turned to leave the room. For some reason, this chilled her mother more than her words had done; Allie was unconcerned by her comments. She didn't appear to even know what she was talking about. This was wholly and utterly consistent with someone truly *listening* to another voice.

But that was patently impossible.

"Honey..." Jillian called after her, only to let her words trail off. Could Elise be right, and Allie did know or sense something about Steven that she herself refused to see? Or was there something else going on here, something related to Dave's death, perhaps a general distrust of everyone?

Jillian wanted to call her daughter back, but didn't. She didn't because she knew that merely summoning Allie back to the entry hall wasn't what she truly needed from her little girl. What she wanted in her heart of hearts was Allie back... period. The way she used to be, filled with giggles and sunshine, light, airy steps dancing through life, the way she'd been for a moment when coming into the house, the way she'd been a year ago.

She turned and met Elise's concerned gaze. She was certain her own was equally troubled.

Elise raised her hands as if in surrender and said, "I'm out of here. But I don't feel good about it. There's more going on around here than *doesn't* meet the eye. And I gotta tell you, I don't like it. Any of it." She looked over Jillian's shoulder, out to the darkening courtyard.

Jillian turned to follow her friend's scrutiny. Steven had apparently paused in the act of loading the piled leaves into a large black plastic bag. His profile was to the house, but something about his stilled hands, his tensed body, conveyed the impression he'd heard every word spoken by those inside. His face seemed even grimmer than usual, and his jaw like chiseled granite, his lips pulled into a tight grimace that could have been either pain or anger.

Jillian couldn't help it; she turned her eyes to that spot in the archway, a place some four feet above the ground, an empty pocket of air, a space where no one stood, but where something had spoken.

CHAPTER TWO

In the glow of the small mock-kerosene lantern on the adobe guesthouse wall, Steven rocked in the old-fashioned chair, his shoulders pressed against the carved oak. His head was bent slightly forward, a furrow on his brow, as he read the book in his lap.

"...that good comes out of evil; that the impartiality of the Nature Providence is best; that we are made strong by what we overcome; that man is good because he is as free to do evil as to do good..."

Steven read the passage again and sighed. Then, aloud, he recited the final line of John Burroughs's treatise *Accepting the Universe*, "...that man is good because he is as free to do evil as to do good."

His words echoed in the small guesthouse, seemed to sweep into the flames of the small fire and crackle and burn there.

Steven sighed and leaned his head against the chair's high back. His thoughts were even darker than usual, and by nature he was inclined to somber reflection. After several long moments, he turned his gaze to the night-stand beside him and stared at the steel blade of the longknife he'd set there earlier.

The weapon was a relic of the fifth century, a gift from someone he'd long ago forgotten. He'd had the knife for so many years, it had become a part of his wardrobe, his life. The blade's polished steel captured the colors of the blaze and held them trapped there.

Like Beleale. Like himself. Both of them trapped in a world not their own. Each wanting, *needing,* the other gone. Brothers on one plane, enemies on another.

Steven stared at the blade as if it would transform, become something other than an instrument of bloodshed. *Once, just once let it be useless.*

But it wasn't useless. It was as sharp as ever, and as deadly.

Steven ran a finger along the knife's thick shaft, the deceptively paper-thin, razor-sharp blade, and the curvature of the handle. Intricate carvings had once adorned the handle, but he'd worn them away over the long, long years.

It was only a knife. Just a simple tool.

He slipped his fingers into the grooves created by his countless years of handling it, and lifted the heavy weapon into the air, turning it, letting it catch the fire's reflection. The blade caught the reds and golds of the blaze, and more, it caught his eyes, as well, shadowed, green, and hard.

Unable to bear seeing his own reflection, he rose and lowered the knife to his thigh, resenting the flow of memories of the innumerable occasions he'd used this blade before. Too many times he'd used it, and afterward, mortals had fallen victim to its bite.

And for the first time in this ten-thousand-year hell, Steven resented knowing the intimacy of the knife, hated the certainty that within the hour he would use it yet again.

He thought of that perfect moment he might offer Jillian Stewart. The day of her marriage? The birth of her daughter, Allie? That summer afternoon she, Dave and Allie had lost their way in the forest and huddled together like nesting cups, a day when her husband had clung to her and told her all the things a husband should?

She might choose any of them. She'd called them all perfect days, perfect moments.

And he wondered, if he had that choice, what moment he would choose. What day, what instance, what timeless, perfect moment, would epitomize his entire existence?

There were none. No perfect moments. No perfect days, afternoons, nights. Only that almost endless stream of war, of living only to fight, of winning only to fight again.

Even to himself, he felt he was little more than an instrument, a machine in human guise, who was forever doomed to search for meaning in immortality, to live vicariously from the perfect moments he reflected back to the dying mortals who allowed him to vanquish one more of the fallen.

But he couldn't even achieve that vicarious joy. He'd long ago realized that only mortals could measure joy by perfect moments. Only a mortal could feel that infinite pleasure of recognizing the brevity of life, of knowing that a single moment, one singular day, one hour, even one second, could put paid to an entire lifetime of pain.

He'd decided that only a mortal being could fully appreciate the notion of perfection of a moment, because, from the moment of birth, mortals were faced with dying. *Carpe diem....* But seizing the day only had relevance when one was tortured by thoughts of the succession of days ending.

Steven's hand trembled slightly as he turned the knife's blade over and again, allowing it to catch his own reflection. He'd held this absolute evidence of his betrayal of humankind a hundred times—a thousand times—before. But it had never troubled him as it did now.

Did his betrayal bother him tonight because this was the final battle, the last one? One of them would win and the other lose for all time. Was he, after all these centuries, learning fear at last? Or was he merely afraid he would never understand the depths that could mean to a mortal?

If only he were simply a man. Just a man. A mortal. If only he could know what a single perfect moment might truly mean.

If only Jillian weren't the one.

Steven slowly crossed the small room to the heavy wooden door. The longknife felt like a lead weight in his hand.

Jillian didn't deserve the gift of the perfect moment, he thought. Not because she wasn't deserving, but because it wasn't fair. She might carry the portals in her, but that was purely a random chance, a once-in-a-hundred-years occurrence. Like the others, the ones before her, she didn't deserve dying. Like them, she had so much good to offer, such a tremendously strong life force in her. But also like them, her creation of the portals, her death because of them, was her ultimate destiny.

What moment would she choose?

Steven started to open the door and hesitated. For some reason, he didn't want to do this tonight. He wanted to wait, delay the inevitable.

In so many of the others, those who had carried the portals, he'd perceived an arrogance, an awareness of their destiny, a brightness honed to the same sharp edge as his blade. Their gift moments had captured times of triumph, achievement.

Jillian was different from these. She seemed too vulnerable for this, too much love lingering inside her.

He knew this. Had seen it, had tracked it for years. Jillian hadn't yet achieved what she could hope to find, hadn't had the time to place her mark upon the world. And she had a child. It wasn't fair that she was the last one to give her life for this too-long, too-bitter war.

But, of all beings, Steven knew that nothing was fair. Nothing at all. Perhaps that was the definitive awareness that an immortal carried... knowing with utter certainty that all life was unfair, an unending stream of imperfections.

He should know. He'd traded his entire being, his existence, for the dubious honor of fighting the fallen, others like himself, but those who had eschewed mortal form. He, better than other men, knew how little of life could be considered fair, because fairness was born of impartiality, of balance, and nothing about mortal life was neutral or symmetrical.

It didn't serve any purpose to hesitate. The rules of this damnable war had been laid down long ago, and were carved in every fiber of his being, in his very soul. One couldn't argue destiny, one didn't dodge fate. Or duty. No matter how little sense it seemed to make, or how much he might be reluctant to act.

Steven depressed the handle of the guesthouse door, and with unaccustomed violence, wrenched it open, the longknife held fast in his other hand.

Like Jillian, he had no choice in his role in this battle. But for the first time in his many years of battle, he found himself pausing, casting about for alternatives.

He knew he had no choice. No options existed for him.

And yet he frowned heavily, his heart pounding roughly in his chest. He knew the reasons Jillian had to die; he knew the consequences of this of all battles.

How was it, then, that even knowing these things, he could feel regret? When had he, an immortal, a warrior, learned remorse?

Jillian drew a deep breath after switching the cordless telephone to the standby position. Glad that Allie wasn't in the kitchen or the adjacent dining room, she simply stood beside the counter, staring at the receiver still cradled in her palm.

"Dark with excessive bright," she murmured. That had been the phrase she'd used after linking eyes with her gardener . . . after losing herself in Steven's gaze. His words, repeated while thinking about his sharp contrasts.

The phone call had come from Elise, who had looked up the odd quotation as soon as she got home and riffled through her battered copy of *Paradise Lost.* The quote was from Milton, she'd told Jillian, taken from the epic poem that wove the tale of the creation of earth and the angels' war over its governance. It was essentially the tale of fallen angels, beings "dark with excessive bright."

Insignificant, inconsequential words, a snippet of a poem written eons ago, yet made somehow important by Elise's agitation over them, her recounting of Allie's strange comment—or rather Lyle's—that Steven wasn't real. Whatever that might mean to Allie.

How utterly ridiculous, Jillian had thought, but, oddly, she hadn't voiced that to Elise.

The phrase had only occurred to her because Steven had said the words a few days earlier. Then, when she was standing there looking at him this afternoon, feeling the effects of that oddly compelling gaze and thinking about her dark, frightening departure into surreal paintings of doorways, she'd thought of them again, felt a connection with them.

Why didn't Allie want Steven in the house, even if such an event was wholly unlikely to happen? Or was she asking the wrong question? Should she alter it to "Why didn't *Lyle* want Steven in the house?"

For the first time since she'd hired Steven, she wondered if she might not have made a serious mistake. And for the first time in his two-week tenure on her place, she wondered if there wasn't more to his being there than his needing a job, than her needing a handyman.

From the first day he'd come and taken up residence in the small one-bedroom guesthouse flanking the main structure, she'd slept a little more soundly, feeling safe because the somber-eyed man was close enough to respond to an alarm raised in the dark, lonely night.

Now, tonight, she thought of that unusual connection she'd experienced when she looked into his eyes, of that taut expression on his face while he was loading the plastic bag with leaves, and she worried that Elise was right, that she'd made a colossal error in trusting him so much.

And, more than her disquiet over allowing Steven such access to their lives, she worried about the wisdom of having admitted Lyle into it.

"This is bunk," she muttered, angry with herself, half-angry with Elise for calling her, scaring her with such nonsense.

What if Allie's right and Steven's not a real person? Elise had asked, her voice hushed with possibility, conjecture and, yes, even a tinge of excitement. The white witch at work, apparently forgetting that she was talking about strange things in her best friend's *house,* not some bizarre event in the abstract.

Jillian shook her head. Milton was a writer of fiction, and hard-to-read fiction at that.

A series of noisy thunks and rattling of shower-curtain loops from down the long, arched hallway flanking the kitchen told her that her daughter was finished with her bath and would soon be ready for the nightly ritual of story and cup of cocoa before bedtime.

She found herself tensing again as she set the milk to heat. Before Dave's death, this had been the best time of the day, the three of them curled up on the sofa, Dave's deep voice bringing a story to life. And even after, it had remained the one sane constant in a world gone awry.

But ever since Lyle had arrived in their lives—or had it come later than that, when Steven had moved into the guesthouse, bringing with him that unusual sense of recognition?—storytime had become something of a torture. She had to share the sofa with Allie *and* Lyle, and had to endure Allie's whispered explanations to the invisible creature—or his to her—and, worst of all, Jillian was all too often asked to blow the imaginary friend a kiss good-night.

The first few nights hadn't been so bad. But one night, just a week ago, Allie had told her that Lyle wanted to kiss her back, that he found her very beautiful. What should have been amusing, even sweet, considering it came from Allie, only made her slightly queasy.

But Allie hadn't said, "You're beautiful, Mommy." She'd worded it differently: "Lyle says he finds you beautiful. Especially when you wear that nightgown."

Something in the peculiar wording, and everything about the adultlike nuance, made her exceedingly uncomfortable. She'd taken to wearing her thickest robe after that, never tucking Allie in while wearing the sheer negligees Dave had so loved, had needed. And she had taken to covering up, not because of Allie, but because of *Lyle*.

She shook her head and shoved the cordless telephone onto the counter without replacing it in the cradle. Maybe the battery would wear down and she wouldn't have to listen to any more ridiculous speculations.

That was exactly what Elise's suggestions were, she thought. Ridiculous. Foolish. And she was the most ridiculous, foolish person of all, for listening to Elise, thinking fantastic and scary thoughts about an imaginary creature. About a gardener who might be unusual, but was still a man for all that. Allie wasn't the only one with a wildly vivid imagination.

She made short work—anger at herself a tremendous spur—of cleaning up the supper dishes, and by the time Allie appeared in her footed pajamas, book in hand, looking like a sleepy-eyed angel, Jillian had her mask of cheer in place. She didn't even wince when Allie stopped the story to point out a few of the more interesting facets of the context to Lyle.

She was even able to answer Allie almost truthfully when she suddenly asked if Jillian was afraid of Lyle. "As long as he doesn't ever hurt you, I guess he's okay in my book."

Allie seemed to accept that, but it made Jillian think. She *was* frightened of Lyle. Not because he came across as sly—which was how his comments often struck Jillian. Nor was it because he seemed too inventive for an eight-year-old—which was most certainly true. She distrusted him because he represented a quasi-tangible problem...another manifestation of Dave's loss, Dave's final abandonment. And every time Allie mentioned him, Jillian was torn between guilt and anguish.

And Jillian felt scared of him because he represented the dark and torturous unknown, an intangible problem existing in her own home.

It was only thinking all this that made her realize what scared her most about Lyle: She thought of him as real, as if all the comments were truly coming from him, and not Allie, as if Allie's newly acquired destructive streak were supernatural, and not the willfulness of a little girl.

Scary stuff, indeed.

She held all this in, as she had every day since that day when Allie had "found" him. With Allie asking if Jillian was afraid of him, however, she had great difficulty keeping her thoughts inside. She wanted to simply admit that the invisible creature gave her the "creeps" every bit as much as he did Elise. She wanted to draw Allie into her arms and tell her daughter that she didn't need some imaginary friend telling her what to do...that she had a mother, for heaven's sake.

But when Allie hopped off the sofa, calling for Lyle, asking Jillian to come tuck "them" in, Jillian remained silent, however chilled. After she managed to blow a kiss to Lyle, she secured the house for the night, and poured herself a rather large tot of brandy. She walked to the French doors and first stared at her reflection, then forced her eyes to see beyond it and into the darkened courtyard.

Steven was nowhere in sight, though if she craned her neck she was able to see the lights on in the guesthouse and the thin trail of smoke snaking upward from the kiva chimney. She could picture him sitting in the old oak rocking chair by the fire, a lamp's glow on the book in his hands. She could imagine his long, work-callused fingers turning the yellowed pages, and wondered what classic, and in which language, he would be reading tonight. What was it about the man that seemed to affect everyone so? Except her.

But that wasn't quite true, either. He did affect her, she just didn't have a name for the feelings he inspired. Gratitude didn't seem to cover her reaction to his dedication, and acceptance of his presence didn't enter into it, either. For she realized now that she always felt aware of him, seemed ultrasensitive to his comings and goings. She had the unusual sensation of seeming to know when he was present, when he wasn't.

Rather than being indifferent to him, as she'd tried telling herself, she was all *too* conscious of him. Was this due to that odd sense of recognition she felt about him? Or was it far more dangerous than that? Was her awareness of him what troubled both Elise and Allie? Were they concerned that Jillian was aware of someone outside her immediate family circle for the first time in a year?

She realized that her fascination with him might be much darker than any of those suppositions. She might deliberately be blinding herself to things her loved ones could see. She might be a textbook case, a vulnerable widow actually falling willing prey to a fortune hunter.

She flicked on the outside lights and studied the courtyard, as if it offered proof of Steven's benign intentions. How different it looked now from the way it had only two weeks ago. Steven had trimmed the trees and evened the lilac hedge, and had gone so far as to rehang the tall wooden gates in the even taller adobe walls. He had seamed cracks and even whitewashed the creamy thick walls surrounding the courtyard.

What was not to trust about a man who did such careful work without even needing direction? Especially a man who took the money she paid him and, without looking at it, folded the bills and casually shoved them in his back pocket? And did this with an apparently deliberate avoidance of touching her.

"I only wanted a place to stay," he'd said that first time, but he had given in to her insistence that he be paid, as well. That sort of indifference to money didn't seem to indicate a fortune hunter. Unless it was part of an elaborate scheme.

The huge flagstones gleamed with some sort of wax or sealant he'd applied, and now looked as though they'd been designed as interior flooring rather than as an exterior patio. The flower beds were turned, mulched and ready for a long winter's nap. The narrow strip of grass had been mowed, the hammock shaken and rolled up and stored for the cold season and all the light fixtures painted and repaired, fitted with new energy-saving bulbs.

Even the pile of leaves Steven had so carefully been raking that afternoon was already gone, scooped out of sight, almost out of memory. He seldom spoke, hardly seemed to move, and yet had managed to make his presence felt in every inch of her property.

She shivered, remembering how their eyes had linked that afternoon...

And how many times in the unknown past?

...but her reaction wasn't based on fear, unless it was misgivings about that odd trembling that seemed to snare her still.

Allie materialized at her side and pressed her silky, still-damp head against her. Jillian ran her hand over her daughter's warm, soft hair, down over her thin, rounded shoulder, and pulled her even closer. This was a moment of total affirmation, of acceptance, of that all-too-elusive concept of "bonding."

Though Jillian knew she should send her daughter back to bed, she couldn't make herself spurn this evidence of Allie's need. And she couldn't possibly have denied herself this precious gift.

"It looks a lot different, doesn't it, Mom?" Allie asked.

"Yes," Jillian said. "A lot better." She felt her chest tighten with love for Allie, love for this fragile child, grateful for Steven's handiwork, grateful that tonight Allie could see good in things again.

"Like when Dad was here."

Jillian forced a smile. "Better, sweetheart," she offered.

She felt Allie tense slightly, and wondered if Allie would ever be able to accept that anything in life could ever be better than the days with her daddy.

"Remember that day when I first found Lyle?"

Lyle. Jillian felt herself stiffen. Was the invisible creature with Allie now? Was Lyle standing behind them at this minute, hovering too close, looking at her curves, eyeing her back?

Jillian craved a moment with Allie, devoid of the ever-present fantasy-inspired companion. And she desperately wanted a second or two when her shoulder blades didn't itch or her skin didn't tighten against that ridiculous, if pervasive, feeling of being watched.

"I remember," Jillian said. Did her voice sound as tightly wound as she felt?

"The grass was really deep, and there were weeds everywhere."

Jillian patted Allie's shoulder. "Quite an improvement, eh, kiddo?" Was she trying to sell Allie on Steven, or to convince herself?

"I was dancing," Allie said, her voice dreamy with memory, her reflection revealing a wistful smile.

Jillian tried to smile, too, remembering.

On that afternoon, Allie's mouth had been working as she sang some melody Jillian couldn't hear. Her hands had been crammed with fading yellow dandelions and dull orange calendula blossoms and had wavered on the air in counterpoint to her peculiar-rhythmed dance.

Totally unaware of her mother's troubled gaze, she'd sung and danced in that neglected garden, a tiny nymph performing a haunting rite of passage on that last day of summer vacation. Jillian recalled how a single tear had carved a hot trail down her own cheek, scalding her with her own inability to stem it, making her thankful her daughter wasn't seeing that fresh evidence of the unassuaged wounds in their lives.

But at that moment, on that afternoon a little over a month ago, Jillian hadn't been crying because Dave was absent. She'd cried because Allie looked so *normal,* dancing in the grass, petals and blossoms in her hands, her hair swaying in rhythm, a song on her full, delicate lips.

Jillian had felt that sense of wonder steal over her and had known that anyone watching Allie, anyone spying that farewell-to-summer homage, would never have guessed the tragedy that had swept through her daughter's world. And the realization of how rarely she'd seen Allie simply being a child had made her almost ill with pain. And the hot tear on her face had carved the first trail of hope Jillian had felt in months, a hope that recovery was finally within their grasp, that Allie would be okay.

Now she thought that her own reflection looked confused, even abandoned, as she—and Allie—replayed a mental tape of that ethereal, unconscious dance.

Jillian said, "I remember wanting to run outside and grab you and hug and hug you."

She found herself wishing that Allie would understand the underlying meaning. Her hands tightened around her daughter's shoulders, holding her very close, the way she hadn't done that sun-dappled afternoon. She touched Allie's hair now, stroking that child-soft face.

She shook with the memory of how she'd longed to smell her daughter's dewy skin, kiss those stained, sticky fingers, but hadn't, because she didn't want to interrupt that carefree dance, that innocent romp, that momentary return to normality.

If only she had.

Instead, Jillian had simply watched, a dazed smile on her own face, as her daughter—unbronzed by the summer sun, fair hair dark from too many days spent inside, knees unskinned from lack of romping outdoors, cheeks free of the normal freckles—had danced in the wilderness that their courtyard had become.

Jillian's heart had wrenched then, and was still torn by the realization that the clear honey-brown eyes had, for a miraculous moment, been unconstrained by the clouded remnants of the explosion that had torn a hole in the very fabric of her childhood universe.

"I was happy that day," Allie said. She seemed to be implying that she wasn't happy any longer.

Jillian murmured an affirmative, but couldn't hold back the frown that her daughter's words engendered. She wanted to fall down upon her knees and beg for the universe to realign itself.

And, for some unknown reason, this thought reminded her of Steven, of the way he stood with his hands splayed, his face to the sun. And the way he'd locked gazes with her that afternoon. She shivered.

Allie said, "I was singing a song. Do you remember what I was singing?"

"No," Jillian said honestly.

She hadn't really heard it, and she'd been too busy reveling in the contrast between the dancing child and the little girl who at night issued long, keening wails, the heart-wrenching screams of an innocent who had witnessed too much, had smelled, felt and tasted the raw, undistilled evidence of her father's last gasp of life, his body cradled in too-small, too-frail arms.

And on that day when Allie had discovered Lyle, Jillian had simply been entranced at the sight of her daughter's dance, calendula stems trailing chlorophyll down soft, rounded arms, joyful that for a blessed moment Allie was simply a child again, forgetful of past or future, just eight years old on a sunny day, singing to flowers, skipping with butterflies and bees.

She hadn't heard the song, but for a truly magical moment Jillian had felt as if she could possibly depress the door's handle, slip down the steps into the brown, untended grass, and join her daughter in that strange and innocent herald to autumn. Her tears had dried, and her heart had pounded in sudden promise. She had felt her fingers tingle in anticipation as they encircled the brass lever.

"That's when Lyle called to me," Allie said. "That was the first time I heard him."

Jillian stared at Steven's miraculously different courtyard, locked in memory, locked in that day only a month old, a day when hope had blossomed and then abruptly altered.

She held her daughter against her now, warm, parental, but on that day, during that moment, her daughter had turned her head slightly, not toward Jillian, but to the overgrown lilac hedge to the left side of the courtyard, the dividing line between their inner courtyard and the other side yard, leading to the guesthouse, the only part of the enclosed patio not contained by the thick adobe walls.

"I remember," Jillian said. "You turned to the lilac hedge, like someone had called to you."

If only she'd called to Allie instead.

"He did," Allie stated firmly. "Lyle called me. By my name. He already knew it, I guess. I couldn't see him at first, but then I did."

Jillian withheld a shudder.

"I wonder why Lyle says Steven is like him," Allie said, her speech slow with puzzlement. "I saw Steven right away."

Jillian didn't answer. She couldn't think of a thing to say to this. Gloria, the ubiquitous grief therapist, had suggested accepting Lyle as fact and avoiding pointing out his obvious unreality. She'd said that Allie needed this invisible friend because he represented something no one could take away from her. But now Allie seemed to be implying that Steven might be a figment of her imagination, as well.

"Well, that's because Steven is a real live man," Jillian said.

Was she saying this a little more strongly than might be necessary? As if to negate Allie's earlier assertion that he wasn't?

Allie shrugged a little, then continued with her story. "I looked and looked in the lilacs...then suddenly I saw him." Her voice rose with satisfaction. "He's *so* amazing, Mommy."

Jillian realized Allie was describing Lyle, not Steven. According to Allie, Lyle was something so beautiful, so incredible, that he was hard to understand at first. She knew how Allie felt.

"Light stands out in spikes all around his body, like fur. Light fur. Rainbow fur," she said, and she always giggled a little. "And his eyes are so green. His eyes are 'xactly like Steven's...only bigger, you know?" She held up her fingers and made a two-handed circle. "*This* big."

Jillian, unable to hold in the shiver this produced in her, as if she almost recognized Allie's description, as if she had seen something like Lyle once upon a nightmare, wanted the conversation over. She was tired of hearing about Lyle and his seemingly unending virtues.

Jillian finished the description abruptly. "And when he moves, the rainbow light moves all around."

She knew her voice sounded flat, even cold, and was sorry about deflating Allie's enthusiastic memory of her first meeting with Lyle, but felt unable to continue the game tonight. It was all too similar to how she herself felt about Steven—all light that moved around. But she was an adult who knew that all things hold contrasts, opposites, and that nothing was ever always "good."

"Remember, Mommy?"

Jillian nodded, having heard the tale before, having witnessed all of it but the "seeing" of Lyle. Allie's beautiful creature still remained invisible to her adult eyes.

Maybe, as a favor to Allie, she'd try again to paint him from Allie's instructions. But she somehow knew that her rendition wouldn't capture him, that she would depict him too "silly." In her rendition, Lyle would appear a toy. *And he's not, Mom. He's something beautiful.*

"He told me he really liked my dancing," Allie said now, continuing with her account of the moment of discovery.

Jillian frowned as she remembered how Allie's hands slowly had lowered to her sides. Then Allie had stood with one leg still slightly raised, as though ready to resume her skipping. But to Jillian she'd appeared a music-box ballerina, wound down and waiting for someone to turn the key. Or maybe she had been so poised because some part of her remained attuned to her mother's warnings about strangers or, suddenly mindful of her own dark memories, had been prepared for flight from the sharp report of a gun, the shattering of glass, her daddy's bleeding body pitching sideways onto hers, the car crashing into an adobe wall. Maybe all she'd appeared was ready to run, to race up the few steps and into her mother's arms for what little safety Jillian could offer her.

And I didn't move, Jillian thought, her frown deepening.

Now, as she had almost every day for the past month, she wondered what would have happened if she had gone ahead and stepped outside, as instinct had told her to do. Would Lyle have simply disappeared at that moment? Would he never have become that unseen presence in their home?

"Where's Lyle now?" she asked. She didn't want to know, not really. But she had to ask.

"Oh, he's over by the table."

The table behind them. Lyle was standing at a place that would account for that itchy, watched feeling prickling her shoulder blades.

"Does he sleep?" Jillian asked.

Allie cocked her head in that endearing considering pose she'd used since she was an infant. "I dunno. When I'm asleep, I can't see what he's doing."

That was eminently logical, Jillian thought with a smile.

"Oh," Allie said. "He says he watches you sleep sometimes."

Jillian's smiled faded abruptly. She felt the heart-stopping sensation that Allie was telling nothing but the absolute truth.

"Why would he do that?" Jillian asked. Her mouth was dry, and her lungs felt constricted.

"He likes looking at you."

If Elise was here, she'd be giving Jillian one of those I-don't-like-this looks.

Jillian heard a faint rustle behind them and swirled to see what caused it.

The dining room table sat empty, its wood grain gleaming in the soft glow of the outside lights. The chairs were all pushed into the table, and nothing moved. For an unbelievably strong moment, she wished she'd housed Steven inside their home and not out in the guesthouse. Then, if she heard a noise, she might attribute it to him, not this invisible Lyle. And, if she heard something, she might call for him to investigate it.

"Mommy?"

Jillian reluctantly turned around, gazed into the reflection to meet Allie's innocent eyes. "Yes, sweetie?"

"Do you still think about Daddy a lot?"

"Yes. Of course I do."

"Lyle says you won't for much longer."

Jillian felt a swift rise of anger. "Well, you can tell Lyle he's wrong about that. I'll never forget your daddy. And neither will you."

"Lyle says a bunch of his friends are coming soon."

Oh, God, Jillian thought, a whole houseful of invisible creatures. Just what she needed.

"He says when they come, you won't remember Daddy anymore. That no one will remember any bad stuff anymore."

"I wouldn't exactly put your father in the 'bad stuff' category," Jillian said, and ruffled Allie's hair to take the sting from her words.

To her relief, Allie smiled. "Me either." Then she added wistfully, "But it would be nice to forget bad things, wouldn't it?"

Jillian felt her heart wrench painfully. "Yes, it would, sweetie. That would be very nice."

"Lyle can do that for you, Mommy. He can just touch you and make the bad things go away."

Jillian couldn't possibly have said anything to that. The idea of Lyle touching her made her skin crawl, made her breath snare in her throat. If she felt even the gentlest of breezes stir her blouse, she would probably scream.

"You want him to touch you, Mommy?"

"No!" Jillian said sharply, then held Allie tighter to let her daughter know it wasn't her she was snapping at. She drew a deep, shuddering breath and tried finding some semblance of rationality. She said, finally, "Allie, the bad things don't just go away by themselves. Or by something like Lyle touching you—"

"They do, Mommy! I know, because—"

"No, Allie. The bad things that happen to us... happen. And we have to learn how to live with them, understand how we've been changed by them. We have to learn how to go on. Like going on without Daddy. We're learning that. If we ignore that pain, pretend it never happened, we can't go on. Do you understand?"

"Lyle made it where I don't have nightmares anymore," Allie said, almost belligerently, as if daring her mother to come up with some other reason the bad dreams were subsiding.

Where was Gloria now? What on earth was Jillian supposed to say to this revelation? She decided to take the coward's way out and say nothing at all. Allie's nightmares were becoming less frequent these days, and had seemingly since Lyle's arrival.

But a year had passed since Dave's murder. She herself was sleeping better lately. Not since Lyle, she thought with an odd feeling of shock, but since Steven had come.

For the first time, she thought she understood Allie's fascination with Lyle. Whenever her daughter talked about him, her features seemed suffused with delight, flushed with pleasure. The invisible, imaginary creature seemed to grant her daughter some respite from grief, some lessening of the hold that fear had over her.

She understood it now, because that was exactly the same reaction she had to Steven's presence. Hadn't she felt that way when she opened the door and saw Steven standing there? Had she felt that first relaxation of grief at that precise moment?

Somehow, the day that Steven had arrived seemed every bit as important as the day when Allie had awkwardly danced for Lyle. And that night, for the first night since Dave had been shot, she'd slept soundly, peacefully.

Jillian stroked Allie's hair, comforting herself as much as comforting her daughter.

"Mommy..."

"Yes, sweetie?"

"What's the equinox?"

Jillian didn't blink at the swift change of subject. Abrupt departures into other topics were the prerogative of children everywhere.

"There're two equinoxes, the spring and autumnal. Those are the first days of those seasons. The summer and winter first days are called solstices."

"Why is this one so important?"

"I didn't know it was, sweetie."

"Lyle says it is. He says that's the day all his friends are coming over."

She'd been mistaken; Allie hadn't changed the subject, she'd only swung back around to an earlier one. "Well, I hope he isn't planning on putting them all up here. We simply haven't got the room. Maybe they can go to one of the bed-and-breakfast places near the Plaza. But they'd better book their rooms now, because Indian Market is that weekend, you know."

As she'd hoped, Allie giggled, covering her mouth with her hand, as she'd done ever since losing that all-important front tooth. Jillian smiled with her, grateful that whatever strange hold Lyle had on Allie, he hadn't totally squelched her sense of humor.

But she'd smiled too soon, for Allie turned abruptly, her eyes unerringly going to that spot some four feet above the ground. Her shoulders tensed, her body stiffened, as if she were trying to hear something far away. Then she looked back up at Jillian.

"He says it's not funny, that we shouldn't laugh."

Irrationally, Jillian felt a strong urge to whip around and chew Lyle out. She said stiffly, "You tell Lyle that I'll laugh whenever I please, and so will you. And if he tells you not to, he'll have to reckon with me. You understand, Allie? You have every right to laugh."

Allie continued looking up at her, as if surprised by her vehemence, stunned by her reaction to Lyle's words. As well she should be, Jillian thought. The source of the words wasn't any creature, invisible or otherwise, it was her little girl. All the more reason for letting her know she could laugh.

A year of darkness was long enough. Allie had to find the brightness again. And Jillian had to help her. Lyle was a dark side of Allie... and she had to serve as his counterpoint. It was a hard role to play.

But hadn't she already felt a difference inside herself? Walking around the grounds with Steven, she'd noticed the condition of the yards for the first time in a year, seen the passage of time in the accumulation of debris. And had felt the rays of the Indian-summer sun warming her shoulders. It was as if his arrival somehow punctuated a change in her, a change in the season, a change in life.

Now she had to convey that difference to Allie, that sense that all things—bad and good—would eventually pass away.

"Allie, has Lyle ever told you exactly why he came here? Came to you?"

Allie tilted her head, making Jillian ache. "Yes," Allie said finally. "To change things."

Jillian felt herself relax. Gloria had been right; Allie needed Lyle. As she had apparently needed Steven. She remembered trying to ask him, that first afternoon, what he wanted, what he needed, but instead she'd only asked if she could help him.

And he'd answered promptly with a simple "Yes," as if that answered everything. Then he said he'd seen her place, and thought he might be what she needed. And she remembered thinking that he'd spoken nothing but the raw truth, that on some deep level she did *need* him.

Was that how Allie felt about Lyle?

Allie was quiet again, assuming her "listening" pose. She nodded once, but didn't translate for Jillian.

Jillian waited, trying to convey love through her touch alone.

Finally, Allie said somewhat defiantly, "If Lyle touched you, you'd know what I mean."

Jillian steeled herself. "Okay, sweetie. Tell Lyle to touch me."

"He can hear you," Allie said. Then, sending a chill of pure horror down Jillian's spine, she added, "He's coming now."

Jillian felt her entire body go cold, suddenly, abruptly, and felt she might faint. Anticipation made her dizzy. This was patently ridiculous, but she found herself holding her breath.

Then, lightly, grazingly, against her loose trousers, just above her knees, she felt a brush of air, a soft, delicate touch.

Lyle!

Instinctively, as though responding to an atavistic knowledge of the rainbow creature, she jerked aside, her mouth wide with an unvoiced scream. Her eyes strafed the reflection in the glass for some glimpse of what—*who*—had touched her.

And saw Allie's hand outstretched behind her. About knee-level. She gulped in air, sagged against the doorway a little, and pulled Allie sharply closer.

"Don't ever do that again!" she gasped out. "Not unless you want to have to run get Steven to pry me from the ceiling!"

"Do you feel changed, Mommy?"

"Do I ever!" Jillian said with heartfelt honesty.

"Lyle says Steven can't change you like he can."

Jillian felt inadequate to answer this, too. She didn't like the implication, and she didn't like knowing that Lyle was wrong. Steven had already changed her, though she couldn't have spelled out exactly how, or why. Just his very presence had shifted her life on a fundamental level.

She remembered how that first day Steven had hesitated before taking her proffered hand, almost as though he were as conscious as she of the significance of their first touch. And she'd lowered her hand, rubbing it against her thigh, feeling relief, because she'd had the singular, staggering thought that their palms were meant to be touching, that she would be safe as long as she remained linked to him.

"Lyle can do anything," Allie said with a matter-of-fact attitude. She even nodded, as if settling some unvoiced question.

Jillian couldn't help but smile. "Anything but become visible to everybody but you," she quipped.

"Oh, Mommy!" Allie said, and then giggled.

Allie's hands dropped to pat her jumper in a parody of an adult performing a knee-slap, only to become serious again almost immediately.

"Lyle says someday soon you'll be able to see him, too."

Jillian felt her smile stiffen. This was a new twist, a turn she didn't particularly care for.

Allie, still smiling up at her, said, "But he can touch you again, if he wants. 'Cause you said he could."

For a glittering moment, Jillian actually thought her daughter was telling her that Lyle was about to touch her. Again. She felt a shudder of horror course through her.

"Well, he can't now," she said through dry lips.

"Oh, yes, he can. He's like a vampire. All you have to do is invite him once."

Jillian heard an odd conversation played in her mind. A friend meeting her on the street, asking how Allie was doing these days. "Oh, she's just fine," she'd say. "She has an invisible friend who is just like a vampire. We love that creature of ours."

"Tell him I *un*invite him."

Allie looked up at Jillian, her expression somber. "You can't do that, Mommy. It's against the rules."

Jillian forced a smile to her lips. "What rules are those?"

Allie shrugged. "*The* rules."

Jillian's back tickled, her skin seemed to contract in on itself. Allie made Lyle seem so real, so *present.* Jillian couldn't hold in the shiver this time. The idea of Lyle's reality thoroughly revolted her.

She wished she knew, with complete certainty, what was real and what wasn't.

At that precise moment, like an echo of her thoughts, she heard the sound of the gate's latch and focused her eyes to see beyond her own reflection.

Jillian couldn't withhold a gasp as Steven stepped through the narrow aperture.

At first glimpse, she was certain he was naked. His bare golden shoulders reflected the dull light from the bug lamps.

Then she saw that he held one hand tightly against his chest and his profile was rigid and stiff. Something was dreadfully wrong.

She realized then, with some relief, that he wasn't naked, only minus a shirt. His golden, muscled shoulders were hunched in obvious pain.

With only the slightest of hesitations, she released the catch on the lock and depressed the French door's handle and pushed the paned glass outward, exactly the way she *hadn't* done the day Allie found Lyle.

"Are you all right?" she called.

Steven looked up, and even through the gloom of the thick, moonless night she could make out his green eyes. *He's in terrible pain,* she thought. She *knew.*

Automatically she reached for and clicked on the back floodlights, the extra lights Steven had installed a few days before. The harsh glare from the floods struck his eyes, and he froze, like an animal snared by a poacher's illegal hunting lights, and yet he didn't look afraid, only vastly wary. His eyes glittered, and her breath caught in some unreasoning atavistic fear.

His eyes are this *big.* She heard her daughter's voice, saw the little hands forming a two-fisted circle.

"Are you hurt?" she called as she watched him fumble closing the gate.

In the two weeks he'd been with them, she'd never once seen him so much as falter; there was nothing awkward about any of Steven's movements. All his actions were ungainly now.

He turned back toward the house and took a step into the pool of light to the house side of the gate. As the light had revealed the green of his eyes, it now refracted off a gash of glistening red on his bared forearm.

"My God," she said, stepping outside and rushing down the steps.

"Mommy—!" Allie called behind her.

"You're hurt!" Jillian cried, hurrying to join him.

Instinctively, she held out her hands to take his arm, to look at it. She experienced a near electric shock when her hands lightly braced his bare and bleeding arm.

He's hurt, she told herself sharply, nearly fiercely, but all she could think about was this odd electrical sensation…and his bared body, heat radiating out from it like a fire.

She had touched him before, she thought inanely, when she had exchanged payment, when showing him the guesthouse and where the lawn tools were stored. But then she recalled how carefully he'd avoided so much as grazing her skin. Nothing in her life had prepared her for the shock of this contact.

Jillian looked up at him, horrified by the wound, more horrified by her reaction to touching him. Her heart pounded in a painful, unsyncopated rhythm.

"I cut it," Steven said unnecessarily. His voice was brusque, scalded with pain.

His eyes met hers, and she could read the tension there. The need. He tried pulling his arm away from her, but she held on, avoiding the wound itself, but gripping him around the wrist and elbow. Her knuckles brushed the hot skin of his flank and seemed branded by the contact.

"Come into the house," she said swiftly. "We'll see what we can do. I'll call a doctor."

"I don't need a doctor," he said, holding his arm higher, as if trying to stem the flow of blood or to pull away from her. Either way, it was a vain attempt.

"I'm sorry," he said then, and she could have sworn he wasn't apologizing for any possible inconvenience, but for something she didn't understand.

Why do I feel I've seen you before? she wanted to ask.

"Nonsense," she said, drawing him up the steps and brushing past Allie, who was half blocking the doorway. "Allie, honey, run fetch a towel out of the bathroom."

For a moment, Steven hung back, still outside, only his hand having crossed the threshold. Blood dribbled over Jillian's hand, hot, smelling of copper, dropping to the floor in what seemed audible splats. She followed his gaze to the swiftly staining hardwood.

Jillian exerted more force, pulling him inside. "Please don't worry about the floor. Good heavens, Steven, you're hurt! Come in now."

When he still seemed reluctant, Jillian looked at him squarely, meeting his unusual eyes. "You need help," she said.

"Yes," he agreed, but not as if he meant with his wound.

He said it coldly, directly. And with greater purpose than the moment seemed to warrant. His words reminded her of the first moment she'd seen him on her doorstep.

Instead of answering him, she simply pulled at him with greater strength, exhorting him to come inside, still cradling his bleeding arm in her outstretched hands. She felt blood seeping through her fingers and looked at him sharply, appalled at how much he must be suffering.

Instead of looking pale and shaken, as might have been more normal, Steven wore a small smile on his lips, and gazed about the room, as if warm for the first time in years of being cold.

Jillian realized that Allie hadn't run for the towel as ordered; she was staring, transfixed, at the blood pooling on the hardwood floor.

Jillian guessed at Allie's dark thoughts—would her daughter ever be able to erase that terrible morning from her mind? She had to break through the darkness and reach her daughter.

"Allie! Quickly, now. Run fetch me a towel. Steven's hurt, but he'll be okay. Now hurry, honey."

Allie gave her a swift, agonized look and whirled for the archway to the bed and bathrooms. Jillian followed rapidly, leading Steven into the kitchen. She held his arm over the sink and turned the cold water on.

"Let's rinse it and see what we need to do," she said, pushing his arm beneath the near-icy water.

Allie returned and, without saying anything, pressed a towel against her mother's side.

"Thanks, honey. Oh, and would you turn on the overhead light, please?"

Allie did so, and the bright glow of the overhead made Steven's wound look even worse, jagged and deep. What could he have run into to cause such an ugly gash?

"You don't need to worry," Steven said. "It'll be all right now."

Something in his words, or perhaps his tone, made her examine him with something akin to suspicion. There was nothing about this wound that could possibly be considered all right.

"The water helps," he said, stepping behind her, allowing her greater access to his arm.

Jillian didn't say anything, but continued to bathe the wound.

"I'm sorry about your floor," he said.

He seemed to be almost whispering in her ear. She shivered in pure physical reaction.

"Mommy—?" Allie asked tremulously.

"It's okay, honey. He'll be fine. Why don't you go on back to bed? I'll come tuck you in again in a minute."

"But, Mommy..."

"Allie," Jillian interrupted. "Go on, now."

"But remember—?"

Remember what?

"What I said this afternoon..."

What had Allie said earlier that afternoon? It wasn't the blood, not the reminder of her father's death, that was bothering Allie.

"Remember, Mommy?"

Then Jillian did remember. What had Allie said exactly? *Just whatever happens, don't let Steven in the house.*

Jillian felt a frozen understanding crack through her.

Now, at her sink, *in her house,* Steven stood staring down at his own blood spattering red upon the white porcelain and swirling to pink in the rush of cold water. An odd, almost bitter smile played on his full lips.

When he looked up and met her gaze, he asked, so softly she had to lean toward him to hear it, "If you prick us, do we not bleed?"

CHAPTER THREE

Steven closed his eyes.

He closed them against the sight of blood, but more against the keen awareness brought by Jillian's touch on his bared arm. And he tried hiding from the truth.

The hydrogen peroxide Jillian poured over his wound splashed, corroded his skin, then burned in terrible fire. It hissed as it bubbled, then burrowed deep to fight the possible germs in his wound. He tried concentrating on the feel of Jillian's hands deftly cottoning the edges of the cut, as she tried to catch the dripping peroxide as it rivered from his arm, but for a single instant, nothing could cut through the piercing torment.

Pain... Pain... Pain...

Spiked, burning, horrible pain.

All-too-human agony, Steven thought, just as intense as it would be for any man. The torment twisted, whetted by acute and fierce demand, and there was nothing at all human about this accelerated incineration. This torture was uniquely his, and the entire universe seemed colored by it, ten thousand years of blood reds, sharp blues. Harsh, dark screams of misery roiled through him.

Then the agony began to slide down that peak of torture. In increments—slow, and as torturous as the initial onslaught of the pain—the torment slowed.

Steven opened his eyes. The world again swam into view, the room into focus, and he could again see the lovely auburn-haired woman tending his arm.

Jillian.

The pain began to ebb almost as swiftly as it had risen. And other emotions swamped him, emotions from Jillian.

She dabbed at his wound, her back to him, her silken blouse, warm body beneath, brushing against his bare flesh. He heard her murmuring, softly, as if he were a child who needed comforting.

Steven swallowed the bitter taste of irony, and wanted to but couldn't smile. He'd craved her touch for so many years, and now that he had achieved this moment, her nurturing touch seemed a travesty of his misbegotten illusions.

He wanted to tell her she could save herself the trouble; the gash in his arm would heal soon enough. For him, physical wounds always did. He wanted to tell her it was the gaping wound inside him that she couldn't heal; no one could.

He closed his eyes again, this time to subdue his sudden longing for the woman so intimately curved against him. This feeling, too, would fade, when she no longer touched him. If only that aching restlessness deep within him could be so easily fueled and so rapidly quelled.

But at this moment, with her hands upon his arm, her back pressed to his naked chest, he couldn't bring himself to step back, to stop the feel of her.

The feel of Jillian.

So soft, Steven thought, and yet her careful fingertips felt like hot steel, branding him, marking him somehow. What would those hands feel like touching him, not as a healer, but as a lover? What would they feel like if she was not a woman simply tending a handyman's wound, but a woman crying out his given name, her hands clutching his shoulders in fierce passion?

The notion was enough to make him groan aloud.

Jillian immediately shifted in the curve of his arms and removed her fingers from the edges of the wound.

He cursed himself and opened his eyes to see her artist's fingers hovering in the air, questing...uncertain. He stared at those slender hands for a second before raising his eyes to hers.

Jillian was scrutinizing him, as if looking for some deep truth. Her lips were parted slightly, and her blue-gray eyes were wide with some unspoken emotion.

His own breath caught, felt trapped in his throat. He'd wanted inside her home, had deliberately sought entry. But now he was sure that some part of him had spent the past two decades imagining her within the circle of his arms.

He knew her, had watched her for so long he ached to be the one she wanted, the one she needed in her life. *I know everything you want,* he ached to tell her. *I know every dream, each longing expression on your lovely face. I know you.*

But Steven knew he couldn't tell her any of this. He couldn't frighten her now, couldn't push her. Knowing her as he did, seeing the look on her face, the vulnerability, the momentary and utterly undeserved compassion, he felt the full weight of guilt, and something else, an anger at her belief in her own safety. Jillian, of all women, was anything but safe.

And he was anything but innocent.

"We have to get you to the emergency room," she said finally, and he had the strong sense that it was not what she truly wanted to say.

Tell me, he urged inwardly. *Tell me what it is you want. You only have two weeks left on this earth.*

"Your arm needs stitches," she said instead. Her cheeks stained a hot red, as if giving the lie to what it was she thought he really needed.

To his vast relief, she looked down at the gash in his arm. The self-inflicted gash.

"I'll be fine," he said, not in any display of bravery, but in raw and self-knowing honesty. She couldn't know that.

She shook her head.

"It already doesn't hurt as much." This was also nothing but the truth.

She shook her head, biting her lower lip. Steven had seen her do this a hundred times before. She'd bitten that lower lip since she was child, just as her own daughter now cocked her head to one side when thinking.

Jillian said, "It's not so deep, but you'll have a nasty scar if you don't have it stitched."

For a moment, he pictured her opening an old-fashioned sewing kit and gently sewing up his arm, brushing her lips against his inner arm as she snipped the thread after the final knot. His entire body tensed at the imagined kiss. This, too, would burn, would sear him, as the peroxide had done, as her fragile smile did now.

He looked from his arm to her and was surprised to again meet her gaze. She was afraid of him, he thought, as she should be. But he knew instinctively that she wasn't afraid for the right reasons. She didn't look at him as her friend did, as a danger, as a threat. Perhaps she did see the mystery, perhaps not. She seemed to look at him as if she would melt into his arms at the merest of touches. It was this she feared, more than she might ever fear what he could do to her.

Steven's breath caught. He knew the bloodletting granted him entry only to the house, not to the woman inside it. And yet...her lips parted, her eyes softened, and to his damnably augmented vision, somehow her skin seemed to grow dewy, inviting.

"Please," she all but whispered, and Steven felt certain that, on some level, at least, she was asking him to touch her.

He could no more have resisted her if he had been wholly human. Almost without conscious thought, he lifted his good arm and lightly grazed her pale, delicate skin with his fingers. He sensed her emotions through his trembling hands, though he couldn't begin to understand them.

In a flash, in that searing, scalding awareness inherent in him, he felt her and, to his shock, he knew the sharp rush of desire, the heady taste of want. Was this from her, or from himself? What was happening? How many years had it been since he'd felt such things? Too many to count.

What was it about this woman, this one woman in all the hundreds of millions of women over time, that seemed to draw him so? It couldn't be only the years of following her, watching her from a distance. And it couldn't be attributed solely to her ethereal beauty, though that was an undeniable fact. And it didn't—couldn't—stem from his burning need to be at this place, at this time, even though that was also a fact.

How much of his want of her was born of her possession of the portals to other worlds? Was his desire created by the inevitability of this final battle? This last encounter. One way or another, the entire war would end at the stroke of midnight on the autumnal equinox, a date less than two weeks away. He'd lived so many years hating the longevity, hating the emptiness, but now that the battles were soon to be over, perhaps some wholly human part of him wanted to live on. And live as a man for a short time. A man with Jillian.

He wanted to close his eyes and drink in her scent, revel in the soft velvet of her skin, the heat of her breath upon his hand. He wanted to take her tightly in his arms and press his lips to hers, to see if she tasted of that mixture of mountain spring and oven-inspired spices that he'd imagined. He wanted this. He *deserved* this.

Hadn't he fought enough battles? Hadn't he done enough? Shouldn't he be granted this one desire, this one wish? A dying man's last request? No cigarette for me, he thought, no last meal. A kiss from this woman... that's all I want. I *deserve* it.

And when she died, he would give her that one perfect moment, the moment she most cherished, he would bring it alive for her, make it fresh, new, *hers* again.

But he didn't want her to die.

The feel of her, the lure of tasting, pulled his wants to the surface, drove thought into the background. Had anything ever felt this wonderful, this sweet?

As if in answer, Jillian released a soft sigh, almost one of resignation, he thought, and her eyes slowly shut. She turned her cheek into his palm so that he cradled her face. Automatically his thumb traced the softness of her parted lips, the rounded line of her chin, her jaw.

The battle he was waging inside seemed far greater than any he'd fought over the countless years. He actually rocked with the rough need to bury his fingers in her silken auburn hair, to pull her sharply to him, to hold her tight against his heaving chest, to take her, to bend her to his will.

A side of him demanded that he stop, that he remember why he was here, why he'd torn his arm, the reason he'd let his blood drop into her home, onto her floor, spill across her hands.

The darkest part of him—the part he knew to be completely divorced from his immortal life—ached to believe he could use the blood tie to coerce her, to flood her with desire. And for a stark, terrifying moment, the dark almost won the inner battle.

He *wanted* her. Feeling her now, that was all that could be allowed to matter. Again he had the bitter notion that he'd somehow *earned* her with all his unrelenting years of war, the years of loneliness and privation. On the heels of that thought he had the distinct awareness that she could be his for the simple taking.

His good hand slid into her hair, gripping it tightly. He closed his eyes, unable to lower his hand, but unable to look at her without giving in to that darker side of himself. What was it about her?

From the very first moment he saw her, almost twenty years earlier, when she was not much older than Allie, he'd felt something unusual, something alien to his being. And he'd spent years watching her grow, always just out of sight, ready to help, if he could, but always unseen, unnoticed. She'd been such an unusual child, adultlike and sophisticated on the one hand, and as giddy and happy-go-lucky as a pixie on the other.

He'd grieved with her at the loss of a childhood pet, the dog, Tippison, she'd loved so much, and had wrestled with the urge to comfort her when she lost her parents in her early college years. He'd tried telling himself he was both relieved and happy when she married Dave Stewart, but what he'd felt most was raw, unvarnished envy. He'd wanted to be Dave, wanted to be the one holding the young and lovely Jillian's hand, wanted to be the one she gazed at with such adoration. And he'd ached to be the one she slept next to at night. He'd wanted to be the one who dried her tears, who told her she was beautiful, who might have loved her as David Stewart never could.

In all the other battles, he'd stayed in the background until the final moments. But this time, this final time, he'd been unable to resist the desire to be seen, the need to talk with her, touch her, hear her laugh, while looking into her blue eyes.

He'd spent these past two weeks, every waking moment of the days and most of the lonely nights, not acting, not doing anything but watching her, waiting, strangely content to simply work in her small gardens, knowing she lingered nearby. Often he'd sensed her eyes upon him, and felt curiously at peace, knowing she watched him. He'd often looked up from some inconsequential task to find her puzzled glance resting on him.

Perhaps he should tell her about the portals. Perhaps that would change the outcome, would allow her to have some slim possibility of survival.

He opened his mouth to do just that, then closed it again. What would he say? *You carry the portals of other dimensions inside you. Even now they are opening. By the night of the autumnal equinox, you will have opened all five. And on that night I will use the portals, and so will another. As in duels of former times, we will battle. One of us will win, the other will cross through. But no one who has carried the portals has ever survived.*

But this time, the war would be over, once and for all. And even Steven didn't know what would transpire then. Ten thousand years of preparation for that moment, and he didn't know what to anticipate as an outcome. Would he simply cease to be? Would he cross back over into his former existence?

Or would he, like Jillian, die?

No perfect moments for him. None but this, none but holding her, touching her. Wanting her.

A soft moan escaped her, and he realized he was still gripping her hair with what must be a painful intensity. He loosened his hand somewhat, but still couldn't bring himself to release her.

"You are so beautiful," he said. Even to him, his voice sounded rough, harsh with want.

Perhaps if he told her all, he would be able to coax her artist's soul to see the portals for what they were, to persuade her to keep the portals sealed. Was that even possible?

He knew it wasn't, and he understood that it was his want for her, this momentary, painful desire, that was driving him to even consider such things.

But if he told her the whole truth, then, at the very least, he might be able to prepare her for the coming battle. She was the innocent, not him. He *knew* what was at stake here. He knew the consequences; she didn't. He should have told her the truth years and years ago, when she had still been a child and might have believed him, might have been open enough to listen to him. But he hadn't, and now it was far too late, and he couldn't think of her as only the carrier of the portals; she was a wholly desirable woman, too.

Had he gone insane? Had his too many years on earth made him more human than he'd ever suspected possible? For in her presence, he found himself craving her want of him, her need of him as wholly human. As if he were just any man, a man she would want to be with.

If only it *were* possible, he thought bitterly, his hand caressing her hair now, rolling it in his fingers, memorizing the silken texture.

But it wasn't possible; he wasn't just any man. If he were just anyone, the entire battle to be waged yet again would never happen, would never be important. And it was important. It was the single most important battle in the universe.

"Steven—?" she breathed. In pain? In want? He forced himself to relax his fingers still more, though he couldn't go so far as to move away from her.

"I can't do this," she said, but didn't step back. "I don't know anything about you." Her eyes begged for answers to questions she hadn't voiced.

"What do you want to know?" he asked.

"Who you are ... many things."

He couldn't answer her without telling her everything, and that telling would take more than a few minutes standing over a sink of running water. And if he did tell her, she would run from him, order him away.

And he couldn't go. Not now.

What could he tell her, anyway? *I'm not a mortal being?*

But that, too, would be a lie now. With her hair in his hand, her scent in his nostrils, he was all too human, and all too conscious of wishing to be even closer to her. And conscious of the end looming around the corner.

Why did this one woman seem so vastly different? What special magic did she possess that she made him feel as a man would feel, think as a man might, made him want things that only a man could have?

But he was a man, he told himself bitterly, however inhuman. He bled like a man, ached like one. Wanted this woman as any man would. Who could pinpoint the difference between all other men and himself? None but he. And it was his hell to know that, no matter how much he might seem the same, he wasn't.

Her lashes fluttered against his skin as his long fingers drew a slow line down her cheek, her jaw. He felt her trembling, a soft infusion of reaction that no mortal could ever have detected. He wanted to stand beside her forever, feeling her confusion, her desire, her want, her fear. If only he could.

But he knew with utter certainty that the moment he took his hands from her the feelings would begin to fade, would ebb, and he would be left with only memory, and faint memory at that. He didn't want to drop his hand, and yet he knew, with the weight of ten thousand years' worth of knowledge, that he had to let this feeling go.

She—and he—would probably never understand how much it cost him to release her.

Seconds, he thought dazedly. He'd only been touching her for seconds.

It wasn't fair, he thought with a dark, piercing ache, even as he lowered his hand. It wasn't the first time he'd thought such a thing, but it seemed to him at this moment that it had become a primal scream of rage somewhere deep within him.

As he had known it would, the sensation of knowing her, the feeling that they were meant to be together, the idea that his body was wholly in tune with hers, slowly shifted, began to ebb, slipped into some distant place. But, puzzling him, startling him, the richness of feeling didn't go away altogether, as it always had in the past.

Something of her lingered, like an elusive scent, or perhaps, more accurately, like the last coal in a fire, an ember, a flicker of life that could be extinguished in time or suddenly spark a conflagration. Was it because the end was so very near?

Drawing a shaky breath, he found that at least now he could think. And he could act. He could bend her now, or he could tell her the truth. With the blood tie in effect, she might believe him. With the look of confusion in her eyes, she might even want to.

"Your arm," she murmured, as if grasping at a lifeline and not out of concern for his well-being.

"I'll be all right," he said, again telling her the truth, though he could see she didn't understand.

She bent over his wound again, her soft auburn hair lightly brushing his bare shoulder. He could feel its silky warmth tickle his skin. He tilted his head slightly to take in the fragrance. It was, as he'd expected, filled with nuances of her day, her night.

"It's not bleeding so badly now," she said. "Maybe you're right, but—"

"I'll be fine," he said, then added, "Trust me."

She stilled then, and looked up, not quite meeting his gaze. That shadow he'd often seen in her eyes hovered there now. She was thinking about her dead husband, Allie's father, the man he'd so often envied. Dave must have said similar words to her at one time, at any time, meaning them or not.

"Mommy—?" Allie said now, coming up behind them. Her voice was as breathy as her mother's had been only moments earlier.

Jillian turned with a look of sharp relief. "Yes, sweetie?"

When Allie didn't speak, Steven looked at her, as well, and had to hide his frown. The little girl, so like the child her mother had once been, wasn't gazing up at Jillian. She was staring at him with something akin to terror. Why?

A bleak fear flickered in him. It couldn't be. Not this soon. Not yet. Beleale wouldn't appear for two weeks yet. But if not, then why would the girl appear afraid of him?

Jillian immediately stepped away from Steven and swept Allie into her arms and hugged her tightly. "Not to worry, Allie. His arm's okay. He'll be just fine. See, sweetie?"

She pulled back a little, and Steven held out his arm, as if she'd commanded him to do so.

Allie scarcely looked at it. "It's not that, Mommy. It's...*you* know."

Jillian frowned and shook her head, obviously puzzled.

"*You* remember," Allie said, then added in that exaggerated whisper reserved for Broadway actors and children under ten, "*What I told you this afternoon.*"

Steven didn't have any idea what Allie might have told Jillian, but knew from Jillian's flash-fire blush that it had something to do with him, something that rendered her incapable of looking at him.

Jillian felt the heat suffuse her cheeks and didn't dare even glance at Steven. Allie's exact words had been *Just whatever happens, don't let Steven in the house.* And he was certainly inside now. And she had allowed him to stroke her face, draw his thumb across her lips, in a gesture as intimate as any kiss might have been, and more so than many. She had leaned against the shocking heat of his body, feeling his muscles rippling against her shoulders, her back. And she'd sensed him waging some internal struggle as he'd gripped her hair so fiercely.

"Come on, Allie," she said faintly. "It's way past bedtime."

She didn't pay attention to Allie's protest, and, still without looking at Steven, she brushed past him, herding Allie to the hallway door. "Just let me get her to bed and get the butterfly bandages. I'll be right back."

Was she telling him to stay in the kitchen? Was she asking him to wait for her? She felt a hundred implications hanging in the air, seeming to assume weight, becoming concrete entities.

"Mommy," Allie whispered as they approached her bedroom, "Lyle doesn't want him in the house."

Jillian felt a sagging tiredness creep through her at the mention of Lyle's name. And a spark of annoyance. "Well, you're just going to have to tell Lyle that his wants don't matter at the moment. Steven cut his arm, and he needs our help. I'm sure that if you explain it to him, Lyle will see that we can't just shut the door on poor Steven."

Even as she said the words, she was aware that she didn't think of Steven with anything remotely resembling pity. He was about as much "poor Steven" as she was "lucky Jillian."

Allie looked crestfallen. Jillian seldom spoke so sharply, and she certainly hadn't in the past year. Was this part of the problem they were having? Had she allowed Allie's grief over Dave's death to rob them of the normal mother-child interaction? Was her lack of parental reprimands part of the reason Lyle had taken up residence with them? Was that the reason for the controlling aspect of his personality? A hopeful thought followed that last question: Maybe Lyle would go away if she reinstated those small but utterly necessary corrections.

"You hop in bed now, Allie," she said, softening the stern words with a slight smile. "I've got to get a bandage on Steven's arm."

"Lyle says—"

"I can't listen to what Lyle says now," Jillian said firmly. "I love you, and good night."

"But Lyle says—"

"*Good night,* Allie," Jillian said. She flicked out the overhead light and left the door standing open to receive the muted light from the hallway. She didn't wait for any further protests, but moved off down the hall to find the bandages and return as quickly as she could.

When she stepped back in the kitchen and he wasn't standing at the sink, she had the oddest feeling that none of the events of the night had actually even happened. He was gone, and perhaps never had been there at all. Perhaps like Allie's Lyle, he was only a figment of her overactive imagination.

"Steven?" she asked softly.

"Here," he said, stepping out of the shadows near the dining room entry.

In its way, the moment was an epiphany, the single word profound. She felt he was granting her some great truth, some prescient awareness of the future. And that prescience flowed on two distinctly different levels. On the one hand, all she could seem to think was that of course he was *here,* here with her. Where else could he possibly be?

And on the other, making her shiver, she felt a dark, almost breathtaking foreboding, as if his words signaled the start of something terrible entering their lives. And it was coming *here.*

She knew she had to break the spell, had to say something, but her mind felt curiously blank, empty.

"Jillian..." he began, his voice as soft and rich as ever, slightly dark with allure, and yet oddly distant, as well.

"I... I have some bandages," she said, holding them out in much the same way Allie had held out her limp flowers to her invisible Lyle. But Steven was very visible.

And very much *here*.

"I'm fine," he said, not moving.

She involuntarily glanced at his forearm. While she could still see the gash, the shadows hid the severity of the wound from her.

"You need to at least bind that," she said, nodding at his arm, not daring to meet his eyes, lest he see more than she wanted him to.

She had stood there and let him touch her, bunch his hand in her hair, run his fingers across her face. And she'd wanted him to do even more. She couldn't allow him to see that want now. Couldn't let him know what a fool she felt like.

She turned slightly, looking for any excuse not to meet his eyes. She stared at the clean kitchen floor, not comprehending why it seemed odd, then realizing that in the space of time she'd returned Allie to bed, he'd cleaned up the mess.

"You didn't have to do that," she said.

"You didn't have to help me," he said in swift response, but something in his tone made her glance at him. His words sounded hollow, like a lie.

"Of course I did," she said, but found her mouth had difficulty forming the syllables. She had to help him, yes, but did she have to stand and invite his caresses? The answer was a resounding negative.

Then, stunning her, he said abruptly, "Show me your paintings." His request sounded like a command, no matter how softly he'd spoken.

"My... what?"

"Your paintings. Show them to me."

She couldn't help taking a step backward. He might have been speaking one of the foreign languages he read, for all she understood of the meaning behind his words now. Why did he want to see her paintings? His arm must still be giving him hell; his face was paler than she'd seen it since his arrival. And it was late. Long after dark. And most importantly...he didn't know her at all well enough to ask to see her work.

And how does he know you're an artist? a small, very Elise-like voice asked insinuatingly in her mind.

"I—I..." She trailed off, unable to come up with so much as a remotely plausible excuse to put him off.

"I'd like to see them," he said.

Something in his tone, or perhaps the expression in his green eyes, sent a shiver down her back. He wasn't talking about the paintings. She didn't know what it was he was after, but it sure wasn't art appreciation.

Her mind flared an image of the two of them walking the long, dark corridor leading to her studio, pictured them standing too close together in the dark, his green eyes the only things visible. And she remembered the almost painful way he'd grasped her hair, pulling her to him, as though fighting with her, fighting with himself.

She swallowed heavily, painfully.

"Some other time, maybe," she said, and was all too aware of how faintly she spoke.

Why did the notion of showing her work to him frighten her? Or was it that she'd already considered showing him her strange, surreal doorways, and hearing him ask now threw her?

Just whatever happens, don't let Steven in the house.

Oh, dear God, was her daughter able to see something in this man that she herself couldn't? Was she being as blindly foolish as Elise implied? She unconsciously stepped back yet another pace and held the bandages pressed tightly against her chest.

Steven would have had to be blind not to see how his seemingly simple question affected her. She was already hard at work creating the portals. That had to be what troubled her. She was opening the portals to alternate planes, other dimensions, and didn't know, didn't understand, what she was generating through her powerful magic. But there was more than this stopping her.

This fear had to be centered on him. His presence, his request at this late hour, the unusual circumstances of his working for her, even the damnable blood tie. But the autumnal equinox was less than two weeks away, and if she had already created the portals, Beleale would be doing all in his considerable power to allow it to work for him, to bring his minions through that slender opening. Calling them forth already, gathering them for the final battle. Didn't Jillian see any of this?

No, he thought. How could she? The world didn't recognize the greatest of its dangers anymore. Newscasts focused on ozone layers, acid rain, incursions between the Serbs and Croats, all serious enough, but nobody did reports on the older races, the bygone powers, the ancient ones. No one but cultists and crazies focused attention on creatures long gone... with the exception of Beleale. And, of course, himself.

"Another time, then," he said, and sadly knew that time would come all too soon.

Then he would see her paintings, see the portals for himself, as he'd heard them during other battles in a piece of music, found them in a poem or an allegory, and forced one of his kind through that portal opened by the composer, the writer, the storyteller. And most of those times he'd won the battle. Sometimes he'd lost, losing the host, losing time, losing himself.

Until now, when only he and Beleale... and Jillian... remained. The last. He and Beleale, the last of their kind. Jillian the last of hers.

He didn't know what expressions had crossed his face at his dark thoughts, but saw that her tension escalated a notch or two. Her eyes took on a guarded, wary look.

"I...I brought some butterfly bandages for your arm," she said.

For the first time in years, he was grateful that his wounds didn't instantly heal, for she stepped closer, peering down at the gash on his arm. But apparently he'd overestimated the slowness of his repair, for she frowned slightly.

"I thought it was...much worse," she said.

She sounded puzzled, even confused. As well she should be, he thought.

"I told you it was fine," he said, then brazenly held out his forearm for her inspection.

"It's amazing," she said softly. "I could have sworn..."

She lowered that tightly clenched fistful of bandages from her chest and started to reach for his arm, then hesitated before continuing to stretch for him. And touch him.

Again her fingertips seemed to sear his skin, pierce his body with her personality, her essence. Would all men feel this way around her, or was it only him, only his unusual properties that would allow such strong reaction?

He clamped his lips together to hold in a sharp intake of air.

To hell with the autumnal equinox, he thought with harsh need. In all these years of battle, surely he could take this one night, this minor respite? Surely he'd done enough, suffered enough. Surely he was entitled to these last two weeks with Jillian. And if not the two weeks, then tonight.

"Will you wrap it for me?" he asked, wanting the moment to extend, craving the lingering of that searing touch.

Even to him the words implied other meanings, alternate possibilities—the night, maybe, or that essence of hers. He wasn't surprised when she looked up to meet his gaze with her own eyes widened and wary. What was she reading from him? Was it anything near the truth?

"Of course," she said, her voice breathless, her lips parted and moist.

With a light and sure touch, despite her obviously shaking fingers, she clamped the sides of the wound with stretchy butterfly clips.

"These will hurt when you take them off," she said, emphasizing her point with a flick of her fingernail across the golden hairs on his arm.

He had to bite back a groan of reaction. She didn't realize how right she was, he thought.

The moment she finished, she stepped back from him, holding the wrapping from the bandages fiercely crumpled in her hand, her fists tight against her thighs. Everything about her spoke of her tension, her wariness.

At the same time, an unwilling desire, a hot, sharp need, stretched to meet him, awakening the passion roughly banked in him, making him aware that while she might be wary of him, might even be frightened, she wanted him.

The moment she eased away from him, the lessening of sensation, the dulling of desire, overtook him. But he remembered. He felt certain he would always remember.

"Such a little fire," he said.

She met his gaze, her own puzzled.

"The pain, or—?"

"'Such a little fire is quickly trodden out—'"

He stopped before saying the rest; it was far too revealing.

He should have guessed she would recognize it. Like him, she'd spent much of her life in dusty tomes, old libraries.

He heard her catch her breath, then caught his own when she completed the lines.

"'Which, being suffered, rivers cannot quench.'"

Steven saw her trembling, knew she was shaken by the unusual exchange, had understood it to her very soul. She suffered that little fire as deeply as he. And he knew that she didn't just know the Shakespeare, but understood *him* as if she'd touched him, not just physically, but on some fundamental level that his kind had long since forgotten, had forsworn millennia ago.

"Who are you?" she asked. Then, confounding him, she added, almost beneath her breath, "*What* are you?"

CHAPTER FOUR

How could he tell Jillian what he was? He was both human and not. He had been on the earth for so many years, he'd almost forgotten his true form, his true nature. Dare he blurt out the raw truth? How could he, when after so long, he wasn't even sure what that truth entailed?

"I guess you could call me a survivor," he said finally, fully aware of the irony. How could he do what was required of him, feeling for her as he did, wanting to know more?

Whatever she took in from his reply must have given her some comfort, for she seemed to relax slightly. "I'm a survivor, too," she said. "It's hard, isn't it?"

She'd never know how hard, he thought grimly. Or perhaps, because of what she'd recently been through, she might have some inkling. She just wouldn't know that terribly darker side, the side that would let death come to someone he cared about.

"At times," he said. *Like now.*

"Yes . . ." she agreed reflectively. "At times."

"How long ago did you lose your husband?" he asked. He knew, but somehow needed to hear her voice her grief over that loss. It might distance him, hearing her love for her husband, might make him feel easier about what he had to do.

"A year now," she said, not looking at him, then slowly turning to face him directly. "Wouldn't it be nice if we could say 'a year...*then?*' As though it were all over, long gone.''

"I'm sorry," he said, and drew some measure of relief when she looked away.

"He had a mistress," she said then, surprising him with her knowledge. He hadn't thought she knew. Her grief had been so intense, he'd assumed she hadn't guessed.

"That must have hurt you," he said. Never had words seemed so inadequate.

"It's funny," she said, and he thought he'd never heard anything quite so much the opposite, "but it hurt me more after he died than it did while he was alive. After he died, I resented the time he'd spent elsewhere, without me and Allie. Does that make sense?"

Steven nodded. He knew exactly. Now that time was so short, he resented every moment not spent in her company.

He said then, "I heard him play one night."

Jillian looked back up at him in what he took as surprise, but might have been hope.

"You did? When?"

He'd heard her husband play half a dozen different times, in different places, during those years of waiting, of trying to guarantee that Jillian would survive all the myriad death possibilities that afflict all humankind, even the one who carried the portals.

"In Washington, D.C.," he said. That answer was safe enough. He'd watched her from two rows back, envying the rapt expression on her face as she watched her husband play. Had she known about her husband's affair then? Had she watched him with such love, even knowing about the betrayal?

He had envied Dave before. He envied him even more now.

"What was the recital?" she asked, a faint smile on her lips.

"He played a collection of Chopin's nocturnes and sonatas."

Jillian's smile widened, and her eyes took on a distant look. "He always loved those pieces."

"That's how he played them," he said, and knew his words pleased her, even as the memory obviously caused her mixed pain.

"So you were in D.C.?" she asked, effectively stemming the flow of emotion.

"Once or twice," he said.

In ten thousand years, cities grew, spread, burned, and grew again. He'd been to Washington, and a host of other places. Over time, such a very long time, they all took on a sameness, a pervasive kinetic energy that seemed driven to spend itself on one too many concrete structures or cement sidewalks.

"And you weren't happy there?" Jillian asked, apparently reading his expression.

"I wasn't any unhappier there than anywhere else," he said, and was surprised at the bitterness and raw truth in his words. What was it about Jillian that made him want to treat her honestly? Had he been lonely so long he craved companionship, ached for questions?

No, he thought sadly, it was just Jillian, her company, her smile, her love, that he wanted. And couldn't ever have.

"You don't give away much, do you?" she asked with a faint smile.

"Not much, no," he agreed.

Her smile broadened and her shoulders relaxed another degree.

"I was thinking this afternoon that there's something rather otherworldly about you. You make me think of characters in old, old stories," she said, and, without waiting for him to ask her how, continued. "Knights, dragonslayers, people like that. I'm not even sure why, you just do. Something in your silences, maybe."

She couldn't know how curiously apt her reading of him was. It was both oddly flattering and strangely disconcerting that she could peg him so accurately. Except that she made him sound vaguely noble, and he knew there was nothing noble about him anymore. He'd given that up for his false humanity.

"You won't even rise to that bait, will you?" she asked, a glint of mischief in her blue eyes.

"I've been told I'm an anomaly," he said finally, hoping in spite of himself that she would probe deeper, pry the truth from him.

He knew this was a damnable game, giving circular, nonspecific answers to direct questions, but in this case, he couldn't give her anything else. Unless he revealed everything, and for some reason he didn't want to do that on this rare evening.

She frowned, even as she smiled. Her delicate teeth caught at her lower lip. The overall image was one of her most endearing qualities, he thought. She gave the impression of serious consideration to his words, while keeping a friendly and open mind to the possibilities inherent in his answer.

Her frown disappeared and her smile remained as she said, "I would have said an enigma, maybe, but you're hardly an anomaly."

It was his turn to frown. Couldn't she see his basic difference from all other men? Couldn't she feel it? He was far more than a mere mystery, some puzzle she couldn't work out. But she had felt the difference. Hadn't she asked "what" he was?

Before he could think of a suitable response—the truth hovering somewhere near his lips—she suggested he sit down.

"You've lost a lot of blood, or at any rate it looked like you did."

She spoke quickly, and a little breathlessly. Was she as nervous as she made him feel? Had she felt that way with Dave? Somehow he wanted to believe that whatever she felt, it was just for him. Him alone.

"Before you came in, I had just poured a glass of brandy. Would you care for one? It'll put hair—" She broke off abruptly, her eyes cutting to the thick mat of gold hair on his chest, then skewing sharply away as a blush stained her cheeks.

"Yes," he said roughly. He felt a surge of joy sweep through him. The blood tie ensured only his ability to come and go at will. It had no power to make her want him to stay. Yet here she was, asking him to sit down, drink a glass of brandy.

He felt ready to do anything to make her calm again, make her relax, her eyes linked with his, her lips parted not in anxiety, but in acceptance. He sat down at the darkened dining room table and lightly rested his forearms against the smooth-textured wood grain. For the first time, he was conscious of his half-dressed state, felt the coolness of the evening playing along his bare skin.

Watching her select a brandy glass, pour a healthy measure of the rich, tawny liquid into it, he realized that after having offered him the alcohol, she was acting as though surprised that he'd accepted her offer, or perhaps she was merely chagrined that he'd done so. He didn't care. He wanted to stay, needed to sit with her a while longer, linger in her home, in her company.

He desperately craved the illusion that she wanted him here for his sake, for basic companionship, and not because he'd torn his arm open to bind her to him, to secure his access to her home so that he could prowl at will, day or night. He wanted, for this one evening, to believe that he was simply an ordinary man, someone who had come to call on her—a suitor, perhaps. Just a man, any man. A man Jillian would want.

He felt the irony ripple over him, seeming to cloud the rarefied Santa Fe air; he was sitting here at her table, trying to make believe that for one evening out of ten thousand years of evenings he was what he had never been and could never be.

She handed him the snifter of brandy she'd warmed for less than half a minute in her microwave oven. Her fingers brushed against his and seemed to set him aflame. The glass, too, was hot to the touch, and the spirits circled around the bowl of the glass and wafted through the narrow aperture, stinging his nostrils with sharp teeth and making him again aware that for him sensation was stronger than for others. Stronger than for any other.

Jillian said, "I learned that trick from a friend of mine. You've probably seen her around...Elise Jacobson?" She smiled and sat down.

God, Steven thought, she was so normal, so easy to be with. Those traits had been uniquely hers throughout her life. She was the pied piper that all others, including himself, wanted to follow.

How could she be one who held the portals inside her? All the others over the countless years, had seemed tortured, haunted by the other dimensions. How could she hold them and not recognize them, not know the dangers? How could she not perceive the fundamental difference in herself as easily as he did? And as he did in himself.

How could she remain so vital, with only two weeks left to live? He felt the worst of abusers, to sit across from her, knowing this and saying nothing, giving her no warning.

"I like it warm," he said, and even to himself the words implied alternate meanings.

He heard her catch her breath.

"So do I," she said, after a moment's hesitation and the deepening of the color in her cheeks. "Maybe it's the idea that something that burns should also be warm to the touch."

I'll burn you, he almost warned her. *Touch me and be burned.*

"You know," she said, a faint smile curving her lips, "I think this is the first time you've been inside my house."

"Yes," he agreed.

Jillian knew it was his first time in her home, he thought. He'd been aware of that lack every moment of every day. He'd told himself that, as he had for the past twenty-odd years, he'd been content to watch her from a distance, but the truth was harsh: He'd needed to make certain the battleground was prepared, ready for him. But now, inside her house, he found he'd most likely acted as early as he had so that he could snatch a few days, a few moments, for himself. So he could sit here like this, drinking brandy with her, absorbing her smile, drowning in the blue of her eyes.

But he'd had to act today, for after he'd linked gazes with her, he'd seen her friend eyeing him with suspicion and been certain he shouldn't wait any longer. And so he'd torn open his arm, knowing she would be too soft-hearted to deny him access, knowing his blood would spill on her floor, knowing full well that his blood would eliminate every barrier to his access. Nothing—not locks, keys or chains—could bar him from her home now.

His blood was on her hands, as hers would inevitably, and all too soon, be on his. But he still had two weeks. Two weeks to dream, two weeks to pretend he was merely a man and she only a woman. Two weeks to grant her whatever it was she wanted most. Before her destiny required the ultimate sacrifice of her. Of him.

By shedding his blood, however intentionally, he had ensured that her home was open to him, free, no corner or closet barred. But, sitting with her now, he found himself wishing that it had been by a completely natural process, that her trust alone had drawn him inside, that her faith in him would be the factor that let him stay, not the spilling of his inhuman blood.

He sighed inwardly. War left little time for wishes and faith, and less than that for finesse. In all his ten thousand years, no one could have known that better than he.

She said something he didn't catch, and he didn't seek elaboration. He was more than content to simply let her soft voice surround him, caress his senses. She spoke with a throaty contralto, easy and rich, and, like her scent, the feel of her skin, her voice touched him on some deep level he couldn't begin to understand.

"Are you in much pain now?" she asked.

He was, but it wasn't any kind of pain he could have described. It was a hunger, a deep, abiding thirst, an ache he had lived with for ten thousand years. But somehow, tonight, the hunger bore her name, the ache her voice.

He shook his head in negation.

In some strange commingling, she became the essence of the emptiness that comprised his very core. She was everything he could never have, the embodiment of his essential lack of humanity, and, perhaps because of that very thing, he was *drawn* to her as he had been to no other before her.

And he was her nemesis, the darkness that would blot out her sun forever. In all those years of war, of battles too horrific even to remember, let alone contemplate, he'd never railed against his lack of choice, never wanted to scream out against his bleak and terrible fate. Until now.

Until Jillian.

"What brought you to Santa Fe?" she asked.

You, he almost said aloud. He caught himself in time. "Wanderlust," he murmured. "I'd never been here."

He wished he could even feel amused by her attempts to probe his past. God knew he wanted to tell her the truth, to reveal the entire next two weeks' worth of truth. But how could he tell her who...or what...he really was?

And looking at her, seeing her vulnerability, her beauty, her intense, if unspoken, passion for life—however much that might have suffered in the past year—he knew that for the first time in his too-long life on this earth, he wanted someone to give that trust willingly, without the desperate demand of blood tie.

More specifically, he wanted *this* someone to do so.

Steven had the sudden, dizzying belief that if he had met her ten thousand years ago, even a thousand, he might have dared to believe that she could be the answer to all the questions in his restless soul.

But he hadn't met her long ago. He'd only been watching her during her short human life, and he was with her now, a scant two weeks before the portals opened, before the final battle began. And there was no time but now, no moment but this short fortnight.

For the first time in centuries, he found himself actually cursing his rival, the world's last great enemy. They had been warring for so long that Beleale had long since ceased to hold culpability in Steven's mind. He was evil, yes, and the last of the damned, but sometime during the lonely years, Beleale had become merely the last opponent, an adversary, not the cause of so much earthly pain.

But now, tonight, sitting with this woman who drew him so, who held the portals within her, who would *die* in two weeks' time, he felt the deep well of hatred that he'd long ago sublimated rise up again. Damn Beleale, damn all of those who had chosen that road of chaos.

Damn them all for years of waste, mountains of pain. But, most of all, damn them for Jillian's sake.

"Are you all right?" Jillian asked him now.

He murmured an affirmative, wondering what had shown on his face to make her ask. He might have known, had he touched her, but she was sitting across from him, both hands clinging to the fragile snifter as if desperate for its warmth, her eyes carefully avoiding his own.

For the flicker of an instant, he wondered what would happen if he simply allowed Beleale to use the portals and bring through the others, the multitude of the other fallen, the legion Steven had forced through those portals over the years.

Was it possible that Jillian could be spared then? He, Steven, wouldn't be forced to see her destruction or, worse, to destroy her himself in his attempts to block Beleale once and for all.

But, even if it was possible, he couldn't do that, couldn't step back from the battle. The battles, and this final one in particular, were his entire reason for being. He might, by ducking the battle, spare Jillian, but what of the rest of humanity? What of this woman's daughter, and a million little girls like her? What would they suffer if he allowed Beleale to use Jillian's portals? He didn't dare consider the possibility.

No, whatever happened to Jillian, the battle must be waged, the war ended, once and for all. And he, as the last champion, the last of the fallen, was the only one left to force the last cast-out one to cross through one of the open portals and leave this plane forever.

"What did you do before you joined us?" she asked.

Fought the battle of the would-be gods, he thought. Forever and ever.

"I've always done pretty much the same thing as I'm doing now," he said. It was true, but it sounded aimless, rang between them like a lie.

"You tended gardens for widows in distress?" she asked, and though her tone was light, her eyes were solemn.

"I haven't done much gardening," he said. Why was he being oblique with her? Why not simply tell her the truth? She would find it out herself in less than two weeks.

He wasn't telling her the truth because he wanted her to trust him, to like him. To relax with him as if he were nothing more than some man come to court her.

She frowned, and the furrows in her brow were as attractive as her smile, and as intriguing. He found himself wanting to reach out and smooth the lines away with a fingertip.

"You've done what you're doing now, but haven't done much gardening... What am I missing?" she asked, and smiled softly, encouragingly.

"I traveled quite a bit," he said.

He felt a stirring of something akin to guilt. While he was certainly telling her the truth, he was still deceiving her on a grand scale.

He took a large swallow of the brandy and felt it sear its way down his insides. It burned as his wound had flamed from the peroxide, as his body had been branded by her touch. For a moment, he felt truly alive—burning, stung by fate, but alive.

"It's interesting," she said quietly. "You put that in the past tense."

What had he said? *I traveled.* Past tense. His hand froze midway from his mouth. The brandy stickily lapped in the glass. This would be the last of his travels. He would win, or fail utterly. One way or another, the war would be over. She would be dead, but he didn't know what would happen to him. He'd signed on only for the war, not for the conclusion. He wondered if that wasn't how mortals perceived death...not knowing what came next.

"I know I asked you before," she said, smiling, "but you have to admit, you didn't give me much of an answer... Where are you from? Originally?"

He wondered why humans suffered such curiosity. It was her friend's overt curiosity—mistrust—that had sparked him into cutting himself. Into gaining entry to Jillian's home. He knew from bitter experience that soon Elise would start pushing Jillian for some kind of background check on him.

He wasn't worried about what would be revealed in any documentation here or there, for the simple reason that there wasn't any. However, in this day and age, that in itself would create a problem. Everyone nowadays had a social security number, a credit history, employment records, and a host of computer-recorded details.

It had been far simpler in older times, in days when honor counted for something and a person's word was his passport and checkbook.

It had been far easier for him to lie then.

But, even as he thought all this, he knew that the real reason he'd cut himself, performed the blood tie, was so that he could have access to Jillian, could come and go in her home at will. He had only two weeks now, and he intended to use every blessed day of them.

"Is it that tough a question?" she asked. "Where you're from?"

"I didn't have a conventional upbringing," Steven said slowly. That was the greatest understatement in the universe.

If anything, her smile broadened. "I suppose I could have guessed that much."

Now he was curious. "Why?"

"People don't normally quote Shakespeare while cleaning out gutters . . . or gashes in their arm."

"Ah," he said, but didn't know what meaning she would take from that noncommittal sound.

"Or recite Milton while clearing out the woodbine."

He found himself actually smiling. The muscles required of such an action felt rusty and unsure. But welcome. Oh, so very, very welcome.

My God, Jillian thought, I'm actually flirting with a half-naked, wounded man sitting at my dining room table. The lights are low, the room is cozy, and the brandy is warm. And I'm flirting.

And he was responding with the first real smile she'd seen on his face in the two weeks he'd been with them.

Jillian felt this was an entirely different man from the one she'd been so steadily observing since his arrival at her home. His features seemed less rigid, his posture more relaxed. It couldn't simply be the lack of a shirt that made him seem more comfortable. If anything, that should have made her more nervous, but, oddly, it didn't. He seemed a great deal more natural to her this way.

In darker times, doctors had bled their patients to release the "noxious humors" in their bodies. It had been a ridiculous practice, but in Steven's case, Jillian couldn't help but be aware of a difference in him following his accident. It almost seemed as though something tense, something dreadfully dark and fierce, had been relieved.

For here he was . . . actually smiling at her.

Just that afternoon, she'd been grateful that he didn't smile. She'd actually been content with his lack of laughter, and, most of all, relieved that no sense of humor remotely reminded her of Dave and the myriad roller-coaster ups and downs of life in the now long-buried past. But seeing that smile now, she realized how much she'd longed to witness it, to catch the lightening of this man's features, the crinkle around his eyes, the softening of his lips.

Her fingers tightened around the brandy snifter, more to keep them in place than from any need for warmth. She had the oddest desire to stretch out a fingertip to his curved lips and actually feel the smile. But she didn't dare touch him again.

Her fingers had brushed against his as she handed him the warmed glass and she had been stunned again at the seeming electric current that sparked between them. Was this purely fantasy, or was there truly something magical that seemed to connect them?

She had jerked her hand back immediately, nearly spilling his drink, and had been grateful that Steven gave no indication of noticing her nervous reaction. Her chemical reaction. Or was it a lonely widow's reaction?

"I've seen your work several times in the galleries," he said now, in perhaps the longest unsolicited statement that wasn't a quote that he'd uttered since his arrival two weeks ago.

And it was the last thing she'd expected him to say. He'd asked to see her paintings, but hadn't struck her as a fan of her work. He'd heard Dave in concert, and now he said he'd seen her work in galleries. A frisson of fear snaked across her back. Who was this man? He seemed to know too much about her, about her life. What did he want?

"Here in Santa Fe, at one of the galleries off Canyon Road, and once in New York, at a little gallery off Twenty-fourth Street," he said.

He certainly wasn't lying about having seen her work. How? He was a handyman, for heaven's sake. How did a handyman get to New York, Washington, D.C., and attend concerts and go to galleries?

Jillian felt immediate chagrin at her inner questioning. He obviously spoke several languages, quoted Milton and Shakespeare as readily as some people quoted from popular movies, and yet because he was a handyman, she'd assumed he couldn't travel, couldn't appreciate art. Art wasn't reserved for the wealthy. When had she become such a snob, so prejudiced? So stupid.

"And I've read about you in a few magazines," he added.

What did someone say to statements like those he'd just made? Oh? Yes, well—? He hadn't said how he felt about them, so a thank-you wasn't in order.

"Did you like them?" she asked, and was immediately aghast at her own temerity. Artists never asked how someone liked their work; it was all too often a devastating experience.

"*The Lonely Unicorn* struck me particularly," he said.

He wasn't lying; he *had* seen her work. But *The Lonely Unicorn* was a piece that had been reproduced in posters. Perhaps he'd seen it that way. He dispelled that notion with his next words.

"You don't often work in oils, do you?"

The Lonely Unicorn had been her only foray into the world of oils. Until now, with her seemingly unending fascination with the surreal doorways and roiling clouds with haunted eyes.

"No," she said faintly.

"You should," he said. "Oils lent a texture to the eyes that few artists can capture."

She couldn't help the swell of pride that followed his words; she was only human, after all. And praise was all too often tepidly granted: "I liked it.... Of course, I don't know anything about art... but I know what I like." Or, worse: "I like it... it would just match my sofa."

"Thank you," she said with sincerity.

"No," he said.

She looked at him in surprise, and a sense of having said something amiss.

Steven's eyes met hers steadily. His granite face seemed relaxed, even calm. She found herself holding her breath, her heart pounding in an oddly unsyncopated rhythm. She had to fight to keep her eyes open; they seemed to want to close, to droop.

She wanted him. Her eyes flew open then, her whole body still with the stunned recognition of what she felt toward him, what she'd been blocking for two weeks, and yet had instinctively known from the moment she opened the front door and saw him standing there.

He didn't smile even the tiniest bit as he said, "Thank *you*. You've given the world a fine gift."

Who was this man? How could he so easily say just the right thing? The very one thing she needed to hear? Dave had never thanked her for her artwork; her work hadn't mattered. Only his. Hers had been a hobby, something to occupy the moments without him.

"What are you working on now?"

Jillian hesitated. He'd already asked to see her paintings, and she'd turned him down. She didn't want to talk about her current work any more than she wanted to show it to him.

But he'd given her a keepsake like few she'd ever received, and he deserved at least an answer in return.

"Dark stuff," she said. "Doors that go nowhere, clouds filled with evil eyes."

She felt surprise that she had told him that much, and was almost too embarrassed to look at him. The silence that followed seemed too long, too uncomfortable.

"What makes you say the eyes are evil?" he asked then.

Involuntarily, she met his gaze. She wasn't sure what she saw there, but she had the feeling that his interest went far deeper than mere curiosity about art, or even curiosity about her. His eyes glittered, drawing her inward, snaring her. Holding her. She thought she read a measure of condemnation there, as if she were being deliberately foolish. And she thought she could read something else, a bleak pity.

"Why do you call the eyes evil?" he asked again.

"I don't know," she said. Her breathing seemed constricted. Painful.

"Eyes are the windows to the soul," he said.

"Blake," she said. "Or Whittier."

"Or FitzGerald," he offered, either correcting her or playing along with the quotation game.

"'Whose portals are alternate Night and Day?'" she asked, and at his nod and slight smile, she shivered slightly. Though entranced by his knowledge, by his uncanny ability to snatch a random quotation and bend it to the conversation, she couldn't help but be disconcerted by it.

"The eyes have it," he said.

She couldn't hold in the laugh at his unusual pun, even as she thought about *The Lonely Unicorn,* the use of oils, the strangely haunted eyes that made that particular painting so memorable.

Her smile froze, then faded altogether. She felt that shocking moment when the cosmic tumblers clicked into place. The *eyes.* The unicorn's eyes were exactly the color of Steven's eyes.

And, according to Allie, the same as Lyle. *This big!*
Emerald green. And glittering.

CHAPTER FIVE

Jillian lingered over her preparations for bed. Her hands shook, her legs trembled. She literally *ached* for something, for a touch, for a whisper. Almost embarrassed by her thoughts, she found that yearning belonged to Steven.

For the past two weeks, she'd found a comfort in knowing that he slept so close to the main house, close enough to respond to a scream in the night, close enough to answer if she called. During those two weeks, she'd been able to drop off to sleep in relatively short order, without the terrible aid of a pill, without having to read until nearly dawn, as if just knowing this unusual man was quartered nearby.

But tonight she felt reluctant to crawl between the cold sheets, suspecting she would lie awake in the dark, thinking about the way they'd awkwardly parted on the back doorstep, the lady of the manor saying good-night to the injured servant. And she knew that the moment she doused the lights, she would conjure his glittering green eyes, with their enigmatic, piercing quality and unreadable messages.

The Lonely Unicorn's eyes. Lyle's eyes. Steven's eyes. Eyes filled with terrible sorrow and purpose. Eyes haunted by demons she couldn't begin to fathom, eyes tempered by dark memory. Green, cold, hot. Glittering, ensnaring.

These were the eyes of her nightmares, the recurring dreams that had haunted her all her life. How had she missed seeing Steven in them before? She *knew* those eyes. She felt she always had. Like the doors in her paintings? Didn't they also strike some chord deep inside her, a triumphant tone of recognition? Was that why Steven had seemed so familiar to her, why she'd had the uneasy sensation of having seen him somewhere before, not just once, but many times?

And thinking such things, and pondering the evening, she knew she would toss and turn, remembering Steven's undefinably accented voice, holding up his unusual statements for analysis, striving to make sense of what patently made no sense at all.

Steven Sayers spoke in riddles and avoided direct answers. He withstood pain as some people swallowed pride. He looked like some statue of a Greek god come to life, and something in his eyes told her that particular life wasn't anything anyone else would envy.

He knew Dave's work, and hers. He quoted Shakespeare and Milton and God only knew who else. He dripped blood on her floor and wiped it up before she returned with bandages. He could touch her and send her into a near-frenetic shock.

Who *was* this so very unusual man, and what place did he have in her life? And why was she so certain that he did have some kind of meaning for her, and that he'd come at this particular time for a very real purpose?

She belted her thick, shapeless robe over the sheer negligee beneath and hesitated before Allie's partially opened door, listening, hoping that this would be another of the rare occasions when Allie slept through the entire night without a screaming nightmare about Dave's death.

She couldn't see her daughter in the gloom, but could detect the steady, heavy child's breathing. Once she would have gone on inside and pulled the covers up to her daughter's chin, kissed that sleep-warmed forehead. But the slightest touch woke Allie these days and would either cause her to half scream in surprise or pout for the next hour because she couldn't sleep.

A flicker of light reflected off something behind Jillian and danced along the far wall of Allie's darkened bedroom, making a prismlike rainbow shimmer for a moment.

Lyle.

Jillian froze in the doorway, her hand half outstretched for the doorknob, her heart suddenly pounding in a furious rhythm.

He's real.

"No, he's not," she whispered aloud.

Why had she let Steven leave? And why was it that every time she concentrated on Lyle, she thought of Steven?

The rainbow light shimmered, dancing across Allie's bedroom wall. Jillian's blood froze.

She forced herself to look over her shoulder, praying she would find something that could be reflecting in the hall lights to produce the rainbow dancing on Allie's wall. A few photographs of her gallery openings, receptions for Dave's concerts or recitals, and even a few of Allie growing up, hung along the corridor leading from the kitchen to her own bedroom. *The rogues' gallery,* Dave had called it, and he had been the rogue who stocked it.

Could the light be dancing off the glass of one of those familiar photos and onto Allie's wall? Please, she begged silently, let that be the solution. Were these innocently captured moments of a better time the source of Lyle's being? Had the very hall light Jillian had conscientiously left burning been the source of Lyle's rainbow fur?

She turned back to the darkness of her daughter's room. Her eyes strafed the ink-black walls, searching, searching. No rainbow danced there now. Her heart jolted once, painfully, then seemed to stop beating altogether.

Then she felt a huge, almost giggly prickle of gooseflesh wash over her as she realized she must have moved slightly, blotting out whatever created the illusion.

She shifted to her right, and the rainbow appeared. She moved again, and it went away. She sagged against the doorjamb in the starkest of relief.

"Lyle," she murmured, smiling, tears of relief stinging her eyes. Her heart resumed a thready, too-rapid beating. "So that's your secret."

She rocked back and forth several more times, creating and obliterating the rainbow on the wall, her smile growing broader by the moment, as did a deep sense of how close she'd come to believing in Lyle, believing he was all too real.

Now, seeing this wholly natural trick of lighting, a purely simple accident of physics, she realized just how dangerously close she'd come to slipping into some strange fantasy zone, a place where invisible creatures lurked, enigmatic handymen possessed electrical touches and her new departure in painting carried mystic significance.

"Sleep tight, Lyle, my rainbow friend," she said. "And take very good care of Allie."

She turned away from Allie's door, the smile still in place, her shoulders lighter, her eyes suddenly and thankfully heavy. She heard Allie noisily sigh and turn over, muttering something unintelligible.

Her own room seemed friendlier now, more welcoming. She tossed the nonsensical, unattractive robe to one side. Now that she felt she knew where Lyle's powers came from, she wouldn't have any further need for such cover-ups. If Allie said Lyle commented on her looks, she'd know with certainty that the source was Allie herself.

Thank God.

She slipped in between the sheets, holding her breath against the sharp chill. She had an electric blanket, but was the sort of woman who preferred the momentary sting of awareness that cold crisp sheets brought to the process of unwinding. First she would stiffen in negation, then she would force her limbs to relax into acceptance, and eventually her body warmth would seep into the blankets. The last would happen about the same time sleep overtook her restless mind.

She should have guessed that she would dream of the man who had shed blood in her house that night, the man who called himself a survivor and quoted the masters. But in truth, she had only hoped she wouldn't again be dreaming about arguing with Dave on the morning he was killed.

"You remind me of knights of old," she said, and knew she'd said something like this before.

She stood facing Steven, but a Steven who smiled, who laughed easily.

Misunderstanding her, or playing with her, he answered, "And you remind me of summer mornings."

She wasn't on a grassy hill somewhere, though she smelled flowers blooming. She stood in Allie's darkened bedroom, reaching out with trembling fingers to a rainbow prism dancing on the black wall. She'd dreamed this moment before, somewhere, sometime.

"I know you're there," she said, and felt a grim foreshadowing at her words. He was there; she just didn't understand how or why.

"Yes," he said, and then he was. And his name wasn't Steven, it was Lyle. And she was afraid of him, yet drawn to him.

He looked exactly like Steven, his golden-blond hair moving in some breeze, and she didn't stop to wonder how Allie's bedroom could carry such a brisk wind. His green eyes glittered brightly, emerald pools that beckoned her.

"Lyle," she said.

"No."

"Steven?" And she felt a surge of joy, of relief. It was Steven she'd wanted to see. It was Steven she wanted to touch her, kiss her, take her in his arms and make love to her.

And here he was, holding out a tanned hand, inviting her, supplicating her.

"Come with me," Steven said. "Show me your paintings, I'll tell you what they mean."

And as she raised her hand to his, she knew that he could explain them to her, and so much more. He was a survivor, a mystery who would be able to reveal other mysteries.

But he looked at her so intently. Why didn't he smile, as he had in her dining room? Why didn't he step forward and touch her face, as he had in the kitchen? Why did he seem like a different Steven, someone else?

"I don't know you," she said.

He neither frowned nor looked disappointed. If anything, her words made him smile now, though it wasn't the smile he'd displayed earlier that night. This smile was different, slightly acquisitive, knowledgeable in an uncomfortable way.

"You are mine," he said. "You invited me inside."

"You were hurt," she said.

"Not I," he answered.

"I don't understand," she said.

"No," Steven agreed.

"Who are you?" she asked.

"Come, Jillian. I will love you as no other could. Come, Jillian..."

"Allie..." Jillian murmured, hedging.

"She's under the haystack, fast asleep," he said.

"What do you want of me?" she asked.

"Your love," he responded. *"Your trust."*

"There's something else," she said.

She thought she was backing up, but found she was walking toward him instead, her fingers stretching to touch his. She ached to feel that shock of electricity course through her again, the trembling reaction she'd felt when he touched her face, his thumb tracing her lips, her cheeks, his hand bunching in her hair.

"You'll open the portals for me, won't you, Jillian?" Steven asked, stepping forward to meet her.

"No," she said as she pulled her hand away from him. She didn't know why she denied him, didn't know why she didn't want him to see her paintings. And she didn't know why she knew it was her paintings he wanted. But she knew anyway.

"Soon," he said, bridging the gap between them and cupping her face with both of his hands. He was cold-hot to the touch, searing her and freezing her simultaneously.

Somewhere far away, she heard someone calling her name, a man's voice, rich, a baritone, filled with anguish and need. He called her like someone seeking a lost child, in a voice thick with torment, with fear.

She shook her head, but didn't know if it was in answer to Steven's *"soon"* or the voice's sorrow.

"Soon," he repeated, and lowered his lips to hers, capturing her. His hands lowered from her face to her shoulders, then lowered still more to her rounded breasts, to cup them, mold them to his large, finely chiseled hands.

Her heart beat frantically, fearfully. His hands were so cold, so very, very cold.

The voice called louder, coming closer.

"Jillian...Jillian...don't believe him...Jillian!"

Steven's hands continued to roam her satin-clad body, shifting the nightgown, stroking her skin, exhorting her to focus her thoughts here, and here only. He frightened her. The intensity scared her. Why were his hands so cold?

"Jillian..."

Was it Dave calling? No. It wasn't Dave. He would never have called her name in such anguish. Over Steven's naked shoulder, she could see a rainbow. Why couldn't she see who was calling her, exhorting her to listen?

She knew the voice, but couldn't place it, couldn't put it into context.

"I have to go," she said, stepping back, but she felt his arms encircle her from behind, wrapping warmly around her. Burning her. This time, all she felt was warmth, comfort. Peace. And she felt more, a restless ache, a desire to simply lean back into him, letting him absorb her.

"I'm here," he said in her ear, confusing her, for how could he be behind her, holding her, when she could see him in front of her, reaching for her still?

"The equinox comes soon," one of the Stevens said.

"Soon," the other echoed.

Jillian woke with a start, her mouth dry, her chest heaving. She automatically reached a hand across the bed, needing comfort, needing reality. Her hand stretched across the cool sheets and, as was usual, as was utterly normal, met nothing, found nothing. Instead of feeling that usual dejection of spirits, of again having to face the reality of Dave's loss, she snatched her hand back and held it against her chest, cold fingers pressed in the warm hollow between her breasts.

Tonight she didn't feel sorrow, she felt relief.

She had the feeling that if she'd continued to search for Dave, she would have found something, all right, but it wouldn't have been something she wanted to find.

She lay awake in the dark, staring into the blackness of her room, her eyes searching the shadows for rainbow patterns, her heart beating unsteadily, painfully.

And she looked for glittering green eyes.

This big.

In the soft morning light, Jillian's eyes felt only slightly less heavy than Allie's looked.

"Didn't you sleep well, honey?" Jillian asked.

Her daughter shrugged listlessly, patently uninterested in the subject. Jillian stepped up to Allie and placed the back of her hand on her forehead and then against her neck. Normal early-morning warmth—not too high, not too low.

As for herself, she felt she'd been wrung out and left on a rock to dry. Remnants of the dream she'd had the night before lingered with her, taunting her with their erotic nuances, daunting her with the slightly frightening quality of the strangely real sequences.

"You'll be careful today, won't you, Mommy?" Allie asked.

Jillian's heart wrenched. Allie asked the same question almost every day, had since Dave's death. She longed to offer promises, blithe assurances—I'll be here for you forever, I'll never go away—but Dave had used those words, and he'd been snatched from Allie. Life didn't hold any guarantees.

"Yes, sweetie, I'll be very, very careful. I'll go back and sit on my bed and not move a muscle until you come home again. I won't even breathe till I hear you come in the front door."

This was part of the ritual they'd developed in the past year. It never failed to bring at least a faint smile to Allie's lips. But not this time.

"No, Mommy. I mean it. Lyle's worried about you."

Jillian thought of her nightmare and of the rainbow dancing on the night-darkened wall, nothing more than a reflection off one of the hallway photographs. She firmly shoved aside the memory of her dream, the rainbow over Steven's shoulder, the cold, cold hands, the other Steven behind her.

"Oh? Why is that?"

Allie shrugged, but not from any semblance of indifference. "I dunno. He's just worried."

"Well, he's going to be here with me," Jillian said, and wished she hadn't, for even knowing for certain now that the rainbow creature of Allie's was nothing other than a reflection from the photographs in the hallway, she felt she was lending Lyle credence.

But Allie brightened somewhat. "That's right. Lyle's here to protect you."

"You bet he is," Jillian said.

She wished it were that simple. A reflection couldn't protect her from the way she'd longed to mold herself to Steven's body in the dream.

"But he can't go outside," Allie said strictly, sounding the fierce parent.

"Okay," Jillian said, playing along.

"He'll get sunburned."

"I guess they don't make much sunscreen for rainbow critters," Jillian said.

Allie giggled and covered her gap-toothed mouth. She turned her gaze to the empty chair beside her. "Do they?" she asked.

"Do they what?" Jillian asked back.

Allie shifted her gaze to her mother. "I wasn't talking to you," she said, and though Jillian knew it wasn't meant rudely or unkindly, she nonetheless felt slightly depressed.

She wanted to tell Allie that her Lyle was nothing more than a fragment of physics, an illusion, something made of light and glass refraction. But, heeding Gloria Sanchez's advice, she didn't. And now that she knew what it was, what possible harm could it do to play along?

If her dream had any logical significance, it could mean a lot, she thought.

"Lyle's really an angel, you know," Allie said then.

Jillian felt a cold shiver prickle down her spine. Elise had said the "dark with excessive bright" quotation focused on the war between the fallen angels.

"An angel, hmm?" she asked. "Does he have wings?"

"No," Allie said easily. "He's not like the Bible school angels."

Jillian was surprised at this answer; she and Dave had decided early to postpone Sunday school until Allie was old enough to make choices for herself about faith, religion, about such matters as angels.

But if Allie was to put any construction on the reflection dancing on her night-dark wall, an angel was probably the most benign of any she might come up with. Elise's strange interpretations notwithstanding.

An angel.

Jillian smiled. "No, I'm afraid he forgot to tell me that he's an angel," she said.

Her hands were perfectly steady as she gathered Allie's empty plate and glass from the table. She wasn't going to buy into any of that this morning. No way.

"You'd better get a move on, sweetie. Your bus will be at the corner soon."

Allie scurried off to the bathroom to brush her teeth as Jillian rinsed the plate and glass and put them in the dishwasher. She quickly jotted a love note to Allie and stuck it in her daughter's bookbag before the girl could return and see her. This, too, was one of the many rituals they'd established in the past year, a small bridge between home and school, a reminder that her mother was thinking of her in the hours of the long school day. And something Lyle was seemingly unable to accomplish.

She tried not to think about Allie's saying Lyle was an angel and tried not thinking about her nightmare from the night before which seemed oddly relevant.

She shook her head. Allie couldn't possibly know that Milton's fallen angels weren't the traditionally conceived biblical angels, winged sexless beings heralding joy and peace. But then, most of the biblical angels weren't that way, either.

Like some of those in the Old Testament, Milton's angels were dark and powerful, kings of tremendous power, forceful and rebellious, capable of complete and utter destruction. They were beings who "changed things."

She shuddered. She wished she could smile at such ludicrous notions. But somehow, after the dream, after thinking about her paintings—*the evil eyes*—she didn't find it so ludicrous at all.

"Lyle says he likes the night better," Allie said as she came back to the dining room and collected her bookbag. "Do I need a coat today?"

"Yes, you do," Jillian said. "I don't want a Popsicle for a daughter."

Allie smiled, then abruptly cocked her head, listening to a voice only she could hear. She refocused her eyes on her mother and said, "Lyle says he likes your nightgown better than what you have on now."

All of Jillian's relief at discovering the source of Lyle's existence abruptly faded....

"He said it feels softer. Silkier. And he says, so do you."

... then vanished altogether.

* * *

With less than two weeks to the official demarcation of autumn, the morning was cold, a heavy, crystalline frost covering the ground, gilding dried flowers and dressing bare trees. When she kissed Allie goodbye, the world had been starkly white. By nine o'clock, the sun had burned the trees back to nudity and the ground to a damp russet; September in Santa Fe, that roller-coaster ride of seasonal changes.

And Steven still hadn't made an appearance.

At nine-thirty, Jillian set her coffee cup down with a sharp clatter and pulled on a light jacket before leaving the house by way of the dining room. She traveled the same path he'd used the previous evening and, in the harsh morning light, saw remnants of his progress the night before.

Dark brownish-red stains marred the brick walkway he'd cleared the week before. Darker splotches had dried upon the gate. If Jillian hadn't known the path to the guesthouse like the back of her own hand, she could easily have found it now, following Steven's gruesome Hansel-and-Gretel trail.

It was no small wonder he'd been enigmatic, she thought, stepping up her pace; he'd lost a great deal of blood. He must have been nearly out of his mind with dizziness.

She chided herself for having given him brandy. She should have given him orange juice, called an ambulance, insisted on taking him to the emergency room. Instead, she'd basked in the warmth of his body against hers, sat talking with him at the table as if they were old friends, however unusual the conversation. Instead of making sure he was all right, she'd flirted with him and, once he was gone, dreamed of melting into his arms, kissing him, aching for more.

She hesitated outside the old-fashioned two-room adobe dwelling. He'd cleared the brush away from it, as well, and patched the few stucco cracks in the thick, irregular walls. Even the vigas, the wooden poles used in southwestern architecture in lieu of ceiling beams, had been trimmed and restained and sealed to stem moisture or dry rot.

When she brought him out here only two weeks ago, the small guesthouse had worn a tired, dilapidated air. Now it looked as solid as its venerable age. It looked lived-in.

The inexpensive curtains covering the windows were open, indicating Steven was up, but the heavy wooden door was shut tight against the chill morning.

Jillian backed up to look at the chimney, seeking a wisp of smoke, a curl of heat distortion, to show he'd built a fire that morning. She could see neither.

Had his curtains been open the night before? Could he have passed out upon returning to the guesthouse? Could the gash have reopened, and he...

She stepped up to the door and knocked and listened for his approach.

...was lying dead on the floor.

She bit her lip and knocked again, more firmly this time.

Still nothing.

She couldn't have said when her heart started to beat in a harsh, painful rhythm, but when she wrapped her hand around the wooden handle, she had to take a deep breath to steady her reedy breathing. The handle lifted easily, and the heavy door swung inward.

Whatever she had expected to see, it wasn't a towel-draped Steven kneeling in the center of the room, in a pool of sunlight streaming in the open windows. His hands were splayed out to either side, his back was arched, and his lionlike head was thrown back, giving great emphasis to his bare throat and chest.

The sunlight danced along his bare skin, lighting the golden hair upon his chest and legs, his mane. Altogether, he appeared as ruffled and sunstruck as a palomino at full gallop on a golden hillside. He was a halo of light on the floor of the old guesthouse.

Jillian's breath snared in her throat at the sight of the nearly naked man, and she froze in the doorway, unable to speak, and equally incapable of retreating. She felt a shock wave of embarrassment wash over her, followed by a crash of sharp chemical reaction, a purely visceral wrenching ache.

Was he praying? It looked far deeper than that. It looked like some form of yoga, but even more. To Jillian, it seemed Steven was performing some alignment ritual, a personal harmonic convergence. It was by far the most private self-communion she'd ever witnessed in another human being.

Allie should see this, she thought chaotically, because this, *this* is what an angel should look like. The notion spiraled around in her mind, making her fingers pulsate with desire to touch him, causing her body to thrum to a hitherto unheard melodic phrase. Her legs felt leaden, her heart was pounding too rapidly.

She wanted to run, needed to flee from this too-intimate scene, and at the same time couldn't have turned away if her very life depended upon it.

Finally her breath returned, adrenaline trickled to her legs and she was able to back up, one step, then two, until she was edging over the threshold.

She knew that Steven hadn't heard her knocking, hadn't given any indication that he could hear anything at all, but the moment her heel crossed to the outside of his doorstep, he raised his head upright and impaled her with his green eyes.

She'd thought herself breathless watching him absorb the sunlight, but she knew that had been nothing compared to what she felt now. For a sparkling moment, all the elements of her dream returned, the fear, the confusion, the aching want, and she felt the rough need to escape.

Not I, she heard, as if he'd spoken aloud, as she had heard him say in the dream.

Jillian needed to drag her gaze from him, but couldn't. Her heart pounded a warning, her mind screamed a command to run. *This is what my dream meant,* she thought. Her ragged breathing sounded harsh to her own ears, and her fingers trembled.

Steven's outstretched hands slowly turned inward, and he sat back upon his bare heels, never taking his eyes from her.

She read desire in them, and something else, a dark knowledge, a tinge of bitter regret. She felt frozen in his regard, trapped in a strange combination of anticipation and dread.

"I...was worried... Y-your arm," she whispered through dry, stiff lips. She tried moistening them with the tip of her tongue, but it didn't seem to work.

Steven still didn't speak. Nor did he look away.

Let me go, she begged inwardly, though on some dim level of awareness she knew all she had to do was turn and leave. He wasn't holding her here, she was. He wasn't keeping her prisoner in his gaze, she was his willing victim.

Allie had told her that Lyle was worried about her. Lyle, the rainbow angel, was worried. With very, very good cause, she thought hysterically.

Abruptly Steven's face shifted, and his lips curved upward in a surprisingly welcoming and gentle smile. He slowly and fluidly pushed to his feet, neither reaching for the loose towel at his waist nor seeming to be self-conscious wearing nothing but that flimsy terry cloth. He stood in that pool of light like a male Aphrodite having just stepped from the half shell.

"Come in," he said.

In her dream, he'd said, *Come.* And she'd wanted to, but she'd been frightened.

She was frightened now, and yet she stepped back inside the doorway. She both did and didn't know why.

"I . . . I knocked," she said.

His smile neither slipped nor faltered. "I didn't hear you," he said.

She knew that, had witnessed his total concentration on whatever he'd been doing, but still didn't understand it. Just as she didn't understand how he hadn't heard her knock and come in, but had seemed utterly aware of her departure.

"I don't have any brandy," he said. "But I have some tea."

He was kidding her. Teasing. As if whatever he'd been doing was nothing. As if standing there half-naked was less than nothing. As if her dream had been nothing. But then, he couldn't know about her dream, could he? Somehow, she wouldn't put it past him to read minds, in addition to all his other odd traits. Or was the whole business with Lyle and her unusual dreams investing Steven with something other than basic human attributes?

Her dreadful attack of fear and confusion subsided somewhat. Had she been fearful of him because of her own unwilling desire for him? She could almost hear Elise's light sarcasm: Now here's an interesting twist to the sexual-harassment issue.

Jillian attempted a stammered apology.

Steven waved her words away and gestured to a rocker beside his bookcase, the rocker she'd pictured him sitting in late at night, some classic and incomprehensible text on his lap.

"I'm fine," she said. "I...I just came to see about your arm."

She could have sworn that for a very real moment he looked utterly blank, as if he didn't know what she was talking about, as if he'd never hurt his arm, didn't remember anything of the night before. Then he turned swiftly and plucked a chambray shirt from the already tidied bed and half turned away from her to slip it on.

But she'd seen what he was hiding from her.

His arm was totally healed.

Jillian told herself she was mistaken. She'd seen his wound the night before. No one could heal that fast. No one.

No one human.

He's not real, Mommy, Allie had said the day before.

Maybe, Jillian thought hopefully, she'd simply forgotten which arm held the gash. But she knew she hadn't forgotten. Her body had curved against his, her back absorbing the warmth from his chest, as she gently cleaned the wound on his left arm.

And now his left arm was bare of that angry wound.

He turned around again, shirt in place, *covering his arm*. His eyes were shadowed, a deeper sorrow present now.

He knew she'd seen.

She hadn't been mistaken. When he knelt in that pool of golden light, his own golden skin bared to her view— all save that hidden by the towel—she'd thought him nearly godlike. No white bandages had marred the overall effect. No butterflies of stretchy adhesive. She couldn't have missed that.

"Let me see your arm," she said. She was almost surprised at the calmness of her tone, the coolness of her command.

"Why?"

"It's already healed," she said. She was accusing him...of what? Of healing himself overnight? Of having powers no one could have? Of being like Lyle*...and therefore not *real?*

"Yes," he said softly. He didn't move toward her. He didn't back away, either.

He should have looked a little silly, standing in nothing but a shirt and towel, but somehow he didn't strike her that way at all. He looked like a lion whose acute hearing has detected another adversary nearby...alert, wary. Ready to pounce if need be.

Unconsciously, Jillian took a step backward, easing herself through the open doorway. And, equally unconsciously, she glanced back at her own large adobe home, looking for something she couldn't even have begun to define. It wasn't help, exactly, though she felt certain she needed it; and it wasn't affirmation that her home still existed despite the unusual morning, for she was sure that it did.

If Steven stood at this particular spot, she thought, he would see my bedroom window. Had he stood in the doorway or at his window at night and seen her light burning well into early morning—two, three, sometimes four o'clock?

If he had, what would he have seen? Her silhouette pacing back and forth, her shadow standing too near the curtains, ready to pull them back to look at the friendly, comforting glow of the lights in the guesthouse?

Now the midmorning sun refracted from the window in a blinding sparkle, creating the illusion of a rainbow on the inside of her curtains.

A peculiarity in the slight breeze or a shadow passing the sun created the impression of the rainbow in motion, the curtains moving aside for someone's passage, as if someone inside her house were looking out. At her.

Lyle. Dear God, he's real.

As it had the night before, when she'd spied that rainbow on her daughter's darkened wall, a frigid wave of fear shot down her spine, through her legs. Adrenaline surged through her, making her fingertips jerk involuntarily and her breath catch in sharp negation.

"What is it?" Steven asked.

She jumped at his words, his voice, and that small motion placed her in a different location, however minutely, and the illusion passed. Her bedroom curtains were still, no rainbow angel hovered there, peering out at her.

She turned to find Steven inches away from her, having followed her gaze to her window.

"Are you all right?" he asked.

She couldn't possibly have answered. She didn't even know what "all right" meant anymore.

"You looked like you'd seen a ghost," he said. Then, confusing her, he added, "I didn't expect you."

Jillian dragged her gaze from her still bedroom window and glanced at Steven. He was in the process of zipping up his trousers. Somehow this simple act of dressing stole some of her fear, some of her sense of unreality.

She thought about his words. He hadn't expected her. They were even; she hadn't expected him, or anything remotely like him.

She couldn't help it—she laughed shakily.

"What's funny?"

"I seem to be jumpy this morning," she said, but couldn't stem the edge of laughter.

"What's wrong, Jillian?" he asked. "It's not finding me in nothing but a towel. Something else. Something you saw just now?"

Jillian looked up at him and began to relax. Something in his understanding eyes, his air of calm strength, and maybe some other undefinable otherness, a part she didn't really want to analyze—*how had he healed his arm?*—made her able to tell him at least a portion of the truth.

"It's just that my daughter has an invisible friend," she said. "And in all honesty, for a minute, I thought I was seeing him." She tried conjuring the laugh again, but failed when Steven's eyes narrowed.

For a split second, she thought she understood how Allie must feel at times; no one would believe her fears over Lyle, her certainty—even for only split seconds—that she'd seen him, felt him touch her. Just as she was certain no one would believe her about Steven, the miraculously healed arm, the illusion of him absorbing sunlight, about the way she wanted him so.

"She says he's made of rainbows," she added. "With green eyes, like yours."

She met his gaze. His eyes seemed greener than ever. Was it her imagination, or did he seem perfectly still, waiting? That lion, ready to pounce, was back.

"Yes?" he asked softly, a nuance of menace in his tone.

He seemed to be reacting as if he were Allie's parent, a father being apprised of a misdeed.

"She says he's an angel."

Jillian heard Steven's sharp intake of air. His breath whistled slightly through his clenched teeth.

She said with a shaky laugh, "I guess she could do worse, couldn't she, than to have an angel as an invisible friend?"

Steven's eyes glittered briefly before he said, "Robert Burton, back in the seventeenth century, said, 'Every man hath a good and a bad angel attending on him…'"

Jillian should have guessed Steven would have a quote from his storehouse of quotations. She didn't have the foggiest notion who Robert Burton even was. She half smiled.

"The trouble is," Steven said softly, his rich baritone voice caressing her, his seriousness frightening her, "with angels, it's so difficult to recognize the difference."

CHAPTER SIX

No matter how lightly he might have spoken, how obliquely, Steven felt as if a cold fist clenched around his heart. For a moment, he wondered how the sun could be shimmering on the highlights in Jillian's hair, when the world had suddenly turned so black.

Jillian's words could only mean one thing: Beleale was already here, in her house.

Like him, Beleale had arrived early. Perhaps Beleale had also felt this final battle was different than all the others. Perhaps, after all, they were not so terribly different, he and his enemy. His brother. Maybe they had both needed to feel every scrap of the final days, to be present for the last few ticks of the earthly clock. For both of them, this equinox would be the ultimate stand.

Useless adrenaline coursed through Steven's all-too-human veins and made his stomach churn with a foreign helplessness. Jillian might call Beleale invisible, little Allie might believe him benign, but neither of them knew him as Steven did, and neither of them had any clue as to what they were dealing with.

But he also knew from Jillian's expression that a part of her, perhaps the part that housed the portals, the part that could see beyond human vision, had either just seen Beleale or come very close to doing so.

She would eventually see him for what he was, of course, because she carried the portals. But to physically see him now? That, too, was unusual, another proof that this final battle was different from all the others.

Looking at Jillian now, he was certain she'd felt Beleale's presence in her home. Many times. What Steven had been attributing to grief, the shadows beneath her eyes, the solemnity of her face, hadn't been strictly confined to thoughts of Dave, but must be at least partially assigned to her discomfort over Beleale.

Steven wondered for a moment how he'd been so blind to the other's presence in her home. Like her, he couldn't see Beleale in his natural state. But, unlike Jillian, he should have felt him. But he hadn't been totally unaware. He'd suspected Beleale's proximity when Allie looked at him with such intensity the night before.

But he should have felt it the moment he knocked on Jillian's door. He'd been concentrating on Jillian instead, looking at her, drinking in her scent, aching for her touch. As he wanted to look at her now. Wanted to touch her.

"How long has your daughter had this friend?" he forced himself to ask, trying to sound offhand, normal.

He wanted to ask much more than this, he wanted to warn Jillian, tell her to order the creature out of her home. But warning her now would do no good. She couldn't *un*invite Beleale. The universal rules couldn't be bent so easily. If that were possible, the war would have ended centuries before. But even in battle, as in all facets of life—and death—rules did apply, and the soldiers struggling to win were bound by them. Even if the surviving players didn't understand those dictates, or believe in them any longer.

"She 'found' him just before school started," Jillian said.

It took him a moment to realize she was answering his question concerning Beleale's date of arrival. How long had the other been watching Jillian's life? As long as he himself had been? While he'd been carefully lurking at the edges of Jillian's existence, had Beleale lurked behind *him,* out of sight, watching as Steven's dreams became entangled with the life force that was uniquely Jillian's? The notion sickened him.

"A month, then?"

"Yes," Jillian said, and smiled crookedly. "Allie found him in the lilac hedge."

No more unlikely place existed, Steven thought. It would have been more appropriate to find him in the sewers, in the deepest pits, in the shadowed corners of abandoned railway stations, where the dregs of society gathered with dirty needles and hopelessness in their hearts.

"Allie calls him Lyle," Jillian said.

Milton, one of those loving someone who carried the portals, had seen him, had written of his given name. And Shakespeare, a descendent of a carrier, had described his fall. Lyle. An apt adaptation of his real name. Beleale was synonymous with destruction, with chaos. Lyle sounded so incredibly innocuous, even playful. A child's story, an infant's toy.

"He frightens you?" Steven asked.

He couldn't resist lifting his hand to her face, tracing the faint shadows beneath her eyes. He felt the shock of contact work through him, burning him, enveloping him. Driving out rational thought.

She lifted her gaze to his. Her lips parted in surprise, or something else. He felt her tremble beneath his light touch, and he trembled in response. Again he had the idea that after all this time, with death so very near, he deserved her, had somehow earned the right to this moment of touching her.

She half smiled in obvious embarrassment, but she didn't step away from his caress.

"Yes," she said faintly. "He does frighten me. Not all the time. Not even most of the time. But I don't like it."

"It?" he asked, trailing his thumb down her cheek, deliberately mesmerizing her, struggling not to succumb to the arrogant certainty that he'd served for so long that he merited this small measure of reward.

But it wasn't small. Touching her now seemed the greatest treasure on earth. He fought against her feelings, her wants, knowing they would overtake him, sweep him away.

"It. Him . . . Lyle."

Jillian's breath came less easily, her eyelids lowered by half. Color edged back into her pale face, and her features began to lose that sharply drawn fear. He could feel a heat washing through her, tingling, bubbling through her veins. He felt it echo inside him. Ah, to be hers.

The wide, shadowed cast to her eyes disappeared at his ministrations. At his touch. For the first time in countless years, he felt the godlike power he had once possessed.

If only he could freeze this moment and preserve it forever. He'd lived so long on this earth, aching for this one woman, this one moment. It wasn't fair to know that soon, having gained some element of her trust, creating a modicum of faith in him, he would use her, destroying her. Something inside him wrenched painfully, and this had nothing to do with mere desire for Jillian, the need to erase her fears, her pain.

Want . . . Need . . . Hunger . . .

The passion seized him, wrestled with him, shaking him. This was gut-tearing emotion, emotion the likes of which he'd only read about, heard about. It confused him, even as it made him angry that it had taken ten thousand years for him to feel such a terrible, wonderful thing.

For it wasn't just coming from her. What he felt from her was confusion, desire, passion. Need, but not anguished need. That emotion was coming from him alone.

"Jillian..." he gasped, needing to focus, willing her to deny him now.

Sparking the horrific sensation was a single question: How could he use her, when she was looking at him with such innocent trust, such confusion in her gaze? *Fix it, Steven,* she seemed to be asking. He would fix it all right, but at what cost to her? He knew the cost, but couldn't afford to contemplate it now.

But he still had almost two weeks to work his own peculiar—and all-too-limited—magic against Beleale...Lyle. And those two weeks might just afford him a clue as to how to bend those unbendable rules of war, lend him some inkling as to how to close the portals and rid the earth of "Lyle" without destroying Jillian in the process.

He'd spent the past ten thousand years wishing to be one or the other, angel or human. And the past twenty years, thanks to watching Jillian, wanting mortal status only. He wondered if he didn't know the secret of it now: Humans always seemed to wish for the impossible, hoping, against all odds, that a dream could come true. As he was doing now.

If those hopes and dreams could make him human, he was fully a man at this moment, for he truly wished for the impossible, hoped for something that couldn't possibly happen.

"Are you trying to seduce me?" Jillian asked him.

I'm trying to find a way to save you, he ached to tell her.

"Would it frighten you if I was?" he asked instead. Everything in him stilled, waiting for her answer.

"Yes," she said simply, sliding a sword's blade into him. Then she added, "And no."

And while the pain was no longer as intense, he still felt the effects of the unwanted wound.

"You are so very vulnerable, Jillian," he said, and meant it from the best part of himself.

"And you are so very alone," she said softly, not having any idea how shockingly accurate she was.

"You don't know how alone," he said.

"Should I be frightened?" she asked.

You should be terrified. You should run as far and as fast as you can, he wanted to tell her. The whole world should be frightened into action.

At one time, long, long ago, when people still carried memory of the old ones, the battles fought below human consciousness, human wars would break out during the time of the portals' openings, innocent families would huddle behind tightly closed doors, sacrificial fires would be lit on open hillsides. But those days were gone.

Now, with only two of them left, Beleale—Lyle—and Steven, the last two of the fallen, the dark and the darker, humankind didn't seem to feel the discomfort of knowing their world hung in jeopardy.

"No," he said, finally, answering her question as to her fearing him, answering his own regarding using her... He had no choice.

"It sounded like it," she said. Her chin raised, and she met his gaze squarely. But her dry lips trembled.

If he alienated her now, frightened her into resisting his efforts to help, attempted to block his access to the portals, then he would have no choice but to force her, coerce her into bending to his will. And he didn't want that, not with Jillian.

"I didn't mean to scare you," he said honestly, and lowered his hands. His entire body ached to reestablish that contact.

"I'm glad."

He wasn't.

Jillian leaned her shoulder against his doorway. The imagery was all too apt—she who carried the portals, leaning on his—Steven thought, but he said nothing as he watched the sunlight picking out golden and red flecks in her auburn hair. She'd been through so much in the past year, must have always felt a measure of separateness because of the portals, and yet she still carried such a life force, such a tremendous brightness inside her. It had to be this he was drawn to, an ancient moth to a new, hotly burning flame.

"How did your arm heal so quickly?" she asked then, but not warily this time. In fact, a faint smile hovered about her lips.

"An old Indian trick," he lied, wanting her smile to stay.

"'Herbs gathered by a waning moon'?" she asked.

"Mary Stewart?" he asked, naming her quotation.

"Yes."

"Something like that," he answered. He felt his own mouth beginning to curve upward.

"I see," she murmured, the smile still in place, her gray-blue eyes warm with mischief. "You're not going to tell me, are you?"

"The truth is," he said truthfully, slowly, "I'm an angel, too."

Her eyes flickered for a moment, but her smile didn't waver. "I should have guessed."

"Why?"

"I'm not sure. I just had a feeling you were something completely different."

"We angels know the secret of speedy recovery."

"Ahh . . ." she said, her open expression holding firm, her smile broadening.

He'd never wanted anyone so much in his years on earth. He wanted to slip into her laughing eyes and stay there for all eternity.

He lifted his hands again, cupping her face with both, holding her still, feeling her life cascading within her.

"Jillian..." he whispered, not asking anything, but needing to say her name while he touched her, while he felt that brightness rising within her.

He could detect her elusive, alluring scent, felt he could drown in the depths of her blue eyes.

"Steven..." she whispered back, her eyes unclouded, for some unknown reason trusting him, accepting him without question.

"We angels know other secrets, too," he said.

His heart pounded faster now, and he felt a tightening in his loins. How could fate, in the final two weeks of his prison term on earth, grant him this rough magic, this bitter taste of utter humanity?

With slow and careful deliberation, he lowered his lips to hers. Her mouth parted, opening to him, letting him taste the sweetness in her. He could feel her heart thundering, could sense, with every fiber of his being, her want of him, her need for a moment out of time, out of logic.

He pulled her even closer to him, burying himself in her taste, in her scent, in the sheer mortal warmth of her. He felt he was dying at last, and, in dying, coming finally to life.

Steven molded her to his body and held her tightly. For a starkly beautiful moment, he was certain they matched exactly, heartbeat for heartbeat, breath for breath.

He'd been no saint throughout the centuries, but he'd never known he could feel as he did now.

"Jillian..." he murmured against her soft lips, then again into her silken hair, her name a prayer of sorts, his need for her an incantation against the dark day to come.

She remained still in his arms, scarcely breathing, her pulse beating a tympani in her delicate throat. He placed his lips over the throbbing vein, feeling her vibrance, her essential humanity.

She shifted in his arms and pulled back slightly. A bemused smile hovered around her lips. Her eyes appeared heavy and unfocused. She held on to his shoulders like a person about to fall. He could feel her body shaking against his.

He relaxed his hold on her and moved back slightly, allowing her freedom, if that was what she wanted, letting her guide him in this novel experience.

She bit her lower lip, pulling on it, studying him with lazy intensity.

He pressed his lips to hers, capturing the moment of consideration, feeling her teeth, tasting her swiftly, then retreating.

She gave the ghost of a chuckle. "Aren't you rushing in where you should fear to tread?" she misquoted outrageously.

Steven couldn't help it—he laughed aloud.

It was the first time he'd laughed outright in a host of centuries.

And he knew what that gut-wrenching feeling had been. Understood it now. In days of old, when poets roamed the earth, painting epic tales of valor and glory, a single line would be added to whatever quatrain blossomed on oilcloth. If any of those poets were alive now, one of them would write, "And a fortnight before the battle, staring into pools of blue, the angel Steven fell in love with the mortal Jillian."

And in that instant of understanding, Steven realized, with a sinking feeling, why he'd followed Jillian's life, why he'd come to her weeks before the equinox.

He'd been in love with Jillian for years.

For Jillian, the following days seemed to slip by on two distinctly different levels. She felt she was two or three alternate people operating in the same location.

On the one plane, she felt a sense of halcyon contentment. She'd found a friend—an unusual one, to be sure, but a friend nonetheless. When she was with Steven, however briefly, she felt she'd truly discovered someone to laugh with, someone to confide her fears and joys to, even if they said nothing important. It was as if a part of her had been searching all her life for a single face, a single touch, and now, finally, at last, she had found him.

She didn't understand him in the slightest, but she felt at peace with him, even when her attraction to him seemed to flame into hotly burning passion.

At the same time, she knew he answered none of her questions, gave nothing away. She saw him daily, talked with him as often as possible, and still knew next to nothing about him. He talked in circles and riddles, and often frightened her with his too-swift understanding and too-intimate knowledge of her life, her wants.

Each passing day lent a new element to her interest in the strange man. Each conversation allowed her glimpses of Steven the man, Steven the worker, Steven the philosopher. He hadn't tried to touch her again, not since that morning in the guesthouse, but she'd been aware of his physical proximity at every moment. And she'd ached for him.

She instinctively knew he was granting her all the choices, all the rights. If she wanted him, she would have to let him know. And she did . . . more than she thought she'd ever wanted anything . . . and she was afraid.

Did her wanting him mean she loved Dave less? No. She had loved Dave, loved him honestly and to the extent that he'd allowed her to love him. But with her husband, some essential, magical ingredient had been absent. He'd felt it . . . hence, his involvement with others. She'd felt that lack, also . . . hence, her guilt when he'd died.

With her husband, whom she'd thought she loved more than life, she had never felt that rush of heat, that nearly senseless dizziness of passion, she felt when Steven stood near her, when Steven gazed deep into her eyes.

She'd never met anyone like him, she thought in the morning when she woke up, and with a smile as she drifted easily to sleep at night. Was that part of the attraction she felt for him, that he was one of a kind, and therefore it was all right that she feel so drawn to him?

She found herself looking up references, honing the old skills, matching him quote for quote, allegory for metaphor. She still knew nothing of his past, but knew him to be remarkably well educated, amazingly facile with words, with imagery. And she believed that in the past few days those dark shadows that lingered in his green eyes had seemed less intense, pushed to some brighter background.

For the first time in a host of years of lonely days and darker nights, she felt alive—achingly, hauntingly *alive*.

In many ways, she thought, coming to a point of knowing Steven, of understanding parts of him, even if she didn't comprehend the whole, should have made her believe that life was coming around, that good things could happen again.

But she found her interest in Steven, her almost uncanny focus on him, couldn't seem to stem the darkness that raged inside her.

She still went into her studio every day, and for hours at a stretch unleashed her uncertainty, her fears, her confusion, on the canvases, creating and recreating doorway after doorway of unfettered malevolence. Thousands of pairs of green eyes peered through roiling, oily clouds, as if looking straight into her soul.

She would work until her back ached, until her hands felt numb and her body shook with exhaustion. After days of work, days of walking and talking with Steven, four paintings stood on four separate easels. And a fifth waited. She knew there was one more painting inside her, one that would be the culmination of this bizarre departure into darkness. Five doorways, five paintings, five . . . aching fingers.

All of the current four were unfinished, and she seemed to work on all of them simultaneously, something she'd never done before. And all held elements of Steven in them, the eyes, the intensity, the ferocity that he occasionally displayed, though never toward her.

And even more disturbing than her bizarre fascination with her unfinished doorways was Allie's reaction to her budding relationship with Steven. For every bit of good it was doing her, her growing connection with Steven seemed to be sending her daughter into darker and darker confusion.

Allie hung back from Steven, giving Jillian accusatory looks, sullen retorts. But when Jillian would question her, try to understand what Allie was thinking, all her daughter would say was "Lyle doesn't like Steven."

And that, combined with the dreams that seemed so contradictory to what she experienced by day, made Jillian begin to seriously doubt her own senses.

The first night Jillian had asked him to join them for dinner, a simple meal of lamb chops and acorn squash—which she'd spent more than three hours preparing on the half chance that he would accept her offer—Allie had stared at the three places set at the table with a puzzled, wary expression.

"Who's coming?" she'd asked. "Aunt Elise?"

"I asked Steven to join us tonight," Jillian had answered, in what she hoped was a steady, pleased tone.

Allie hadn't said anything then, only exchanged glances with her imaginary angel. Or at least that was how it had looked to Jillian; she, of course, hadn't seen Lyle.

Allie had been quiet all through dinner, but the sullen, ofttimes baleful looks she cast her mother had sent Jillian's pleasure in the evening drifting from high to an abject low.

Steven had departed early, only staying long enough to help her clear the table and rinse the dishes for the automatic washer. She'd wanted him to stay, but had to admit to a sense of extreme relief when he left.

Story-and-bedtime hour was a torture that night.

"I told you," Allie had remonstrated, "Lyle doesn't *like* him."

"What about you?" Jillian had countered. "Do *you* like him?"

"That doesn't matter!" Allie had insisted, almost tearfully. "You don't do things an angel says not to!"

That had only begun Allie's rebellion and her rejection of Steven. By and large, the things she did seemed the perfectly normal reaction of an eight-year-old trauma victim faced with change. Jillian tried seeing it that way, tried believing it was the truth.

Gloria Sanchez said to be patient, but cautioned Jillian against moving too quickly herself, warned her against giving her heart too soon, especially given Allie's overt dislike of the man.

Jillian had wanted to argue that it wasn't Allie talking, it was Lyle. But she'd managed to bite her tongue. To admit such a thing was tantamount to admitting insanity. She might as well have said Steven was as much an angel as Lyle; it was equally ludicrous. Equally insane.

And yet for her, in his way, Steven was far more an angel than Allie's invisible creature. An angel who struck her as completely human in his secretiveness, his withholding of his past.

But the greatest difficulty she experienced during that time didn't come during the days, but in the lonely nights.

There, in her dreams, Steven changed, altered, compelling her forward, even as he repelled her.

In the throes of nightmares, he became two Stevens, one she recognized from somewhere, always protective, loving, warm, the other cold, frightening and, strangely, every bit as alluring as the former. As always, when she had the dreams, she couldn't tell the two apart, and both snared her with glittering green eyes and called her name.

With only a week left before the official beginning of fall, Jillian felt a strange sensation of some dreaded event coming her way, coming for her. The house seemed to pulse with awareness of it. Allie seemed even more on edge than usual. Even Steven seemed tense, poised, as though he were hearing something she couldn't.

And outside, the elements warred and buffeted the house with a ferocity abnormal for this time of year. A warm afternoon followed by black, angry clouds that spewed forth sleet, then Ping-Pong ball-size hail, and the next morning a soft, wet snow that melted by noon. The winds howled and whistled in the corners of the courtyard and seemed to whisper pleas for entry in the fine cracks in the window seals.

Like her dreams, like the uncertainty and tensions surrounding her now, the weather was hot, then cold, light, then dark, shocking in its abrupt transition and contrasts.

She didn't know what she should do. She wished she were psychic and could see what the future held, six months from now, six years. It was a coward's wish, a desire to know which decision would prove the correct one: to accept Steven, to turn away from him.

By all rights, she should listen to Allie, to Elise, even to Gloria, and walk away from whatever it was she was feeling for Steven. Everyone else who mattered in her life didn't trust him, didn't seem to even like him.

She didn't know how she felt. She wanted him. She craved his company in a way she'd never craved anything before. He looked at her with love evident in his eyes, but where had that love come from? From that same strange and mysterious place where her attraction to him had risen? Like her, he had to know practically nothing about who and what she really was.

She called Elise, hoping she would come over and spend an evening with them, look at Steven over the dinner table, see him as a man and not as a threat. Jillian suspected that seeing him through someone else's eyes might help her confusion. Disappointing her, Elise was too busy gearing up for her new semester to come by, but—shades of Gloria—she made it all too clear she thought Jillian was making a mistake by trusting Steven so much.

"For God's sake, Jill, don't get too close to the man. Whatever you do, don't start having him in to dinner, and acting the lonely widow looking for someone to play doubles with. You'll never get rid of him. Remember, honey, you're about as vulnerable now as a human being can get."

Elise couldn't know that Steven had said nearly the same thing himself. And didn't know that Steven had kissed her, then let her go, leaving her the freedom, the space, to think for herself, to choose him . . . or not.

Elise continued, "If he so much as catches a whiff of your cooking . . . and your money . . . he'll be there till his dying day. I'll come by next week, after the freshmen find which advisor can give them the easiest classes. You call me if you need anything, hear?"

Jillian hadn't told Elise that Steven was already eating with them every night, and sharing coffee with her in the mornings after Allie left for school. And talking with her in the afternoons beneath the falling leaves of the old cottonwood. Or walking with her beside the *acequia*, the old abandoned walled waterway that ran behind her property.

How could she begin to describe to Gloria, to Elise, and most especially to her daughter, what it meant to her to see two sets of adult footprints in the snow? Where could she start to explain the feelings that Steven instilled in her? She felt herself blossoming, stretching, striving to reach the light he seemed to offer her. Not since Dave's death had she felt like a woman, and not since long before that had she felt so alive herself, so intrinsically valued, just for herself, not as an adjunct, a helpmate.

Was she playing the fool? The two people she most cared about in the world—Elise, the steadfast friend, and Allie, her own daughter—didn't seem to trust Steven. Didn't *like* him. Shouldn't their opinions matter more than her own desire to spend time in his company? Were they able to see what she, in her newborn awakening, was unwilling to view?

But if she caved in to their mistrust of Steven, her dreams' warnings about him, backed away from him, went back to how it had been in the beginning, watching him from a distance, never seeking him, would things go back to normal...whatever that was? Or would she always feel a pang of regret for not having pursued an elusive something important, a something beautiful she felt whenever in his presence?

"What's wrong, Jillian?" Steven asked now.

They were in the dining room, as had become usual for them in the middle of the day while Allie was in school. A week in his company, and already patterns had been established, habits had sprung to life. And Jillian knew from bittersweet experience that it was the little things, the small, habitual routines that created a backdrop for a relationship, that could create the strong foundations for a future.

And she knew nothing about him. Nothing.

Jillian didn't answer him right away. She'd risen from the table and gone to the French doors and was standing looking out at the well-tended courtyard. She'd known him less than a month, and yet everything in her life was different now, the tidy grounds, the midnight dreams, the longings.

She wanted to show him her studio today. She wanted to show him her paintings. In this past week, no matter how much she might have thought about doing so, she hadn't taken him down that long hallway to her north-windowed room. It was her most private place, her singular most intimate and revealing spot. She wondered if this wasn't the reason she'd avoided taking him there, but suspected the truth could be found in fear of what he might say, what he might think of her work.

And because of the dreams.

Jillian closed her eyes, feeling him step behind her, knowing he was close enough to simply lean into. As always, she felt him drawing her like a magnet. And, as she'd forced herself to do every time she felt this, she stood firm, wanting to give in, afraid to do so.

"Jillian—?"

She loved the way he never shortened her name, didn't reduce it to a cute half, or third it to a rhyme for silly. Somehow his full use of "Jillian," particularly the way he spoke it, his accented baritone voice pronouncing it with care, made her feel special, unique.

"I was thinking," she said.

He didn't comment, didn't question. He simply waited for her to continue. That, too, was refreshing. Others might have quipped—*Should we call Guinness?* A few might deride—*Don't think, Jilly. Whenever you do, some disaster happens.* But Steven only patiently waited. Somehow he conveyed the notion that he would wait for her forever.

"I really don't know anything about you," she said finally.

In essence, that said it all, even as it seemed to say nothing.

"You know everything," he said, then added, "You just don't believe what you've heard."

For some reason, his words struck her like a blow. Did she truly know anything about him? Did she, as he suggested, know *everything?* Was she trying so hard to be the good mother, the dutiful friend, that she was deliberately blinding herself to him?

It wasn't true, she realized. She didn't know everything about him. She knew next to nothing. She still didn't know, for example, how he'd healed his arm so quickly, and after that one morning had never mentioned it again, though she dreamed of that cut often. And she didn't know what peculiar spell he'd woven over her to make her accept him so readily, to ignore all warning signals.

She wasn't finished; she needed to tell him the rest. "I've been having dreams," she said slowly, still not turning around, still not allowing herself to lean back against his golden body. She hadn't yet, and couldn't now.

And still he waited.

"I dream of you at night," she said, and heard his intake of breath.

Any other man would have put his arms around her then, would have taken her words as some sort of invitation. Not Steven. Someone else might have asked her what she dreamed, but he didn't do that, either. Again, he simply waited.

"In the dreams, I hear you calling for me."

And still he said nothing.

"You call... and I come to you." Her voice sounded far away, as if she were back in the dream world. She felt that jagged dream spearpoint of fear pricking her now. "And you take me in your arms."

She could hear his quickened breathing, and her own breathing accelerated in response. Her body seemed to grow heavy, and her fingers trembled with the need to simply reach behind her, feel his solid presence. Only inches from him, close enough to feel his body heat, hear his change in breathing... She knew all she would have to do was tilt no more than a fraction and his arms would be around her, holding her, as they did in the dreams. Did she want that? Did she dare try?

"And I... kiss you, and I feel I'm drowning in the warmest, best waters I've ever been in."

And still he didn't so much as touch her.

It was as if he understood that what she was saying now was more important than anything they'd talked about before. Because it was true, all true.

But there was more, and if she didn't say it now, she never would. And if she never told him about the dreams, she would never give in to the desire to be in his arms.

"Then I open my eyes. In the dream, I look up and meet your gaze. And you aren't the same person. You look like you, but your eyes... they're yours, I mean they're still green... but they're so cold. It's like plunging into a mountain lake. And your hands feel like... *ice*... on my skin."

She shivered, remembering. She wanted him to touch her now, to erase that part of the dream, to put the nightmares to rest.

"Jillian..."

"Yes?" she asked breathlessly.

"Turn around."

"I'm afraid," she said. "I'm really, really afraid."

"I know."

"Are you?"

"More afraid than I have ever been," he said, with such intensity that she knew he spoke nothing but the raw truth. A painful truth.

She opened her eyes and turned around.

In the warm, afternoon light, Steven's eyes weren't cold at all. They were hot, fiery. Hungry. They were the deepest part of the flame, a bright green blaze.

CHAPTER SEVEN

Jillian didn't feel herself moving into his arms, she simply *melted* into him, molding herself to his golden strength. *This,* she thought, is where I wanted to be, where I need to be.

Steven's hands were far from cold, as in her dreams. They slowly poured over her like liquid steel, hot, molten and fluid.

A moan escaped her, and he caught it, took it inside himself, breathed a sigh in response. She tasted coffee and an aftertaste of herself. She smelled the outdoors, cold and smoky, and felt the rough-soft texture of his golden skin.

Her hands stole into his thick blond mane and tangled there in silken bonds. In some utterly removed part of herself, she thought she could feel each separate strand, each golden thread, and she pulled him closer still.

Right or wrong, future or not, she wanted this moment, this foray into the ultimate mystery of Steven. Here she could forget Lyle, forget the pain of Dave's death, the many sleepless nights. And she could learn Steven, know him through her fingers on his burning skin, his fiery hands on her.

As if sensing her decision, her surrender, his fevered hands intertwined in her hair, bunching it, gripping her and fiercely pulling her tighter. His hot tongue warred with hers. Fast, furious, passionate beyond all bounds. Alluring, exciting, terrifying.

This has to be wrong, she thought, but didn't understand why, couldn't think of any reasons. Nothing had ever felt so right before, so purely tempestuous, a raging river gone totally wild, utterly free.

She felt as if a doorway opened somewhere deep inside her and a hot, violent wind swept through, clearing out the past, obscuring the future, negating any and all pain, masking all guilts and recriminations. *This* was the moment, and it was singularly theirs.

His hands lowered and, no less fevered, stroked her face, her neck, molding the hollows of her collarbone to his firm and trembling fingers. The fact that he also trembled humbled her somewhat, and fanned the flames of her own passion. He wanted her *that* much.

He trailed his hot fingers lower still, to the curve beneath her shoulders, and then to her breasts.

She felt him hesitate, seemingly frozen for a moment, his hands lightly pressed against her breasts, flattening them, making them full with need, making her arch against him, aching for more.

Rays of dappled sunlight broke through the low-hanging clouds and pierced the glass at the French doors, lighting Steven's hair, throwing his golden face into sharp relief. His green eyes were half covered by heavy lids, and desire was the only thing she could read in them.

She'd never seen anyone so thoroughly in tune with his every touch, with each stroke she returned. It was as if he existed for this moment alone, as if he'd spent his entire life preparing for touching her, making love to her.

And because she felt some of this, also, knew the sharp need to live in the present, to forget the past, to let the future take care of itself, she found herself grateful for his single-minded attention. No apologies, no questions. His focus was fully and totally on the moment, wholly upon her.

No music played save that of their mingled breathy sighs, their light moans of pleasure and want. Nothing intruded on this time. It was as if the world ceased rotating on its axis, halting the clock, stemming all concerns save those of coming together.

She tilted her head back when his fingers stuttered at unfastening the top few buttons of her blouse and closed her eyes at his sharp intake of air when he spread the collar wide, exposing the rise of her breasts to his intense gaze, to his inflamed kisses.

He roughly dragged the still partially fastened blouse from her shoulders, and yanked her brassiere straps free, also, pinning her beneath his gaze, his nearly desperate onslaught. Jillian shivered as he ran firm hands down her bare arms, molding her to his palms as if memorizing her, as if trying to absorb her the way he'd appeared to take in the sun.

His fingers shaped her collarbone, the hollows above and below it, as if he were a blinded man discovering a wholly new sensation. Like a sculptor, he pressed his palms to the rise of her breasts; then, gently, questingly, he lightly traced the cups of the brassiere, held in place now only by the fullness of her aching breasts.

She shivered a little at the teasing, tickling touch, breathing so rapidly, so shallowly, she felt dizzy. Her legs nearly buckled as he hooked a finger inside each cup and gave a swift, sure tug to free her breasts from their final barrier. A moan escaped her.

His strong hands immediately cupped her breasts, holding her erect, keeping her from falling, testing their weight, kneading them with a deliberate, sure touch. He bent to snare first one hardened nipple, then the other in his mouth. His hot tongue encircled the sensitive areolas and flicked at the nipples. His sharp teeth lightly grazed the turgid tips, making her cry out, not from pain, but from the shock waves rippling through her in reaction.

He kneaded her breasts with deeper passion, molding her, shaping her to his touch. Again she had the notion he was memorizing the feel of her.

His golden hair brushed against her shoulders, her chin, and she again sank her hands into that mane and held him tightly to her, kissing him, arching to meet him, feeling certain she could die at this moment and die happy.

"Jillian..." he murmured, making her name a rough benediction.

"I want you so," she whispered back. And knew it was the deepest of truths. Whatever Elise, or even Allie, might think of Steven, however much they might dislike him, this was right for Jillian. Only for Jillian.

He straightened then, pushing her away from him roughly, and holding her at arm's length, pulling at the air like a man going down for the third time. His entire body shook with the force of his desire. She could feel the shaking echoing inside herself. His fingers dug into her naked shoulders, and his eyes blazed green fire at her.

She shivered and murmured his name.

He was asking her something, and all she could think was that he was nothing like her nightmares, nothing at all like the cold, confusing dreams.

"I'm not what you think me, Jillian," he said. His voice was harsh with all he was holding inside, and his hands were fierce with unassuaged need.

"None of us are," she whispered. "You're here. I'm here. Isn't that enough for now?"

His eyes didn't so much as waver from hers. His fingers tightened, though she scarcely felt them.

"I've lived ten thousand years of hell," he ground out.

Jillian placed her hands on either side of his face, feeling the sharpness of his granitelike cheeks, the harshness of his features.

"I don't care about the past," she said. "Or the future. Just love me, Steven. Today. Now."

Even knowing she was misunderstanding him, not hearing the truth of his words, Steven could no more have denied her request than he could walk away from the final battle in one week's time. It was unfair of him, and wrong...damnably wrong...but he couldn't let her go and walk away now. Not after having tasted her kisses, touched her breasts, felt her hands running through his hair. And not after having her ask for his love, ask for his touch. Not after that. He was human enough to know that no man could have turned away now.

His entire body resonated with her essence. He felt her caresses to his very soul and his veins seemed to be pumping champagne instead of blood, effervescent and heady, making him drunk with need of her. And he felt a strength like none he'd ever encountered, a deep, reverberating power, an all-encompassing need, building in him, growing, demanding.

As he felt his wound, as he felt the hell in which he lived, he felt her with an intensity that transcended human awarenesses. Every pore of his body opened to her, all of him reached for her. Ached for her. And still he held her at shuddering arm's length.

"Jillian...I have to tell you the truth about me," he said.

"I don't care," she whispered, then added in an agonized and broken voice, "Please..." A single word that almost brought him to his knees.

He'd tried, he thought weakly, desperately. God knew, he'd tried. But only a saint could have walked away from her now. And he, of all people, knew he was no saint.

He swept her into his arms, folding her to him, holding her tight, tighter still. He murmured her name over and over, kissing her, thrumming to the sensation of her kissing him. He wished he could draw her inside himself to hold her safe there forever. And he wanted to bury himself in her and lose himself in her beauty, her warmth, her passion for life.

He bent slightly and, with a swift flex, lifted her into his arms. He held her against his chest, nuzzling her bared shoulders, savoring her weight, closing his eyes against the sensuous feel of her hair trailing down his arm.

He carried her through the kitchen and down the hallway to her room. Though he'd never been there before, he'd gazed at its exterior a thousand times in the past three weeks, had sent his thoughts questing there nearly every night, had intruded on her during her sleep.

Now the room was cool and curtain-darkened. He hesitated before lowering her to the bed. He thought of Beleale—Lyle to innocent Jillian—and he knew, with utter certainty, the evil in that creature would run and hide from this soon-to-be-union. For the very reason that it would be union. And *union* represented light and caring and everything Beleale most feared and hated. No, Beleale would not disturb them. Not here. Not now.

Steven was reluctant to so much as let her go for an instant, afraid the strong ripples of emotion would ebb at the instant of separation, as the burning of wounds would ebb too swiftly, the closeness of a kiss would fade within seconds.

Not with Jillian, he vowed. It couldn't happen with her, not this time. But he wouldn't take the chance.

He lowered her to the bed, and himself with her, stretching out beside her, keeping his hands upon her trembling body, his lips upon hers.

He felt her fingers against the buttons of his shirt and had to bite back a groan of pure anticipation. She peeled back the soft material of his shirt and slipped her hand inside, her knuckles brushing the mat of golden hair on his chest, her fingers both cool and hot to the touch, inciting a riot of sensation throughout his body.

All his years on earth coalesced and focused for him, and he knew that he would spend every second of that hellish time over again if they led to this one moment with Jillian. Ten thousand years of hell, for one moment of heaven.

His heart pounded with the intensity of his feelings for her, his want of her, and his mind and body grappled with the need to make this time seem to last forever.

One way or another, he would be gone in a week, having destroyed her in the process. This realization sent flash fires of horror ripping through him, and he pulled her roughly to his chest, cradled her there, as if he could deny the future, protect her from her own destiny.

"Oh, Jillian..." he murmured, as much from agony as from desire.

This moment had to put paid to all debts, all sorrows, all empty futures. By some miraculous stroke of luck, the Fates had granted them both this brief time together, and he knew he had to make this union with Jillian a heaven for them both, a glorious universe of human perfection.

He groaned aloud as her lips found one of his small, hardened nipples and she grazed it lightly with her teeth. This was what it meant to be human, he thought. Loving her, feeling her, wanting her against all odds, knowing the ultimate costs. Knowing that being with her was heaven on earth, because all would be lost forever in that week-hence tomorrow.

He refused to think about that dark day, about the terrible future lying in wait for them, the worst of all possible traps. He would think only of this moment, this time. This lovely, lovely woman.

He slid to his side and propped himself on his elbow while slowly stroking her with his free hand. He ached to drown in her, but wasn't about to do so at the expense of missing a single nuance of her taste, her scent, her touch.

She moaned and rolled onto her back, baring herself to him, allowing him access to her remaining blouse buttons and the fastening of her loose trousers. As if reading his mind, as if by some miracle she knew he needed to be in constant connection with her to maintain the heightened intensity, she rested her fingers lightly on the back of his hand as he carefully undid the final few buttons of her blouse and unhooked her pants.

He swept the blouse and brassiere free of her arms and pushed her free of the restrictive trousers and underthings. Now she lay bare to his avid gaze, open to his touch, her body dewy and warm, inviting and trembling.

Her eyes were wide now, no longer hooded, and she looked at him somewhat shyly, he thought, as if uncertain again, afraid.

His entire being raged against the unfairness of having spent thousands of years on this earthly plane without Jillian, of having encountered her only now, just days before he would lose her forever. She embodied the spirit of what he'd fought generations to preserve, to protect. It was unfair to take her from the world in order to save it.

It was unfair to lose her now.

He felt the rage boiling in him, demanding action, needing release. Again, as if sensing what was going on inside him, Jillian lightly traced his lips, defusing the terrible anguish roiling in his heart, in his soul.

He pressed his lips to her finger, acknowledging her attempt to silence his dark thoughts.

I love you, Jillian, he thought, but didn't say it aloud. The murderer might make love to the victim, but only a fiend would also bind her with words, give her the false promise of a future.

He lowered his lips to hers and kissed her with a hot and urgent need to still his rage, as if when he kissed her, her returning caresses would render him senseless, mindless. He kissed her until he lost himself in the kisses, finding again that molten purity of need, that liquid heat of raw desire.

Her hands gripped his shoulders fiercely, as urgently as his hands strafed her body, and she pulled him down to her in swift, compelling want and held him locked in her embrace.

Jillian struggled against the seesaw questions of right and wrong, wanting to ignore everything but Steven's fevered touch, the heat of his tongue, the passion in his hands. Who was he? Why did she have the sense that he was seeking some absolution from her, that in an odd way he was asking her forgiveness before even having done some misdeed?

Or was she projecting, and it was really her who sought compassion, forgiveness for her abject loneliness, her doubts, her fears of Lyle, of Steven, of Allie's need, Elise's opinions, and the crippling weight of life without Dave?

She knew that with Steven's hands upon her, his lips pressed to her throat, a golden vampire with the gentlest of deaths in mind, she shouldn't be thinking of Dave. But she also knew that in a very real sense Steven was, in some odd way, giving Dave back to her, pushing the horrible details of the past year into some recessed place and allowing the best knowledge of Dave, the best part of herself, to take wing again.

Now she could call on the loving side of her nature, the forgiving side, the part of her that could forgive Dave for dying and herself for resenting him for going away. He was giving her back that part of her that could give her-

self wholly and readily to this unusual man, this mysterious, beautiful stranger.

Wrong? Quite the reverse. His was the greatest of gifts,
the freedom to live again, to give, to love. She wanted to
be able to tell Steven some of this, and perhaps would
some day, one day in the far-flung and nebulous future,
but now... She stretched beneath him, arching upward
from the bed to meet his roaming hands, lifting her lips
to his, pulling him with her, demanding that he match her
stroke for stroke, kiss for kiss, love for love.

Steven felt her coming alive to his touch, to some inner decision she'd made, and wished for a moment that
they had never begun this, had never succumbed to the
passion that flared so seemingly effortlessly between
them. He felt the most base and unfair of creatures, loving her now, knowing what she couldn't possibly even
guess of her dark future.

But everything in him cried out for her, throbbed for
her, demanded that he give her every single drop of his
being. And this demand was made, even knowing she
would, one day very soon, hate him, when the portals
opened and the battle raged again. The final battle. The
end of the long, horrible war.

He shifted and trailed his tongue down her torso,
needing to escape her hooded gaze, the eyes no longer
wary now, no longer shy. He was too afraid of what she
would read in his eyes, was scared she would read the future, would know that he did this, loving her, all the while
knowing he would be using her all too soon.

And then, as his tongue tasted the slightly salty tang of
her delicate skin, felt the satin velvet of her inner thighs,
he forgot everything, everything but her. And him.

The past became cloudy, insignificant, the future was
forgotten. Her taste, her scent, her silken caresses, became the entire universe.

He parted her legs, touching her, watching her reaction, staring in awe at her goddesslike body, her lush warmth. He felt nothing but the purest of desires, the most intense of wants. I would give you everything, he thought.

Everything.

She moaned softly as he lightly brushed the crisp hair at her apex, and her entire body seemed to shiver as he trailed his fingers down, dipping into her very core. He'd wasted years of bitterness over his neither-one-nor-the-other state, not wholly human, not what he had once been. Now, seeing Jillian respond to his touch, seeing her body arch, her hands grasping at the comforter, hearing her breath drawn in between her teeth, he knew, for the first time, that he hadn't forsaken one for the other. He was ultimately both. And Jillian's pleasure was his reward.

Lucretius said it best, he thought as he lowered his lips to finally taste her. "When immortal death has taken mortal life." Love for Jillian transported him from his immortal hell to that fragile sense of mortal heaven.

She bucked beneath his questing tongue, then seemed to freeze in midair, her entire body focused on his caress, on his touch. This sudden stillness of hers lent him power, awe, and the deepest, most profound sense of at last doing one perfect thing in this world.

He slipped his fingers into her warmth, sliding them to the rhythm of his tongue and the rocking of his body. She moaned his name and began to rock with him, opening to him, relaxing to his touch, even as her body stiffened, seeking more. He felt her fingers tangle in his hair, pulling him, pushing him away, but didn't—couldn't—stop.

He needed to feel her peak, crest that pinnacle of human bliss, as much as he'd ever needed anything in his entire existence, on this plane or any other. At that moment, he would know trust, true trust, and would know some measure of utter human triumph. *He,* Steven the man, would have done this for her. *He* would have taken her there.

She cried out his name, and her legs pressed fiercely against his shoulders. He slipped his other hand beneath her, raised her slightly, caressing her rounded fullness, kneading her with the same rhythm he applied elsewhere. Her skin was damp and dewy, her body hot and fluid. He had never wanted anything so much as to make her insane with his touch, delirious with his kisses.

She released a soft, mewling sound and arched her body sharply, suddenly. She seemed to stop breathing altogether, and she pressed against him, stilled, suspended on the edge of that precipice known only to lovers.

"Steven!" she cried, and her voice tangled on a choked sob. And still he wouldn't stop. Then he felt the first wave of spasms pass through her, tightening, spiraling, pulling at his fingers, drawing him even deeper inside her.

She called his name again, and thrashed beneath him, caught in that other universe, that place that has no name beyond that of culmination.

Jillian's entire being shook with the intensity of her release, and she clung to Steven as the only anchor in a world that had suddenly exploded into a million jagged bits. Instead of stopping immediately, he stilled his fingers, slowed his tongue to the gentlest, softest, of laving strokes, easing her back, bringing her home with paramount generosity.

She felt tears gather in her eyes and let them slide onto her temples, into her damp hair, unconcerned over them, for they weren't tears of sorrow, or even of joy. They were the cleansing tears that wash away loneliness, erase too many days and nights of emptiness. They were tears of life. This, too, he'd given her.

"Steven..." she said softly, her body having now been gentled back to reality.

He lifted his head, his eyes glazed with his own want, the glittering green turned inward, still caught in her climax, her passion.

"Please come inside me," she said, spreading her arms wide, inviting him, begging him.

Agonizingly slowly, his throbbing manhood beating a drumsong against her as he rose, he crawled up the length of her until he held himself over her, propped on locked arms, green eyes gazing down at her, golden body blotting out the ceiling, the room.

"I don't carry any viruses," he said harshly, as if demanding she understand the truth about him.

Strangely, on some dim level, she thought she did. This was the Steven of her dreams...one of them. And this was the moment she'd craved.

"It doesn't matter," she said.

"With anyone else, it would," he said, but he looked sad.

"I'm not with anyone else," she answered softly, surely. She looked deep into his eyes, letting him see the truth of her words as he'd wanted her to see his.

He whispered her name in supplication, in need, and she raised herself to meet him, wrapping her arms around his shoulders, her legs around his buttocks, ending all argument by taking him swiftly and deeply inside her.

"Ahh! *Jillian!*" he cried as he entered, sounding in the most severe pain, his body shaking as they met, apex to apex.

But despite his cry, despite the harsh frown on his face, the lips pulled back against his teeth, Jillian knew he wasn't in pain, he was drowning in pure ecstasy. She rocked against him and felt his shuddering response.

He murmured words she could barely hear, didn't bother trying to understand. Some were in English, others not. All spoke of need, want, even love. And all were delivered in harsh, raw gasps, muttered with every deepening thrust.

She lowered her hands to his buttocks, pulling him even more deeply to her, needing the union, craving this melding of two separate bodies into one.

She pressed against his locked arms and took his weight gratefully, desperate for that evidence of this reality, feeling that this pressure against her lent a solidity to their union, a concreteness. A rightness.

He thrust his arms beneath her, raising her shoulders, kissing her deeply, thrusting faster now. Deeper. With hard, sure strokes, he pulled back, slid home, parted, returned, rocked and stilled.

Jillian thought nothing in the world could take her beyond that edge a second time, but she was wrong. With every thrust, he pushed her a notch closer, calling her name, pulling her with him, exhorting her, challenging her, rocking her. He enticed, teased, tormented. He shook, made an earthquake of the bed, made her body an instrument for his fine playing.

She stayed with him, riding the dragon, caught in the tempest of his passion, storm-tossed and more vibrant than at any point in her life. Never had she tapped such passion, felt such power and raw intensity of emotion.

Faster, harder, and calling her name over and over, he moved, blistering her with his heat, scorching her with his white-hot passion. Fevered, he met her in ardent, scalding need. Sure, swift, demanding. Faster and faster. Harder and harder. Passion growing and growing, deeper and deeper, until he suddenly and sharply stilled, muscles rippling, his eyes clenched shut, his jaw rigid, his face a rictus of agony.

And she felt him around her, fiercely gripping her, and felt him inside her, throbbing, pouring himself into her in hard, fierce and glorious release. And as he groaned aloud, his chest heaving against her, she plummeted with him, taking him deeper inside, holding him there, lost in that spiraling alternate universe, and yet wholly with him, as well.

In that other plane, they seemed to spiral together, then drift apart, lost in that universe of primal need. Slowly, slowly, he relaxed against her, easing his tense body more readily and gently onto hers.

Again tears formed in her eyes, but these were different, filled with relief and joy. She was whole again, and made fully female by his ardency, by his release. She ran her hands along his back, soothing him, bringing him home as he'd brought her back earlier.

He shuddered again, convulsively, and she murmured his name against his hair, soothing him, comforting him, making her lips an anodyne against separation, an antidote against that time when doubts and questions about him would return to haunt her.

He moaned, and she shushed him, stroking his face with fingers that no longer trembled, that couldn't shake now. "It's okay," she said, as though he'd been hurt.

It was the right thing to say, the right way to act, for she felt him relax still further, and could tell by the shift of his body that he'd come back. He raised slightly, allowing her to breath again, and looked down at her with an inscrutable expression.

She remembered a time, some days earlier, when she'd felt he was trying to memorize the feel of her hair, the touch of her skin. She had the feeling again now. He was recording her, memorizing her. Trying to take her inside himself somehow. So that he could keep her with him forever.

"It's okay," she said again, not quite knowing why she felt she had to say something.

He shook his head a little, his blond hair tickling her shoulders.

She tried smiling. "All right, then, it's not okay."

"Jillian," he said heavily.

"I'm right here," she answered, lightly stroking his face.

"As much as it is humanly possible for me to do so, Jillian," he said roughly, with deadly seriousness, "I love you."

Jillian's breath snagged in her throat. No, she wanted to cry out. Don't say this. Not now. Not yet.

Before she could speak, he added, "And hearing that, you will never know how thoroughly I've just wronged you."

CHAPTER EIGHT

"You haven't 'wronged' me, Steven," Jillian said unsteadily, still reeling from his words about loving her. *It couldn't be; why did it feel so right?*

"Quite the reverse, in fact," she added when he didn't say anything further.

"You don't know," he said, and would have pulled away from her, separating them.

She held him in place against her, unwilling now, more than ever, to let him slip away from her. "Don't," she said. It was far more than a plea, it was a primal need to have him stay with her.

He looked at her for a long moment, and then, as if he understood her, he stopped trying to pull away, even if he didn't relax.

"I told you I'd spent ten thousand years in hell," he said. He shifted enough to lightly stroke her hair from her forehead. "I was telling the absolute truth."

Jillian held her breath, wondering what, exactly, he was trying to tell her. It was obviously important, moved him deeply, but she couldn't understand, wasn't even sure she wanted to hear any of his words.

"I've spent quite a bit of time in hell too," she said.

"No, Jillian. I meant it literally."

She didn't know what to say to that, so she said nothing.

"It will all be over soon," he said.

"What will?"

He ran his fingers through her hair, trailed the tips down the curve of her cheeks. His eyes, usually so filled with fire and glittering brightness, now seemed shadowed, tinged with a sorrow deeper than even she could fathom.

"I would trade every year I've lived, every good thing I've ever done, for this time with you," he said.

Jillian tried to smile. "Even I don't charge that high a price," she said. As an attempt at humor, she could see it fell very wide of the mark.

"I need more time," he said. And something in his tone sparked Jillian's earlier sense of foreboding that some darkness was coming soon, something that would destroy her life.

"I'm not in any hurry," she said, unable to think of anything else, but wanting to ease the sadness in his eyes, the tension in his shoulders.

"Ah, Jillian . . ." he said, lowering his lips to hers, as if tasting her for the last time.

She met his gentle farewell kiss with a need to erase that thought, that fear. She kissed him fiercely, deeply, clinging to him with determined promise.

To her surprise, she felt him growing within her, passion rising to meet her fiery demand. He ground out her name, rolling her over, atop him now, matching her fierceness now, strafing her naked body with bold, strong hands.

"I can't let you go," he growled, as if angry with her, or as if angry with something she didn't understand.

"I don't want you to," she murmured, riding him, digging her fingers into his shoulders, rocking her hips sharply against him, craving his renewed passion, shocked and gratified by her own.

"It's not fair," he muttered, but she didn't think he was talking to her, though on some level it had everything to do with being with her.

His hands molded her breasts, her narrow waist, and dug into her buttocks, holding her closer, thrusting deeper, growing stronger, harder, rocking faster.

"To know you now," he muttered. "To know... this...*now*. Jillian, I feel like I'm dying."

So did she, dying of such exquisite beauty, such incredible passion, that she never wanted it to end. Never.

"I didn't know," he said. "I never knew it could be...like this."

With each word, as if punctuating his awareness, he thrust even more deeply into her, raising them both from the bed, arching her into the air, making her fly with his desire, making her soar with his need, with her own.

He sat up abruptly, holding her to him, one hand on her buttocks, the other behind her head, kissing her deeply, staying with her, as if melding with her, joining her, permanently and desperately so.

She felt she couldn't breathe, couldn't think. She clung to him as he sent her spinning into a universe of lights too bright to look at, sensations too intense to comprehend.

"Don't leave me," she cried, not even knowing exactly what she meant by the words.

"I promise you..." he said, "I will...be with you until the very end. The very end, Jillian. That...if nothing else...is the absolute...truth."

And as if his promise, the words that said everything, triggered a primal freedom inside her, Jillian felt herself flung over that precipice once again, losing him out there in that soaring beauty.

She gloried in the sensation, even as she sought to find him again. She couldn't think what he meant, didn't understand what he was telling her, wanted to believe, was afraid to. She only knew that whatever sprang between them, chemistry, electricity, beauty, was something so rare, so incredibly special, that she couldn't turn away from it.

He beckoned to her like a lighthouse on a storm-tossed shore, calling her safely home, bringing her back to port. To life.

Steven cried out her name and shook with the force of his need for her, filling her yet again with his longing, rocking her with the force of his desperation.

He'd told her nothing but the truth. He'd never known what loving could really be, hadn't understood it at all until now. What she gave him was far beyond anything he'd ever imagined, ever dreamed of.

But even as he lost himself in the perfection of loving her, he knew he hadn't told her everything. He'd promised to be with her till the very end.

And that end was less than a week away.

He pulled her to his chest, roughly, desperately, wanting to deny the future, wanting to run away with her, hide her, somehow, by some miracle, keep her safe. Let her live.

He wasn't aware of time passing, had no idea how long he held her, how long she lay quiescent in his arms, but knew when he felt her finally stir that their precious, stolen time together was at an end.

He wanted to buy time, to steal it from one end of his too-long life and give it to her now. He cursed himself for not coming into her life sooner, for not taking every moment of every day that he possibly could have.

He had guessed, but he hadn't known. Couldn't have known what it would be like to be with Jillian.

He couldn't have known what love really felt like. He felt something inside him shift forever, changing him, altering him for all time. He would never again be the same. He would never again think of daylight without equating it with Jillian, think of music without hearing her name, think of living without knowing her taste, her touch... her loving.

And in a week that would all be over, all be gone.

And when he pulled away from, was no longer touching her, he would forget this joy, forget the intensity, forget what it was like.

No, he thought fiercely, stroking her still and velvet-soft body, he wouldn't forget. He would never, ever forget, not if he lived forever. Jillian was a part of him now. As real as the body he had now, as real as his former essence. As real and paramount as the battle soon to come.

"Allie will be home soon," she said, and he knew she was telling him that they had to move, had to part and rise, had to separate.

He ached to buy a little more time, wanting to say a hundred different things, knowing that when she learned the whole truth, when she understood, she would, in all likelihood, regret this afternoon.

But he needed more than seconds clicking on the clock to give him enough time. He needed a lifetime, a span of years, a host of nights, mornings and hours spent like these. He needed Jillian. She was the secret to humanity, the secret to life.

How could he let her die now?

Jillian ached for more time. She needed to remain in his arms, and at the same time needed space from him, needed enough time to recover her scattered wits before trying to understand his cryptic words, the intensity of his passion, of the passion he brought out in her.

Steven didn't move for a moment, for which she was profoundly grateful, but then, as if reading her renewed uncertainty, her fear of Allie arriving home and finding them together in her bedroom, he sighed heavily and lightly patted her shoulder.

Jillian felt tears sting her eyes at his touch. It was an oddly familiar and intimate caress, as if they'd been coming together like this for years and years. It signaled closure and safety, a gentle continuity. *Future* times.

She released her hold on him, and he rolled them both to the bed, holding her still, then, with another sigh, releasing her and shifting onto his back. He hesitated there, neither restfully nor with any degree of certainty.

"Steven," she whispered.

He uttered that uniquely male grunt that seems to mean anything from acceptance to denial, a deeply hummed question mark.

She needed to tell him how very, very special this time with him had been. She needed to say something that would make him understand that he'd taken her beyond the stars, beyond the known planets. Unfortunately, there weren't any words to convey such a tremendous journey of body and soul. Of heart.

She took a deep breath and said, "I want you to know this wasn't casual with me."

Jillian was sure she didn't have to say it; he'd surely guessed as much the moment he touched her, had to have discovered it when she arched against him, trembling, aching, dying for his caress. But she instinctively felt that something as incredible, as confusing, as her time with him needed words to underscore the feelings, to define them in some small way.

She ached to simply turn her head, to catch some glimpse of what he was thinking by looking at his chiseled profile.

"I know," he said heavily, as if this knowledge rested on him like some great weight. He sighed again, then said, as if confessing some crime, "It was anything but casual for me, as well."

She wasn't sure what she'd expected from his response, but she knew it wasn't this incredible, almost liquid relief.

"I know," she said, also.

Until he said the words, she hadn't realized that it wasn't merely important to her that he felt something during their time together...his feeling something special had been paramount.

She had understood that she hadn't merely been making love to him, she'd been reaching out for life, reaching out to another human being again. She'd lowered her guard enough to let another human being in. It was that important.

Making love to Steven had been everything. Was everything.

She lay next to him, confused, uncertain, fulfilled, and wishing she could figure out which confused her more, not knowing how she felt about Steven, the man with whom she'd shared such a gloriously intimate exchange, or not knowing how she felt about tomorrow, when debts were rendered, when she had to face how she might feel about a stranger named Steven.

"I wish..." he began, then trailed off.

"Yes?" Jillian wondered if her voice was hopeful.

"I wish I had known love could be this way," he said. Reminding her of his touch, his voice was firm and delicate at the same time. Intangible.

Jillian wished she could smile, wanted to believe that he meant the words in the most positive light. But something about the way he'd said them set an edge of sorrow on their sharing, made her feel a barrier being raised between them.

"You make it sound as if it's too late," she said, finally, not certain if she was asking for affirmation or denial.

He sighed again, and the breathy sound made her feel sad, abandoned already.

"Too late? Yes," he said. "For centuries, philosophers have pondered the notion of being free, of a man's—or a woman's—freedom."

Jillian frowned, trying to follow this odd digression. Instead of answering, she slid her hand to lightly stroke his flank, felt him flinch, as if her touch burned him. Then he moved closer, as if having decided he needing searing.

"Do you believe a man is free to do either good or evil?"

"Yes," she said simply. "Though I don't believe in evil per se."

"You should, Jillian. It exists. It truly and sadly exists. You've seen it. You've felt it. You'll know it again soon."

She rolled to her side and rested her hand upon his chest. She reveled in the way he held his breath as she shifted, and the sudden rise of his chest as he relaxed into her touch. In time, she knew, their passion might be superseded by familiarity, but now, at this moment, desire still knew the gasping, questing rush of ardor that every touch, every look, created.

She waited until she felt the steady rise and fall of his breathing. She gazed at the rigid jawline, the green eyes staring straight up at the ceiling. She had the feeling that while he was every inch in tune with her, he was at the same time miles and miles away.

"You seem so certain," she said, "that evil exists."

"I've seen it too many times," he answered. He sounded trapped between anger and sorrow.

"What are you trying to tell me, Steven?" she asked then, for instinctively she knew it was something important. And with equal certainty, she was more than a little bit afraid she didn't want to hear his answer.

His hand rose to cover hers, holding it tightly against the mat of golden hair on his chest. "If you had a job to do, a duty, something you'd sworn to accomplish... and then you met someone who would be hurt by your doing this job, this duty...would you turn away from that task?"

Jillian thought for a moment, trying to understand this unusual man who drew her so. "It would depend on what the task was, why I had sworn to do it, who the someone to be hurt was, and what that hurt would entail."

She saw Steven's lips curve in a slight smile, but not one of amusement.

"Good response," he said softly. "But no answer."

"Was this a test of some kind?" she asked.

"No. The question was real enough."

"What about you?" she asked. "If I asked the same question, what would you answer?"

"I don't know," he said. Surprising her, he elaborated: "That's the whole trouble. I just don't know. And even if I could walk away from the job, abandon the duty, I don't know if that would solve anything."

"Steven, I'm not following you."

"No," he said, half angering her with his easy acceptance of her lack of understanding.

Jillian wondered what pulled her to him so. He was so terribly complicated, so caught up by moods, by a darkness in him that she didn't, couldn't, fathom. He held a passion inside him, *with her,* that she couldn't seem to grasp.

Dave had been passionate at his piano, but away from it, even with her, he'd been refreshingly open, a uniformly happy soul. And she had loved Dave with all her heart, even if she'd never managed to bridge the gap that separated them, even if she had never been the one woman in his life, the one passion that he craved.

With Steven, she had the instinctive surety that he would give her that intensity of feeling, would love her to the exclusion of all others, and love her with an unmatched, undying depth of passion.

All she'd ever wanted was to love and be loved. So why was she drawn to this unusual man, with his moods, his quotations, his otherworldliness, his dark side? Why did he pull her so? That intensity of emotion? That almost desperate sincerity of feeling?

She thought about the moments locked in his arms, the catapulting over that precipice of passion, the feeling that all desire in her soul, her body, her heart had culminated in one exquisite moment, and found she didn't care what pulled her, she just knew that she had to be with him. To try. To love.

Without rhyme or reason.

As if reading her mind, he said, "It doesn't matter, Jillian," he said. "What we have here is a question that no one can answer. A riddle that has no solution."

"Every problem has some solution," she said. And meant it. "Maybe we don't see the solution immediately, and it could be that the solution might take years to discover, but it's there, part of the pattern of the universe, part of the intricate puzzle that awaits us all."

"You are such a rare and beautiful woman," Steven said. He smiled a little, but again it wasn't a smile of amusement, and his tone was sad as he continued. "I wish I could believe what you say about solutions."

Jillian didn't feel she'd made a mistake in being with him—far from it. But something in his words, in the way he spoke now, made her feel horribly confused, as though the loving of him brought out this dark side of him, this self-questing need in him.

She hadn't known him long enough to know if these dives into moodiness were something that was common to him. And if they were, she wasn't certain how she would feel about it. She was prone to high and low edges herself. Dave had once said she held a corner on that particular market.

How could two introspective, moody people hope to weather the bad times, face the good ones? Didn't at least one of them have to be set on a course with an even keel?

"Autumn will be here soon," he said, and the way he said it made Jillian feel a frisson of cold prick along her spine. "The equinox is next week. Everything will change then. Once and for all."

Hadn't Allie asked her about the equinox only the week before? Hadn't Lyle said something about inviting friends in?

His words—and Allie's and Lyle's—made the innocuous event sound ominous, fateful. And somehow he made her feel that by speaking the words aloud, he was bringing them both closer to the edge of some impending disaster. And for a moment she clearly felt as though her time with him, time altogether, were somehow marked, targeted for doom. She shivered in that dark foreboding yet again.

As if he felt it, too, Steven sat up swiftly and swung his legs from the bed. He paused there, his broad golden back to her. She could see the room now, could see a rainbow prism dancing angrily along the edge of the window, bouncing from the wall to the curtain and back again.

For a moment, she tensed, unwillingly drawn to that rainbow, imagining the impossible, resenting its intrusion on her privacy. Then the curtains stilled, the breeze dissipated, and the rainbow disappeared.

At another sigh from Steven, she turned her gaze to his golden back. She almost gasped aloud at the sight of the multitude of paper-thin scars webbing his broad shoulders, his tapered back. She hadn't noticed them the evening he cut himself, and they were so finely etched she hadn't felt them while loving him.

Automatically her eyes dropped to what should have been his injured arm, but wasn't. A thread-width white scar was the only mark on his left forearm. No wound, no scab, no evidence that he'd been cut anytime in the past ten years, and certainly not just a few days earlier.

She reached out her hand to touch him, then hesitated just before laying a finger against one of the tiny white scars. *Ten thousand years of hell,* he'd said. Were these scars testimony to a portion of his metaphor?

She pulled her hand back and closed her fingers against her palm. Her heart beat irregularly, her body felt a coldness stealing into the room, separating them.

Steven cleared his throat, and when he spoke, his voice was full, heavy. "I've spent years trying to discover what it is to be a man," he said.

He stopped and gestured in a large, sweeping circle with his hand, though Jillian couldn't begin to guess at the meaning of his words, the nuances of his gesture. She didn't prompt him, even when several long moments had passed. She took a cue from the way he patiently waited for her to speak, and waited. She knew that to explore one's basic humanity was deep discovery indeed. And to share the knowledge found was even more profound.

"You make me feel I almost understand it now," he said softly. Reverently. "As if I could reach out and grasp the understanding in my hand."

Jillian had no idea what to say to this, how to respond. She also felt changed. He'd granted her life again, the taste of loving, and the sweet lassitude of joining. In some kind of miracle, he'd given her back her passion. She felt reborn, restructured, offered the glimpse of a second chance.

"I don't understand," she said, finally. "But you make it seem the greatest compliment."

He pushed to his feet, unabashedly naked, not trying to cover any part of his glorious body. He turned then and looked down at her. His eyes met hers with uncanny precision.

"I had to tell you how I felt now, Jillian. I may not have another opportunity, and I may not even be able to feel it later."

His words should have hurt, and on some level might even have caused sharp pain. But somehow, seeing the shadows in his eyes, the pain etched on his features, she knew he was only trying to speak the deepest of truths. The words weren't intended badly, only honestly.

When she might have spoken, he waved his hand and frowned heavily. "I know you don't understand. That doesn't matter. I'm not asking anything of you now."

Jillian frowned. He was right, she didn't understand.

His green gaze burned down at her, branding her, holding her impaled. She couldn't have moved if her life depended upon it. "I told you I love you, Jillian Stewart. I meant it with every part of me. I think I've probably loved you for years."

Jillian felt her breath catch in her throat again. She suddenly longed for a sheet, a towel, anything to hide behind. This disclosure came too soon, too suddenly. He couldn't love her; he didn't know her any more than she knew him. And yet a very real part of her soared in swift and sharp joy.

He *loved* her.

Despite the dryness of her lips, she managed to say his name. "Steven—"

He interrupted her with a chopping motion of his hand. "You don't have to say anything, Jillian. You don't know what I'll be asking of you. You don't understand what I am, what I need. I barely understand it now myself. I thought I did. I even thought I'd come to terms with it. But now, I don't know. I just don't know."

Before she could say anything else, he scooped his clothing into his hands. He turned to leave her bedroom and stopped in the doorway to turn one last time.

"The worst thing to realize is that there are rules to everything, Jillian," he said. Then he added as he left the room, more to himself, she thought, than to her, "Not even angels can be allowed to break those rules. Not even for the best of causes, the best of reasons. Not even then."

CHAPTER NINE

Jillian sat in the middle of the bed she used to share with Dave, the bed that now seemed transformed every bit as much as she felt changed herself. She ran a hand along the comforter, feeling the warmth in the valley Steven had left behind, feeling a chill where he hadn't lain.

Steven couldn't love her. He couldn't.

But somehow she knew he did.

And this knowledge only confused her, because she was more than half-afraid that locked in his arms, feeling his heart beating against her chest, feeling his breath upon hers, she herself had been all too close to falling over the precipice of desire into the deep and very dark abyss of love.

She told herself that she understood nothing of his words, save those relating to loving her, and even those sounded ominous, dangerous. Warnings of sorts. But on some level, a level she usually experienced only in her artwork, she thought she did understand, that some of what he said made perfect sense. Terrible sense.

What on earth was she supposed to do now?

Steven stood in the waning sunlight, his palms outstretched, his head back, trying unsuccessfully to feel warmth from the faint ultraviolet rays. He could still feel them, but they seemed muted, insubstantial.

Jillian had marked him, and he couldn't forget the delicacy of her touch, the wantonness of her loving. He hadn't touched her for an hour or more, and yet she lingered in his memory, in his heart. She occupied all his thoughts, his longings.

He had no choice but to follow the dictates of war, the rules set down long before humankind had even begun scratching records for history. His course was set. He had no choice.

But he hadn't known Jillian then, in that nebulous place where time had no meaning, where a linear sequencing of days meant less than nothing. He hadn't known what pain he would feel at the thought of losing her now.

Because now he knew her, had tasted her, had drowned in her kisses, and risen again at her sigh. He wasn't the same anymore. Because of her.

And because he wasn't the same, he wanted the war to be different, also. Because he felt as if the universe had shifted on its intergalactic nexus, he wanted all the rules to bend, as well. He wanted to be free of the constraints that had bound him for so long, bonds he'd taken willingly all that time ago but hadn't known would cut so deeply.

Jillian carried the portals, had already created most of them. But, unlike him, she hadn't asked for this fate, hadn't demanded to be the one who would lay down her life for a war she didn't even know about. He had. He was duty bound, destiny bound.

He should never have touched her, let alone buried himself in her. It was inevitable that after having done so, he would seek a way out, a loophole in those cosmic rules, a way to allow Jillian to live.

Because having loved her now, he didn't know how he could stand by and watch her die, give her that final moment and assist her as she left him forever.

Jillian spent the remainder of the day in a daze, replaying the afternoon over and over, as if by mentally reviewing every moment she would understand what had transpired between them, understand any of what Steven had tried telling her.

Her heart seemed to wrench painfully each time she remembered how his touch had burned her, scalded her every pore. And how perfectly they had been matched, how poignantly the passion had fused them. And with each mental replay, she found herself wanting him again, and aching to go to him now and tell him.

This, too, was part of the gift he'd given her, a freedom to express herself, a desire to let her wishes be known. He said he loved her, and though she didn't understand how or why, she believed him. On some utterly honest plane, she knew he meant what he'd said.

Did that mean he'd told the truth about the other things? The ten thousand years of hell? The questioning of what it was to be a man? Somehow, even this last seemed appropriate to Steven. A man who read every classic, every philosopher, was a man who had spent a lifetime in search of answers, a man searching for humanity, a man of metaphors and allusions.

If she spent his ten thousand years trying, she doubted she would understand everything about him. And, in thinking this, she found herself smiling a little. For the first time in a year, she was thinking into the future, wondering about someone else, looking forward to the quest for a mysterious Steven, an enigma, a man who loved her as she'd never been loved before.

And she still hadn't shown him her studio, hadn't let him see her own mysteries, her nowhere doorway paintings.

Jillian decided later that it had been utter naiveté to assume that Steven would appear at dinner as if nothing had transpired between them. She'd seen the depth of his passion, the totality of his feelings about her, and heard from his own lips the depth of his confusion about her, and still she'd set three places for dinner, waited for him to join them until the hour hand on the clock passed another half an hour.

He didn't answer his door when she went out to the guesthouse to call him in, and no smoke rose from his chimney.

For the first time since the afternoon, Jillian felt the chill of self-doubt, the coolness of apprehension. He'd said she didn't understand what he would ask of her. Had said he might not have an opportunity later to tell her he loved her.

Had she so blinded herself to the meaning of his words that she'd neglected to realize they might be taken literally. Was he gone for good? She was stunned by the degree of anguish that fear raised in her.

Standing outside the door to the guesthouse, Jillian understood for the first time that afternoon just how far she'd traveled into the future, how deeply she'd responded to his lovemaking, to his passion, to his words. Gone for good? If he was gone, there was absolutely nothing good about it at all. Nothing.

Though Jillian couldn't seem to summon an appetite, Allie had eaten her dinner with renewed alacrity and maintained a light, rollicking conversation utterly at odds with her behavior the past few days. She'd talked about school, about her teacher, and, it seemed to Jillian, incessantly about Lyle. Lyle was excited about autumn coming, she'd said. Lyle couldn't wait until the twenty-first. Lyle was inviting some friends over for a big party.

"What friends?" Jillian had asked.

"I dunno. Lyle's friends. Some other angels."

Angels, Jillian had repeated inwardly. Rainbows of light, ribbons of color, coming to keep Allie company.

"Sounds pretty," Jillian had said absently, thinking that while her daughter could only talk about Lyle...Lyle...Lyle...she could only think about Steven, what he was doing, why he hadn't come for dinner, why he was staying away from her, now especially, when she felt most vulnerable to him.

Jillian felt as though her heart grew heavier by the quarter hour, until by the time the story-and-bedtime kiss arrived, she felt as though she had gained a thousand pounds, that if flung into water she would sink like the proverbial stone.

Tonight, she couldn't even call up her atavistic reaction to Lyle, was almost unconcerned with his troublesome presence. She only felt the lack of Steven's. How could he tell her he loved her, then just walk away, abandon her?

By ten o'clock, a measure of anger was stepping in to supplant her doubts and fears. And by midnight, she was a statue of indignation. But by two o'clock, when the guesthouse remained dark and her bed dreadfully empty, she only felt small and forsaken.

When she finally crawled beneath her cold sheets, trying to think of anything but Steven Sayers, she was fighting back tears of betrayal, tears of insecurity. He'd given her the greatest of gifts that afternoon, and was stealing it back by the ticking of the clock, by each small movement of the second hand.

By three, still wide-eyed, and in greater pain than at any time in the past year, she tossed the covers aside and angrily, hurtfully, dragged on her old bathrobe and marched down the darkened hallways to her studio. Only with brush in hand would she be able to release the confusion in her soul, the chaos in her heart.

Halfway down the hall, she noticed a soft glow of light coming from her studio. Had she left the lights on earlier? Had she even been in her studio earlier today?

She slowed her progress until she was practically creeping up on her own doorway.

Finally there, she stopped just inside the entry, feeling a breaker of emotion wash over her, a whitecapped, red-hot shock.

For a single, staggering moment, she hoped she was still in bed, having a nightmare. But she could feel the cold floor beneath her bare feet.

Steven Sayers stood in the semilight cast by a single lamp, staring at the four doorway paintings resting on their easels. Like a living statue, he was perfectly rigid, his profile to the door. He seemed both alien in this room and, at the same time, utterly at home.

Jillian couldn't have spoken, but didn't need to. The sudden flare of the lights made him turn. His face was taut with whatever emotion held him in its thrall, his emerald eyes tortured, haunted by terrible, horrific thoughts.

But whatever he was thinking, whatever he was feeling, it was nothing compared to how she felt when he moved. One of his muscled arms was held behind him somewhat, and he shifted now, revealing too much. A tensed and very tanned hand clamped around the handle of a long, vicious knife.

She stared at that blade for several seconds, then shifted her questioning, uncomprehending gaze to his tormented eyes.

"I don't understand," she said. It was nothing but the truth, and yet it didn't seem to say anywhere near enough.

"Jillian..." he rasped, as if he hadn't spoken since he'd left her that afternoon, as if whatever despair held him in thrall had robbed him of normal voice.

Jillian experienced the oddest duality of contrasts. Despite the knife in his hand, despite the tension and horror etched, *grooved* into his face, and overriding the threat of the violence he was obviously prepared to enact, on what—her? her work? her paintings?—she nonetheless felt a rush of relief at seeing him here.

He hadn't gone after all.

And, following that sharp, sweet tang of relief, she knew that even thinking such a thing was pure, undiluted lunacy. Whatever was going on here was outside rational thought, outside the give-and-take rules of relationships. A man didn't come courting with knife in hand.

Jillian conceived the half-hopeful notion that this Steven wasn't *her* Steven, that this troubled man before her was the dark Steven of her dreams, the one who kissed her with cold passion, the one whose hands felt like ice upon her skin.

But she knew she was lying to herself, and understood with deepest anguish that she'd been doing this all along. This was Steven, all right. The Steven of the afternoon *and* the Steven of her warning dreams.

Sadly, agonizingly, she knew now that all the Stevens were just one man. This man.

And she also knew that this Steven was a very, very dangerous individual.

Unable to keep silent, she again voiced the only thing she felt capable of expressing, "I don't understand."

"Jillian," he said again, his voice harsh, hoarse. Raw with scarcely controlled emotion. And it sounded exactly the way it had this afternoon, when he'd been locked in her embrace, when he'd cried her name like an incantation, a talisman against dire consequences.

"What is going on, Steven?" she asked when he didn't explain, didn't move. Her heart was pounding so painfully, so rapidly, she was half-afraid he would hear it, would know how frightened she was.

"I know you don't understand," he said, "but I came in here to see the portals. I had the idea I could change the rules, bend them somehow."

"What rules?" she asked.

He shifted a little then, waved his hand slightly. The evil eye of the knife snared a ray of light and glinted sharply, ominously.

To her astonishment, she realized that Steven seemed unaware of just how dangerous he looked, what a threat he was presenting. She toyed with the notion of pointing it out to him, but couldn't make the words rise to her throat.

"Don't you see, Jillian? I can't let you go now," he said. And he looked more than anguished, he looked *mad.*

"No," she said, unable to hold all the pain inside, as if by repeating this single denial, she could set the world to rights again, turn back the clock, not see what she was all too clearly witnessing, not feel the chaos she was feeling.

Slowly, achingly slowly, he lowered his hand until the knife flat-bladed his thigh, the thigh she'd run her hands over just that afternoon, the muscled thigh that had pressed against her own.

"No," she murmured again, her voice weaker this time, though inside it had become a scream, a keening wail of negation.

I can't bear this! Jillian thought. She wanted to beg him to magically explain his presence here, explain the knife away, to *take* it away, to make everything all right again.

Her heart pounded, scudded against her rib cage. Her veins felt injected with ice water. She wanted to sink to her knees and cry out in rejection. How could he explain it? *I thought I heard a bad guy? I saw a mouse? I was guarding your paintings?*

None of those were even logical, let alone likely. There was no rational explanation he could offer as to why he would be in her studio, staring at her paintings, with a knife in his hand. Not one possible good reason. There were only hosts of bad ones.

But she desperately needed to hear him try. Because of the afternoon, because he'd told her he loved her, she had to believe that he had good cause for being there, that he was tortured by something that she would eventually understand, that she would be able to see clearly.

"What rules?" she repeated. He'd mentioned rules this afternoon. And he'd asked her about duty, a responsibility to a task that involved hurting someone.

Was this the cause of dark foreboding she'd felt? Had she dimly understood that Steven was so utterly different, so completely divorced from all she'd ever known, that he was capable of bringing a darkness into her home, into her life?

"There are...were...others before humankind," Steven said then. He stared at her, as if willing her to believe him, compelling her to follow his odd statement.

She didn't know what to say. She felt she'd just wandered into a nightmare.

"I see," she said, and hoped the words didn't sound as patronizing, as terror-filled, as she felt inside.

"No, you don't!" he barked at her. Then his face softened. "How could you? I must sound crazy to you. Out of my mind." He swept his free hand through his golden hair and looked away from her in something like shame. Or frustration.

He'd told her he loved her. And if she was to cling to those words, hang on to that thought as a drowning man clutches at a broken log in a raging river, then she had to try, had to force herself to listen to any explanation, any possible explanation.

But even he knew how this must look to her, how he sounded. There were others before humankind? What kind of lunacy was this? A dark, terrible kind.

So much was made clear to Jillian now. Too much.

His gaze shifted back to hers. His eyes burned with sorrow, with dreadful need. "A long time ago, millennia ago, Jillian, we began a war. It was a war over the earth, over freedom."

Jillian wanted to fling herself at him, arms flailing against him, beat him for her own foolishness, storm at him for betraying her trust. Most of all, she realized, she wanted to lash out at him for not being what his kisses had promised, for not being the person she'd wanted him to be.

But overriding all of this was the thin, rapier awareness that she had to placate him at all costs. She had to make certain that knife stayed lowered and at his side. She had to ensure that blade wouldn't find its way into her own body or—God forbid—into Allie's.

What have I done? What terrible danger have I brought down on us through my own unwillingness to listen to warnings from Elise, Gloria, even Allie?

Please, please, she begged silently, *just let me get through this. Let me get rid of Steven.*

Her heart breaking, her blood seemingly frozen in her veins, she said with confusing honesty, "I still don't understand."

"Listen to me," he snapped. "I'm telling you the whole story, the absolute truth. I told you that you didn't know who I really was, *what* I was, and what I would be asking of you. I'm telling you now."

Jillian wanted to ask if the knife was necessary to the tale, but couldn't bring herself to mention it.

"Tell me," she said, and was inordinately relieved when his shoulders seemed to relax a single notch.

Again his hand raked his hair, as if that rough gesture would bring him clarity of thought. There was no clarity possible, she thought sadly.

"We aren't like you," he said.

Don't say anything more, Jillian begged silently. She didn't want to hear anything further. This was too crazy, too irrational.

"A rebellion started. It was simple at first, just an infraction or two, a slipping from the old ways. But soon, more and more began interacting with your kind, trying to control you, win your trust."

He stopped speaking, still looking at her with that forceful gaze. Was he waiting for her to say something? What on earth could she say to such an outlandish story?

"You seemed human enough today," she said finally, far more coldly than she'd intended.

Surprising her, a wry smile tugged at his lips. "Today. Yes. I need to explain about today, also."

"I think so," she said.

But he didn't—he continued with his tale. "Soon, the rebellion developed into a full-scale war. There were two sides. Those who wanted to use humankind for whatever purpose, and those who believed humankind should be left alone."

"Which side—?" Jillian had to ask, not believing the story, not wanting to even hear anymore, but because she was unwilling to see that knife blade raise again, and because of the afternoon she'd spent in his arms.

"I was...*am*...on the side of allowing humankind to find their own way, to live without controls."

"I see," she said, knowing she was lying.

He apparently did, too, for he frowned heavily. "Five portals were created. And those who wished to leave were told to choose one of those five portals, so that they might exist in a different plane. One of the portals led to earth."

"But I thought—" Jillian began, only to break off, aghast. She'd actually been about to argue a point in his outrageous story.

"Those who wanted to be a part of this earth could choose that portal...only to change completely, become human themselves."

He had an answer for everything, she thought. Insanity bred its own form of logic. "And you're one of those," she said.

"No, Jillian. When the portals were opened, many fled through, off to other dimensions, other worlds. But some, the most rebellious, refused to abide by the council's decisions, and swept through the portal into this world. As themselves, not as humans."

Jillian didn't say anything. She couldn't. In her mind's ear, she heard her daughter telling her that Lyle had had a home once, a long time ago. She heard Allie telling her that Lyle said Steven wasn't real. And she heard Allie's eight-year-old innocent voice saying that Lyle was an angel.

Her heart thudded painfully. Her mouth felt both overwet and too dry. Her hands and feet were cold, not because of the early-morning chill, but because of the pervasive cold inside her.

"You know how this sounds," she said.

"God, yes, Jillian. Don't you think that hasn't been driving me out of my mind? I can see it in your eyes now. You think I'm crazy. But 'There are more things in heaven and—'"

"I know, I know." She finished for him. "'And earth, Horatio, than are dreamt of in your philosophy.' But somehow, quoting Shakespeare now doesn't make everything okay, Steven."

"Oh, Jillian. I know that. But you have to hear me out. There isn't much time."

"Why?"

"Why what?"

"Why isn't there much time?"

"Because when the others passed through the portals all that time ago, the council resolved that once every century the portals would open again, and those who had gone through would be hunted down and forced to leave, to go to one of the alternate dimensions. Each century a human is born that carries those portals inside their soul. That human opens the portals."

"And you think my doorway paintings are the portals."

"I don't think it, Jillian. I know."

"You still haven't told me why there's so little time."

"The portals always open on an equinox, on a date when the earth aligns with the sun."

Jillian felt a cold chill sweep across her back, down her arms. Allie had said Lyle was planning a party on the equinox. She shook her head.

"That's a week away," she said.

"But a week's not long enough, Jillian."

"What else aren't you telling me?" she asked, knowing there was more to this madness, knowing with utter certainty that his insanity hadn't yet revealed the final denouement.

"The carrier of the portals..."

"That would presumably be me this time," she said, amazed at how reasonable she could sound under the circumstances. How collected. Calm. A voice of reason in the face of abject dementia.

Steven closed his eyes, sharp pain etching every granitelike element of his face. As if the words were dragged from him, he said, his voice filled with terrible anguish, "None who carry the portals inside them have ever survived the battle."

CHAPTER TEN

Steven could guess at the thoughts racing through Jillian's mind. Her beautiful eyes were wide with horror, her mouth was tight with shock. He couldn't help but admire her poise, standing there confronting what she must assume to be a madman, her slender shoulders thrown back, her chin up, her lips quivering. Sweet, doomed Jillian.

"That's why I said I couldn't lose you now. I came in here to try to destroy the portals, hoping that would stop the battle."

"You were going to use that knife on my paintings?" she asked in thin, taut fear.

"You don't have to be frightened of me, Jillian. I would never hurt you."

"You wanted to destroy my paintings, you tell me I'm going to die...but you don't want to hurt me? Oh, Steven—" Her voice broke on a choked off sob.

He started to take a step forward, but her hand shot out in front of her, stopping him as effectively as a bullet might have anyone else.

"Don't," she said. "Don't come any closer."

"I thought I could change the rules," he said urgently.

"The rules..." she repeated dully, her voice hitching with her fear, the pain he must be causing her.

"The portals, Jillian. Remember when I told you that the rules couldn't be bent? I realized this afternoon, after we parted, that the rules could change. That you had changed me. And if I was changed...then I could make other things change too."

"And...that knife was going to help you bend the rules?" she asked. He saw the effort she used *not* to look at the knife.

"Not the knife itself, Jillian. I told you, I thought I could destroy the portals," he said. He heard the desperation in his voice, was unable to quell it. He had to make her understand. To believe.

"Oh, Steven," she said, and cut herself off before adding what would naturally follow... *How could you?*

He could hear the sorrow in her voice, the sense of betrayal. She thought him insane, he thought with a dull feeling of hopelessness. Insane.

"Jillian, you have to listen to me."

"Okay," she said, and he could tell she was only humoring him, that she was petrified enough to agree with him on anything now.

"You don't have to be frightened of *me,* Jillian," he said urgently. Earnestly. He knew better than to advance so much as a single step. One false move, and she would bolt.

"Okay," she said again. Placating him. Her tone was patronizing, condescending, even if her pitch was uncertain and thready.

He held the knife blade out and felt her instinctive flinch to his core.

"I love you, Jillian. I never expected to, I didn't even know it was possible for one like me to love a mortal. But I do." He felt a measure of anger at her, no matter how utterly justifiable her reaction might be after catching him in her studio, a knife in his hand, an insane story spilling from his lips.

She didn't even blink, and Steven realized she was too frightened to even close her eyes to him for a second.

She'd found him in the dark, in her studio, in her *private* place, ready to destroy her beautiful, if disturbing, work.

But she wasn't listening to him, wasn't hearing the truth. She didn't know what she'd created. Didn't understand what the paintings were.

"It's late," she said, and it tore him apart to hear the note of constraint, of terror, in her voice. And more so to see it mirrored on her face.

"Jillian—"

"It's okay," she said swiftly, interrupting him. "No damage done."

A thousand deep wells of damage had been done, he thought with anguish. All because he'd decided he could try to bend the rules, to try to alter their mutual destinies. All because he hadn't been able to bear the thought of Jillian's death.

How to convince her? How to tell her about the battles now, when her eyes were wide with horror, her body was tense with fear?

"This isn't a game, Jillian," he said.

"No?"

"Of course not!" he snapped, then stopped. He drew a deep, steadying breath. "This is hardly the time for games." He spoke as slowly and as steadily as he could, given the circumstances. The urgency.

He said, "I have to think of something, anything, that will change your destiny. Our destiny."

He could see all too easily that whatever he said now, she wouldn't want to hear it, that his talk of destiny was only pushing her farther away from him, deeper into denial.

And worst of all, by the shadows on her face, the heaviness of her eyes, he could see that the worst truth was that she was thinking she'd given herself to him unwisely. That he was crazy, and she'd been crazier to love him during those halcyon afternoon hours.

"I'm not crazy, Jillian," he said. "I know it looks that way, but you have to believe me. I'm telling you the truth. He's after the portals, because that's what he has to do. That's what I had to do. And in less than one week, you will have them all opened. I thought if I destroyed the portals, you would be safe. You see, when the portals are all open, either he will be pushed through . . . or I will. I thought I could . . ."

He trailed off, unable to continue while she shook her head slowly, left to right, negating him, negating his attempt.

"He?" she asked in a small voice.

Encouraged beyond measure, he answered her directly. "Beleale. The last of those cast out. What you think is an invisible friend of Allie's."

"Lyle."

"Yes, Lyle."

"He's after my paintings, too."

"No, damn it," Steven snapped and brought himself up short at seeing her flinch. "He knows you have the portals. He's only waiting for the fifth one. And then he'll try to use them to bring his minions through the portals."

She didn't move, her eyes didn't meet his, in question or even in rejection. She stood there, bare feet upon the cold floor, her eyes dull with pain.

"His . . . minions. Like demons or something. Legions."

"It's the truth, Jillian," he said. He put every bit of persuasion in his voice that he could possibly muster. She had to believe him. Had to understand why he'd been willing to destroy her work.

"The truth," she repeated finally. Dully.

Amazingly, he could see that a part of her wanted to believe him, wanted to listen. But when he saw her eyes slide from him to the paintings, now behind him, he suspected she was only making conversation to stall him, to keep him from using the knife on her, on her child.

Guilt flayed him raw, made him angry with her for misunderstanding, angry with himself for having believed the emotion of the afternoon might last, might stay with him . . . might stay with her. But it had stayed with him. It was with him now.

"Look inside yourself, Jillian. You have to face what's happening here. This is real, Jillian. All too real."

He couldn't restrain himself from taking an angry pace, but he halted immediately at her reflexive retreat.

"Jillian. You *know* about Beleale. About the one your daughter calls Lyle. You *know*. You couldn't have created the portals otherwise. Somewhere deep inside you, I know you can feel the truth of what I'm saying."

He felt a tremendous surge of relief as her eyes again cut from his to her paintings and back. Her lower lip slipped into her mouth, thoughtfully, reflectively.

"You *know*," he said again, stressing the word.

"Beleale—?" she asked softly, and perhaps, he thought hopefully, with a note of recognition in her voice.

"The last of the cast out. You've read Milton. You *know*."

She released her biting hold on her lower lip. "I see," she said. "He's one of the fallen angels." Her voice might be dull, but he could see a glimmer of understanding in her eyes.

"Exactly!" he barked in triumph. "Allie's creature, Lyle, is none other than Beleale. Look inside you. You *know* him."

She frowned slightly, and again he felt encouraged. She *was* going to listen, would understand.

"And you have to know what I am. I chose to be the one who came after those who sneaked through. I went through the portal, also. I am both mortal and not. Both.''

She shook her head slightly, her eyes wary.

''This is the last battle, Jillian. Maybe the rules can be bent. Not even I know what's possible now. Maybe if we prepare, come up with a plan...something. Anything. Maybe things don't have to be the way they always were.''

He hated seeing her hand steal upward to clasp the lapels of her bathrobe tightly together. But at least she was listening, was partially taking in his words, even if only at a subliminal level.

''The battle...'' she repeated, even more dully this time.

''Jillian,'' he said, agonized.

He'd never tried spilling the truth to the portal carrier before. Most understood the other dimensions without his ever having to say a thing. Jillian was different. And he was different now, because of her.

''Don't you see?'' he asked desperately. ''Once I'd been with you, once I'd felt what I did, I had to try to change the rules. For ten thousand years, my only goal was to stop those like Lyle from using the portals. Now there's only Lyle left. And me. I came here knowing I had to stop him from bringing forth all those I'd already pushed through those five entrances to alternate universes. That's my destiny. My duty.''

''I see,'' she said. And her dull tone told him she saw something, all right, but perhaps not what he was trying to get across.

''You don't,'' he said. ''But you must. We only have a few days left before the autumnal equinox. And I'll be damned if I'm going to let you be killed in this battle.''

He didn't know exactly what he'd said, but she jerked as though struck. Her eyes flickered, her back stiffened even more. Her eyes cut to her paintings, the four portals.

"You can even see those waiting to come back through. You painted them in."

Again her eyes flickered, but whether it was in comprehension or some other emotion, he couldn't have guessed.

"I came in here wanting to destroy them, aching to slash the portals to ribbons, but I couldn't."

Her eyes slowly moved to meet his again.

"It wasn't your coming in here that stopped me, Jillian. I wasn't able to do it. I felt blocked by something... maybe those rules I swore to uphold. Maybe it was love of your work, love of you. Maybe it was because there are only four. I don't know. I just know I couldn't do it."

A shudder worked through Jillian. He ached to hold her, comfort her, assure her that everything would be all right, that she could trust him. But there were no assurances, and, in all likelihood, she would be dead within the week.

He began, "This afternoon—"

"Don't." She cut him off as her eyes snapped to his. Her chin was set, her lips were pressed tightly together. He could read her cold anger, and something else. A dark sense of betrayal.

"Don't talk about before," she said through clenched teeth. "This afternoon has nothing to do with this."

"Don't you see," he said slowly, "in very many ways, loving you today has *everything* to do with this? I couldn't both love you and let you be destroyed."

He saw that whatever anger had snared her dissipated at his words. Her eyes slid from his, and a deep sorrow marked her delicate features. And a terrible fear etched her lips.

"I... It's late," she said finally. She tried a smile, but it slipped woefully.

Steven needed to take her in his arms, comfort her, find the magic they'd found earlier, find it again in his body, his soul. He took another step forward, but stopped when she backed away an equal distance.

"Jillian..."

Her fingers tugged convulsively at her robe's lapels. Her knuckles looked a bloodless white in the harsh light of the overheads. She shook her head slightly.

"Can we talk about this in the morning?" she asked, her eyes just past his shoulder. "If we have a...battle to plan, I'd just as soon do it by light of day."

Steven tried feeling a measure of hope at her words, but didn't. He only felt the cold certainty that she was humoring him, attempting to get him out of her house. Ironically, that was something she couldn't possibly accomplish. The blood tie would prevent that.

"I'm tired. I can't think very straight," she continued, speaking a little more rapidly, as if trying to convince him.

She was the one who needed convincing, he thought bleakly. But all he said was her name. "Jillian..."

"Please, Steven," she said, a little more sharply now, her eyes snaring his.

What he read in her gaze silenced him more effectively than any words might have done. He could too easily see a sickened despair, a desperate need for distance. And he could read her torn emotions, a faint wish that what he was telling her might hold some grain of truth, because then she wouldn't have to feel that everything he'd said to her had been a delusion, that all had been lies.

"I wasn't lying to you, Jillian," he said.

She said nothing, but her head turned sharply away from him. Denying him. Denying the afternoon in his arms. Wishing, perhaps, that it had never happened.

"Tomorrow," he said finally, feeling the emptiness of that hope.

"Tomorrow," she agreed. She backed through the door, and he followed.

Jillian didn't know how she managed to walk down the hallway. Her legs felt numb, disconnected. Her shoulder blades ached with atavistic reaction to his gaze upon her. Her throat fought with the choked-back tears threatening to escape. Her eyes burned with the need to cry.

She could hear him walking behind her, could feel the warmth radiating out from him, and knew he was close enough to touch, close enough to lean against.

Never again, she thought despairingly. Never again would she be able to touch Steven.

Because Steven Sayers was crazy. Certifiably, dangerously crazy.

She just wanted to get down this hallway and get him out the back door without incident. Once he was gone, and the doors were locked and barricaded, she would give in to the need for tears, the compulsion to give in to the tidal wave of horror and shame that ripped through her.

A step, another, and another. She should have listened to Elise. She should have taken Allie's warnings at face value.

All those words this afternoon, those beautiful, beautiful moments with Steven...all the goodness he'd given her, those wonderful perfect moments, meant nothing now. Less than nothing. They had been reduced to ashes and, as a result, her heart to rubble.

Because she'd wanted so very much to believe. *Had* believed.

Oh, Steven, she thought as her breath caught on a sob.

Feeling as if the walk took hours, as if it were measured by the torrent of tears welling inside her, she almost cried out in relief when she reached the dining room. She stepped back from the sliding glass doors as he approached them. She couldn't, didn't dare, meet his eyes. If she did, he would read every bit of her fear, every nuance of the sickness that roiled in her now.

"I meant what I told you this afternoon," he said softly, his rich baritone sending ripples of reaction down her back.

She could see his rigid body just inches from her. She couldn't raise her eyes. Wouldn't.

"I... did, too," she managed to choke out. He was killing her. Wasn't this nightmare ever going to end?

"Jillian..."

Ah, this is pure torture, Jillian thought. In a voice that sounded anguished even to her own ears, she couldn't help blurting out some of her pain.

"Please, Steven. I can't even think now. I'm too tired. It's too late. Tomorrow. T-tomorrow will be s-soon enough to talk. *Please.*"

She felt hot tears spilling free, and carving trails down her cheeks. They felt like molten lava against her cold skin, and she had the idea that they would scar her permanently, be forever etched on her face, a testament to the extent of her present pain. Markers of the destruction of joy, the loss of faith.

"Just go, now," she begged him. "Oh, please, Steven."

"Don't cry, Jillian," he said.

"Now..."

She stilled herself for his touch, and was half-afraid she would scream if he so much as brushed his fingers across her cheeks. The tears belonged to him, but she couldn't bear it if he tried to claim them now.

"I'll be back in the morning," he said, and to Jillian it sounded more like a threat than a promise.

You won't, she wanted to say, needed to say. But the long-bladed knife still clasped in his hand rendered any argument mute.

"We're connected now, Jillian."

"I know," she said, and in some odd way she knew that, if nothing else, was the utter truth.

"I'm sorry," he said. And, strangely, she believed he meant the words. Meant the sentiment, and meant it absolutely.

"I know," she said.

But she didn't feel she knew anything at all. Her entire world was coming apart at the seams. How could he sound so eminently sane and so crazy at one and the same time?

"You have to listen to your heart, Jillian."

Her heart had listened that afternoon. Her heart had heard what she now had to throw away, had to close off forever. This was the time to listen to reason. Logic and cold, rational thinking were all she had left.

No matter how many of his comments seemed uncanny echoes of things Allie had been saying lately, no matter that a few of them even made a rather alluring sense, she had to think coolly, analytically. There was a perfectly rational explanation for why some of the things he said matched those Allie had said: He was the one feeding Allie's stories, Allie's belief in Lyle. Because *he*, Steven, believed in Lyle.

"I'll listen," she lied.

He touched her then, his hand cupping her face, his palm wiping the hot tears from her cheeks, her throat, smearing the tears to a film of betrayal across her features. She clamped her tongue between her teeth to hold in her agonized groan.

Her body, her betraying heart, wanted to lean into him, to give in to the promise of his touch, the tenderness inherent in the firm stroking. Her mind screamed denial, raged at the betrayal, the hurt. The pain at having chosen so terribly unwisely. She closed her eyes, squeezed them against the suffering, the longing, the confusion.

Making a shock wave of desire-etched terror crackle down her spine, he lowered his lips to hers, covered them, pressed lightly against her unresponsive mouth. His kiss deepened, as if commanding acknowledgment, demanding that she find a measure of the emotion she'd felt only that afternoon.

If he only knew, she thought. Adrenaline coursed through her, a dark heat sweeping across her as a fire charges across a dry prairie.

"Jillian..." he murmured, his lips finding that pulsing throb in the sensitive curve of her neck.

In spite of herself, despite her knowing this was wrong, that *he* was wrong, that he was *crazy,* her head tilted back slightly and a moan of weak acceptance escaped her lips. Dear God, she thought, even knowing what he was, even *knowing,* she wanted him. Ached for him.

At her moan, he raised his head swiftly and lowered his lips to hers in a seemingly desperate appeal. He would never know what strength it took her not to give in to every blessed promise in that kiss, in his hot lips against hers. Fleetingly she had the despairing notion that if it were only her, if she didn't have Allie to consider, she might give in to this craziness, might actually turn her back on rational thought, and accept whatever bizarre course he set her.

And with that notion, the kiss turned bittersweet, tasting of betrayal and dreams gone astray. The passion flared, only to give way to the aftertaste of what could have been and now could never be. For a final second, the promise lingered, strove to hold true, then slipped, faded, and he pulled away from her, setting her free. Leaving her alone in a backwash of bitter regret.

"Until tomorrow," he said then, and dropped his hand.

She felt so cold. So very alone. It wasn't fair, she thought. She'd railed against fate when Dave was taken from her. Had raged against fate when Allie cried out in the middle of the night, and when she herself had reached for Dave's warmth and found nothing but cool pillow next to her. But this, this wasn't fighting fate. This was fate slapping her directly in the face. In the heart.

Still without opening her eyes, as if by not watching him leave she wouldn't have to absorb every nuance of his betrayal, his insanity, Jillian listened as he depressed the handle of one of the French doors. Abruptly she felt the sting of cold air sweeping over her, startling her, needling her.

She held her breath as she heard him step through the aperture and outside. She kept her eyes closed, scarcely breathing, hoping the nightmare was ending finally, and suspecting that on some deep level it never would.

"You know the truth, Jillian," he said then. The cold wind followed his words, snaking around her bare feet, her legs. "You know what I really am."

She did, she thought. She knew all too well.

After a second's hesitation, he shut the door, snicking it firmly into place.

A sob that seemed to come from her very soul escaped her then, rocking her. She opened her eyes and stared through the shimmering tears to the empty courtyard beyond the French doors. The film of tears made rainbow prisms in the reflection on the glass, as if Allie's angel had come to commiserate with her, as if Lyle were offering the protection Allie claimed he would.

She should have listened to Lyle, she thought hysterically. She wouldn't be standing here now, feeling as if everything in the world that most mattered had just been rent into a million pieces.

Steven had said she knew the truth about him. He was right. Sadly, horrifyingly, she knew the truth all too well. Not his truth, not the truth that could make a man sneak into her house late at night to destroy her paintings. But she knew truth, nonetheless. And the truth was starkly simple: Steven Sayers was insane.

Oh, dear God, she thought, in the darkest despair she'd ever known, could ever have imagined knowing. Of all the things she'd ever encountered in her life, this knowledge was the worst of all. It surpassed hearing about Dave, went far beyond loneliness or fear of the future. This was the death of dreams, the end of second chances.

She slowly lowered the burglar bar on the inside of the doors and clicked it into place. With numb fingers, she flipped the lights from bright to dark. She pulled the curtains across the doors, something she hadn't done for years.

None of these small but significant actions against a repeated intrusion gave her any sense of security. And none of them made her heart any less heavy, her mind any easier.

She moved to the countertop, stared for a moment at the intricate and brightly colored pattern of the Mexican tile, remembered the first time she'd seen it. She let her eyes roam across it, as if trying to find deeper meaning in the vine motif.

But it was only a curling vine with thick green leaves. And Steven was only a man with insane green eyes.

Jillian lifted the telephone receiver from its cradle, and as though she moved through thickest, coldest water, she slowly pressed an oddly steady finger against three of the raised buttons.

"Please state your emergency," a female voice demanded.

"My name is Jillian Stewart," she said. Even to her, her voice sounded calm, collected, and oh, so very far away. She provided the woman on the other end of the line her address and gave a concise explanation of the easiest way to reach her home.

"And the nature of the trouble?" the woman asked crisply.

A broken heart? Betrayal? A bit of both. A lot of cold, stark and terribly lonely reality.

"A man who has been working for me broke into my home tonight. He had a knife." It was the truth, and yet nothing had ever tasted more like a lie.

A few moments later, Jillian hung up the receiver. The tears were gone now. The pain she felt inside went far deeper than tears. That pain stretched cold, numbing fingers throughout her body, cutting off all sensation.

She didn't look at the clock, but knew only minutes had passed before she saw the blue and red lights circling the room and heard a staccato pounding on her front door.

Like an automaton, she crossed the room to the front door.

Help had arrived. The drawbridge was lowered. Her castle would once again be secure and she and her daughter safe.

So why did she feel she was the one doing the betraying? Why did she feel such a cold, dark despair?

CHAPTER ELEVEN

With achingly dry eyes, Jillian watched the police transform, chimeralike, from stolid, large and oppressive figures into dark shadows that stole along her courtyard and beyond, to the gate where Steven's blood still marked the wood and around and behind the lilac hedge—where Lyle had first spoken—and to the guesthouse.

Horrified, she saw one of the shadows circling in from the front yard, edging alongside the guesthouse with his spectral gun out before him. Another swung around from the right. Facing each other, on opposite sides of Steven's door, they advanced, shades with extended instruments of death silhouetted on the guesthouse walls, apparitions with violent intent to combat violence.

Jillian stepped through the French doors. "Wait!" she called, but no one seemed to hear her.

She hadn't meant for this to happen. This wasn't why she'd called the police. Naively, she had only called them to be safe. She hadn't considered the repercussions. She hadn't wanted to ever again walk into a room and see a man with a knife standing before one of her paintings. But she certainly hadn't wanted anything to happen to Steven, either.

It was as if there were two men, the man with her this afternoon, and the man tonight.

She felt a chill wash along her shoulders. She'd dreamed of two Stevens. Two entirely different Stevens. But dreams weren't reality, and those subconscious thoughts had no place in the shadow play taking place now.

She'd called the police because Steven had been talking irrationally, and because that damnable knife had terrified her. She'd only done what she had to do to protect herself...protect Allie, *her daughter,* who had already been exposed to too much horror in her young life.

She wanted to close her eyes, shut out the sight of the men surrounding the guesthouse. Surrounding Steven. But she forced herself to watch, to remain where she was. If she turned away now, didn't stay in place for this betrayal, then she would never again be able to look at the guesthouse without anticipating him, she would never be able to walk out the back door without turning her head to look for a man who stole into her dreams, into her heart.

And she would never again feel certain she wouldn't walk down that dark corridor leading to her studio and flip the light switch, only to find him standing in a golden pool of light in the center of her private domain, fist curled around a knife, glinting blade upraised.

That's why I called them, she wanted to call out now, wanted to send the words winging across the grounds to the small guesthouse—warning him?—letting him know what she'd done. And why. But words wouldn't blanket the gun-laden shadows on his walls. It was far too late for warnings. Far too late for apologies.

The deed was done.

And whatever rare and unusual connection she'd felt with Steven had to be done, as well. For good. She shuddered with a cold that seemed to seep into her very soul.

She'd been brutally, blushingly honest with the police, telling them of her foolishness, her reluctance to listen to her friends' advice, her daughter's warnings. Fighting guilt, she'd implied she'd made a grievous error in trusting him. And the whole time she spilled this sordid story free, she'd suffered. Because she still trusted him, still wanted him. She feared him, yes. She knew what he'd been about to do, but she nonetheless believed in him—not in his words, but in him, Steven.

She'd seen by their shifting gazes, by their uncomfortable silences, that the uniformed officers filling her house at first assumed she was the source of the problem. Exchanged looks, chiseled, tightly rigid mouths had let her know that admitting to having spent "time" with Steven was tantamount to admitting that she'd given him carte blanche to do anything he wanted.

Cool nods and sharper questions had allowed Jillian to know that having loved Steven that afternoon, however euphemistically she'd described it, made her suspect. The police questioning her apparently believed that as a lonely widow she'd given in to the advances of a randy gardener, then regretted it. One of the policemen had even asked if she'd called them out of retribution.

"You know, Mrs. Stewart, maybe you were attracted, and then afterward got to wondering what your friends might think. Maybe you decided to call rape then."

Jillian had remained calm and largely turned a deaf ear to most of the questions, but this last had needed addressing. She'd turned a hot, burning face toward the officer who had asked it.

"I didn't say Steven raped me. He did no such thing. I only called you because I found him in my studio tonight with a knife in his hand and saying some pretty strange things. I don't think he wanted to harm me or mine. I just think he needs help. What people think, one way or another, is neither here nor there," she'd said. Her icy voice was a dramatic contrast to the heat in her face.

At another skeptical look, she'd followed her statement with "If I'd been so worried about my precious reputation, I doubt I would have called the police, and I certainly wouldn't have admitted to...to an attraction to Steven."

But, horrifying her, making her feel even worse—if that was possible—their faces had solidified into granite blocks when they realized who she was, when they asked a few questions about the fact that she was the widow of a man shot in a drive-by shooting only a year earlier.

They might as well have voiced their thoughts; she could read them clearly enough on their faces. *Maybe the shooting wasn't as random as everyone thought. Maybe she'd been at something back then.*

But when she repeated her description of what had transpired in her studio—Steven's words, his knife, his whole demeanor—their attitudes had shifted, metamorphosed into something akin to understanding. She'd seen in their eyes what Steven had undoubtedly seen in her own: The man in her house tonight was crazy.

Crazy.

"Are you pressing charges, ma'am?"

The question had sent chills down Jillian's spine, driving home the full weight of guilt, of fear. Fighting back tears, Jillian had asked what her options were.

"Well, ma'am, we need to know what it is you want us to do. Are you officially firing him? Are you asking him to leave your property? We can escort him from the premises, if that's what you want."

Fire Steven? She hadn't even considered him an employee for almost as long as he'd been on her property. He'd struck her more as the earth, the sky...part of her life.

"That's about the most we can do, if you don't press charges. We'd just be telling him to clear out. And we'll keep a report on him, so that if he pulls something else, we'll have a file on him.

"On the other hand, ma'am, if you press charges for assault—and don't kid yourself, that's what it sounds like he was about to do, either to you or your paintings—then we take him in right now."

Her head spinning, all Jillian had thought was that she hadn't asked for any of this. And moreover, confusing her, driving logical thinking into the dim recesses of her mind, was the afternoon spent with Steven, spent loving him, spent being loved. As the officer waited for an answer, she had found that the afternoon lingered with her like bittersweet aftertaste.

She didn't understand what Steven was about, what he wanted from her, but when the officer asked, "Which is it to be, ma'am?" she'd finally said, "I think he needs help. I just want you to...to help him somehow."

"So you want him off the property, is that what I'm hearing, ma'am?"

"I have a little girl," she'd said, as if that were the only rational argument. As if it explained everything. Or apologized for anything.

"Yes, ma'am. So, do you want him off the premises...or do you want to press charges?"

She didn't want either one. Not really. Not, as Steven had once said, in her heart of hearts.

"Off the property," she'd said finally, in the smallest of voices, the smallest of admissions.

What had she done? Why was this happening?

Bam! Bam! Bam!

Jillian jumped, and her hand covered her mouth.

One of the shadows flanking the guesthouse had slipped forward, was pounding on Steven's closed door. She couldn't make out the features on the officer's face. Was he the one who had accused her of crying wolf, or the one who had presented her with those horrible options?

The officer banged on the door again and stepped back out of the way, once again becoming nothing more than a sinister shadow. Jillian couldn't withhold a whimper of hurt.

It wasn't her own pain. She felt as though each sharp rap had echoed in her soul. On some track inside her mind, she heard Steven's afternoon words replayed, his rich voice telling her that he loved her, had probably loved her for years.

"I had to tell you how I felt now, Jillian. I may not have another opportunity, and I may not even be able to feel it later."

Had he had a premonition of the night's activities? Had he known what she was going to do? She hadn't understood him then. Didn't now. But he'd been right; he would never have the opportunity to tell her that he loved her again.

Given the circumstances, the police outside surrounding the guesthouse, this realization should have relieved her. But it didn't. Not at all.

What had transpired between her and Steven shouldn't have ended this way. They had just come together, just found each other. They should have had the time to discover love, discover mornings together, afternoons spent in leisurely desire, evenings spent reading, playing music, laughing over one of Allie's antics. They should have been granted the time to find those myriad little things that would bind them, habits and sayings, routines that would make them a couple, a unit.

Instead, they'd only had the one glorious afternoon, and then Steven, in a darker mood than any she'd ever encountered before, had turned the darkness loose.

She heard a loud, booming voice call out, "Mr. Sayers? It's the police, Mr. Sayers. Open the door, sir."

The cold night seemed to catch the words and fling them at the stars. How far away would that controlled, strong voice be heard? A hundred miles, a thousand miles? *Ten thousand years?*

Only that afternoon, after loving her, he'd said he'd spent years trying to discover what it was to be a man. His hand had circled in the air, seeming to create a wheel out of the curtained-darkened bedroom.

"Mr. Sayers, if you don't open this door immediately..."

"You make me feel I almost understand it now," he'd said.

What would he understand when he opened the door of the guesthouse to uniformed police and guns held at the ready? Would he feel even a measure of the betrayal she'd felt when she flicked on the overhead lights in her studio and found him standing with his knife's blade poised above her most recent painting?

No, she wanted to call out, wanted to say to the police, to the man in the guesthouse, she hadn't called the police out of any desire for retribution, not from any urge to make him feel the same pain she'd felt upon seeing him in her studio. She'd called the police out of preservation only. Her own, perhaps, but, far more importantly, preservation of her daughter's life, her daughter's sanity.

A sob again threatened to rise to the surface. Or perhaps it was a scream.

The uniformed shadows inched closer and closer to the doorway of the guesthouse, until the two silhouetted pairs of hand-held guns met in a strangely symbolic gesture, directly over the center of the wooden door.

A third shadow materialized again and, with horror, Jillian realized that one of the officers had positioned himself in a low-slung, poised crouch directly in front of the guesthouse door. Now, like the others', his hands were stretched out before him, wrapped around each other, supporting the weight of a .357 magnum.

No, no, no! Jillian cried inside. Frozen, unable to move, she begged aloud, "Stop this! Dear God, stop this!"

But her voice was little more than a whisper.

"Police, Mr. Sayers. Open the door. *Now!*"

Jillian waited for the guesthouse door to open and flinched when a narrow crack of light appeared in the darkness.

At some time, in some myth, a nervous Pandora must have waited to see what poured from that long-ago box she'd opened, despite all advice to the contrary. And she'd set the evils of the universe loose upon an unsuspecting world.

In this time, in this all-too-harsh reality, she, Jillian, felt she'd opened a similar box of horrors. Had she done it the first day Steven knocked at her door? The night he cut himself? Those afternoons they had walked together? This afternoon, falling over that precipice only he could have created?

And once opened, the box couldn't be resealed, closed away, flung back into that nebulous sea. The evil damage was already in progress, the horror loose.

Jillian held her breath as the guesthouse's heavy wooden door slowly opened. Steven stood framed in the light, a golden man, his body oddly striated by shadows of guns, arms held doubled at full length. He didn't look crazy. He didn't look threatening now. He looked as he had the first time she'd seen him, neither subservient nor arrogant. He looked most like a dream.

But she knew now he was a dream that couldn't last.

Tears again burned Jillian's eyes, washing his image away. She couldn't hold in the soft whimper of pain she felt seeing him blur, knowing that his green eyes would be turning in her direction.

She remembered him joking in that very doorway, on a golden morning about a week earlier, "The truth is, I'm an angel, too."

Irrationally she thought if he really was some kind of an angel, then they wouldn't be able to make him leave. Wouldn't be able to take him away. And for a moment, she wished that, by some miracle, he could be that very unreal creature, that unbelievable demigod.

But it was her daughter's invisible, imaginary friend who claimed that particular purview. And Lyle didn't even like Steven, had warned against him. Lyle, whom she had distrusted, whom she disliked and was afraid of.

And Steven was only a man who had tried to steal her heart, and who, in his thieving, had accomplished far more than he might have wished.

Again she was struck by the singular unfairness of it all. Why couldn't he have been what she wanted? Not an angel, but a man she could trust, a man she could believe in. Why couldn't he have been what he unspeakingly promised?

But, as if answering her own unspoken wish, she watched as he answered the policeman's questions, alternating nodding or shaking his head. She couldn't hear his rich baritone voice, could only see his actions.

She angrily, agonizingly, brushed the tears from her eyes. She had to *see*. Had to be certain he understood how desperately she'd needed to call the police, had to know that she'd had no choice.

He stepped forward, his hands held out to his sides, empty, nonthreatening.

"Don't fight them," Jillian murmured. "Just do what they say."

Guilt made her dizzy, made her sway on her feet.

She couldn't hear what the police were saying to him now, but he suddenly called out, his voice rough with his need for her to listen, harsh with his want.

"Jillian!"

"Ah, no," she ground against her hand. "Don't do this." A sob escaped her.

"Jillian! You have to listen to me, Jillian!"

"That's enough, Mr. Sayers!"

Steven ignored the command. His eyes continued to look in her direction, his face blazing golden in the light spilling from the guesthouse.

"Jillian! Everything I told you is real! Lyle is *real!* The portals are *real!*"

The police closed in on Steven, restricting him without touching him, but Jillian could see that he was scarcely even aware of them, that all his attention was on her. One of them moved close, and Steven shook him off with an impatient, almost negligent shudder.

More loudly, he called, "Jillian! We weren't brought together only to be torn apart! We *can* change the rules! We have to! It's the only way!"

Jillian was certain she would die if he continued.

"Jillian!"

"Sayers! The lady wants you out of this place. Now! You can either do that, or we'll have to do it for you!"

"Jillian! Whatever you do tonight, don't paint the fifth portal! You can stop it, Jillian! I couldn't destroy the portals because the fifth one wasn't there! They can't open without the fifth!"

Jillian felt he was flaying her with his shouted agony, with his insanity. With his chaotic, nonsensical words. If only he didn't sound so passionate, so convinced that he made sense. And if only his words didn't now make some peculiar sense to her.

"Jillian!"

The meaning of his words impinged upon her full consciousness now. Got through all the way. Deep inside her, they seemed to strike a chord of memory, a chord of recognition.

He could have destroyed her work, she thought numbly. He could have easily. Because the fifth painting was already complete. He just hadn't seen it.

"Oh, Steven," she murmured, in more pain now than at any time in her life.

"Jillian, tell them to go away! Tell them it was a mistake. They can't save you. Only I can do that!"

"Sayers, one more outburst from you, and we'll have to take you in."

"Jillian! Lyle's here for one reason, and one reason only—"

"Okay, Sayers, have it your way..."

Two of the officers swamped Steven, hefted his arms painfully high behind him. Again, Steven didn't seem to pay the slightest bit of attention.

"He's here to use the portals! He'll bring all the others back through! You need me, Jillian! Without me, you're going to die! He'll use you, then kill you!"

"That's it, buddy!" one of the policemen barked, and muscled a pair of handcuffs on Steven.

Steven didn't fight them with any degree of ferocity, but it took three of them to wrestle him down the pathway and around to the back of the house, presumably to their waiting units.

Jillian didn't move. She couldn't. She felt she was rooted to this spot, this point of betrayal. She slowly dragged her fingers from her frozen lips, the mouth that had kissed him with such passion, had drunk a matching desire from him.

She'd felt she died herself when she had to make the funeral arrangements for Dave. And she'd felt helpless and angry in the night, rocking Allie's nightmares away, soothing her little girl's terrors and tears.

But nothing she'd ever done, ever felt, could compare with the sense of loss, the dark sense of having committed the greatest crime of all, that of calling the police, that of turning her back on a man she could have loved. Had loved that very afternoon.

She could still hear him calling her name. But far away. Distantly. "Jillian!"

The officer with the harsh questions stepped up the stairs at the back door and said her name softly. No doubts lingered in his eyes now, and his face was rigid with scarcely controlled emotion.

"Mrs. Stewart?"

"Yes?" Jillian asked numbly. Nothing the man could say to her now would make things right.

"We're going to book him for verbal assault. And for threats on your life."

Steven hadn't threatened her life. He'd claimed to be trying to save it.

"Mrs. Stewart? Do you know this person Sayers was screaming about...this Lyle person? Has he been troubling you, also?"

Jillian felt something break inside her, an undefinable something that she really hadn't even known existed until it broke. Whatever it was, a wall, a sheet of glass, it had served her all her life, separating reality from unreality, life from death. That barrier had let her feel pain without knowing despair, feel anger without rage. But it was gone now, shattered into a thousand pieces, and all she felt was cold. Very, very cold.

She turned to meet the officer's eyes.

"Lyle is my daughter's imaginary friend," she said. She sounded like a robot, her voice a lifeless monotone. She felt that way.

"An imaginary friend?" The policeman looked shocked, then puzzled. "That guy was claiming some imaginary friend was out to get you?"

"Yes," Jillian said. Her shoulder blades itched.

"Crazy as a bedbug. What was all that crap about portals and stuff?"

"The paintings he wanted to destroy are of doorways."

Any moment she would feel that brush of nothing, that shifting of air against her legs. But this time Allie's outstretched hand wouldn't be reflected in the windowpanes.

"Well, we got him in custody now. I don't think you'll be hearing from him again. When we get through the paperwork and he spends a night in the cell—or gets a visit from the shrink—we'll make sure somebody comes with him to get his things."

She'd made certain Steven was out of the picture.

"Thank you," she said dully.

"Unless you want to call somebody in to pack them up. That way, he'll have no reason to ever come back here. If I was you, I'd do that, and I'd call an attorney in the morning to slap an injunction on him."

"Thank you," Jillian repeated, letting her gaze drift from the policeman to the guesthouse. The door to the small adobe still stood open.

She felt oddly disassociated. All she could think about was the fact that Steven's books, his old, old classics in their variety of languages, would be ruined if it snowed. They'd taken him away without a coat.

Did he have a coat inside? Should she have this policeman take it now?

"Could you close the guesthouse door for me?" she asked. She still sounded as dead as she felt inside.

"Sure thing. Oh, and I really think you should press charges now. It'll help keep him away from here."

"And get his coat for him."

"Ma'am?"

"He wasn't wearing a coat."

The policeman gave her an odd look, but nodded anyway. "Are you all right, ma'am?"

"No," Jillian said steadily. "No, I'm not all right."

The officer shuffled from one foot to the other. "You want me to wait while you call someone?"

"No," Jillian said again. "Is it possible to let him go now?"

The officer looked scandalized. "No, ma'am."

"I'll call a friend, then."

He looked dubious. "Well, all right then, ma'am. You lock up now. I'll just close the door and—"

"And get his coat."

He smiled crookedly. Nervously, she thought. "And get him a coat. Okay. Somebody'll be calling you in the morning."

"Fine," she said. But it was a lie; nothing was fine.

"Don't worry, ma'am. I don't think you're ever gonna see that guy again."

That wasn't what Jillian was worried about. Quite the opposite.

Steven knelt upon the cement floor of his narrow cell. He couldn't feel the cold, and he shut his mind to the sharp pain in his bent knees. He rested his palms upward on his thighs, though no sunlight offered ultraviolet sustenance. He tilted his head back, keeping his eyes closed, stretching his mind, his heart.

He ignored the steel bars of his jail cell. In one way or another, he'd been behind bars all of his earthly existence. He wouldn't be here long, just as he felt certain his time on this plane was nearly finished.

Jillian didn't believe him. She would paint the final portal before the equinox. She had to, because it was her destiny. And he would be there to see her die. That was his curse.

He could hear the sighs, groans and complaints of the others inside the Santa Fe jail. He heard the low conversations in Spanish, followed the muffled phrases in Navaho, and even those lilting words in Acoma dialect. And he could smell the astringent tang of disinfectant, urine, and even blood. All his senses felt assaulted by this fresh evidence of life, of mortality.

None of the odors or sounds, none of the textures or tastes, broke through his concentration. But, concentrate as he might, he couldn't reach Jillian.

After what seemed hours of futile effort, he sank back on his heels and felt his aching shoulders bending forward.

He wasn't afraid of being kept in the prison. A simple cut of his flesh would open the door for him. Another cut, and he would pass through the outer doors.

And he had already ensured his entry to her home.

It wasn't the mechanics of getting out of the jail cell that troubled him. It was getting to Jillian. The heart of Jillian.

Someone with heavy footfalls walked slowly down the cement hallway on the other side of the barred cells. The footsteps stopped outside Steven's cell.

Steven opened his eyes and stared through the steel grid before him at the nonuniformed man on the other side.

"Steven Sayers?"

"Yes," Steven said. He didn't feel any resentment toward this man, or any of the others. They had only done what they'd been called to do. Called by Jillian.

In their way, they were after the same thing he was: keeping Jillian safe. Hence the bars on these cells, hence the questions. They couldn't know that Jillian wasn't safe without him. They only assumed, as he had done all of her life, that he was a threat to her.

He knew differently now. Had known it all afternoon. Had realized it after loving her, after burying himself in her very essence, after touching that life force that was so uniquely hers.

He knew now how he could change the rules, alter the course of events set forth thousands and thousands of years before Jillian. It was so incredibly simple, he felt ashamed of not having realized it before.

But then, he'd never been with a woman like Jillian before. He'd never *loved* a woman before.

"Seems we've got us a little problem, Mr. Steven Sayers," the man in the sports jacket and chino trousers said. His smile was pleasant enough, but didn't reach his steely eyes.

"How so?" Steven asked.

"Well now, I'll tell you. It seems we can't find a single record of a Steven Sayers that matches up to you anywhere on our records."

"And yet I'm here," Steven said.

"We found a couple of Steven Sayerses, all right, but one of them is in his mid-eighties, and the other's a college student in Omaha."

"And me."

"No, sir. That's the interesting part. See, we couldn't find you."

Of course not, Steven wanted to say, already tired of the game. He didn't have the time for trivialities at this juncture. He needed out of here, but couldn't do it as long as this man stood outside his cell.

It wasn't casual for me.

As if she were right there in the cell with him, he could hear Jillian's voice, telling him that what had transpired between them had mattered, had impinged upon her heart.

He'd known love had brushed her then, had felt it to his core. And he hadn't been touching her. And he'd still felt it when he answered. Amazingly, against all precedents, against the acquired knowledge of ten thousand years' worth of too swiftly lost emotions, he felt that love still.

He hadn't known it would last, hadn't believed it was even possible for him to feel that intensity of passion, compassion, love. He'd tensed, expecting the feelings to fade, but they had lingered, as strong as when he'd held her close to his heart.

He'd realized the feelings weren't ebbing sometime during the evening and, stunned, had huddled like a lost child, savoring the newfound feelings, the unexpected depth such emotions wrought. He'd been frightened and exultant. Terrified and free for the first time in this earthly body.

And in those moments in the twilight, he'd suddenly understood what he never had before. Loving Jillian was the only secret, the answer to how to bend the rules. Because by his loving her, but continuing to feel that love, even when not touching her, the universal rules were *already* irrevocably altered.

And if the rules could change that much, they could be altered in a thousand different ways. Lives could change, destinies could alter, fate could be shoved aside.

If one such as he—a *man* now for all time—could love, could feel the total joy and pain of that love, then all the rules were mutating, shifting. The battleground was different, the framework had been redesigned, the focus altered.

"Mr. Sayers? Could it be there's another name we ought to be looking for?"

"No," Steven said simply.

He could have given the man half a dozen names. But none of them would check out, either. And it was unimportant, anyway. He had only to get the man out of there, and he would leave, and there wouldn't be any mysterious prisoner for them to check out.

He didn't need keys, permission, or bail. He only needed the blood in his inhuman veins.

"You know, according to the officers at the scene, you were spouting some pretty crazy-sounding stuff when they picked you up."

Steven knew better than to say anything.

"Seems you said some things about killing Mrs. Stewart."

Steven opened his mouth to protest, then closed it again. It wouldn't do any good to argue with the man. He was here now because he'd argued, because he'd been so stunned that Jillian had so thoroughly misunderstood him that she'd called the police to restrain him.

How ironic it was to think that, having finally glimpsed the ultimate secret of humanity, having finally tasted the truth of human love, he had lost it upon the instant.

"Want to tell me about that, Mr. Sayers?"

"She misunderstood. So did your policemen," Steven said.

"You didn't want to hurt her, is that what you're saying?"

"That's right," Steven said.

The man reached inside his jacket pocket and withdrew a small spiral notebook. He flipped it open and riffled through a few pages. He stopped and read the notes inside.

He looked back up and said, "Just what did you mean when you told Mrs. Stewart, 'He'll use you and then he'll kill you'."

Steven only vaguely remembered saying anything like that. He must have been more panicked than he'd realized.

Now he said, "Lyle is Jillian's daughter's imaginary friend."

"Now that's interesting, Mr. Sayers. That's exactly what Mrs. Stewart said."

"You make that sound like an accusation," Steven said.

"Well now, Mr. Sayers, I'm finding it a little difficult to swallow that a lady like Mrs. Stewart would call the police because her gardener's saying that her daughter's invisible friend is a bad guy."

Steven couldn't help smiling a little. This plainclothes detective, if that was what he was, would never know how big a bad guy Lyle really was. Or the man would, if he didn't get out of the hallway and let Steven do what he could to set things right.

The man outside his cell asked, "You know what the most interesting thing about this whole shebang is to me, Mr. Sayers?" When Steven remained silent, the man continued, "It's that Mrs. Stewart refuses to press charges against you."

Steven felt a sharp twisting deep inside him. Jillian refused to press charges? Why?

"And I'll tell you something else. She was insistent the sergeant bring your jacket in. Now I wonder why she did that, hmm? First you threaten to slash her paintings to ribbons—and by the way, I checked up on her, too, and it seems she's a pretty damn good artist, or at least she makes a decent living at it—and she calls the police.

"So far, I'm with her a hundred percent. But then, when the police get there, and you start yelling all sorts of crazy stuff, presto changeo, she goes all squishy, won't press charges, and even worries about you catching a cold. Now, tell me, Mr. Sayers, what kind of a hold do you have on the lady, or what exactly were you threatening her with out there?"

Did she understand? Had his words triggered some glimmer of understanding in her? Belief in him? Or was he being foolish to even hope such a thing was possible?

But she'd sent his coat. She refused to prosecute.

She might not love him as he loved her. But what these two things told him conclusively was that she didn't *hate* him. Couldn't hate him.

Because of the afternoon. Because of the walks. Because of the magic that flared between them. And maybe, just maybe, because of something she knew deep inside her, buried within her unconscious, hidden in the dark corners of her soul. If he could see her now, he would surely be able to convince her to work with him to try and rid the earth of Lyle once and for all... and save her life in the process.

"I'm not sure what you're asking me, exactly," Steven said now, rocking back on his heels, letting his hands lie flat against his thighs. "Mrs. Stewart misunderstood my actions in her studio. Your policemen misunderstood, also, when I was trying to explain to her what I was doing."

"Well, Mr. Sayers, I wish I could believe you. I really do. But I have to tell you, some things you yelled, combined with the fact that it seems you never even existed, makes me just a little bit suspicious. So I'm proposing you stay with us here a while, until we get a clearer handle on all this."

Steven didn't answer, merely looked away, hoping the man would take this for a refusal to say anything more. Apparently it worked, for he listened to the man's heavy footfalls walking away from the cell.

The man called out, "Have a good night, Mr. Sayers. Room's not fancy, but it's free."

A heavy door opened and slammed shut.

Steven sat there a moment longer, half anticipating the man's return, as if the detective could read Steven's intention to escape.

He thought of Jillian. Of the way she felt in his arms, the way she smiled, the fear in her eyes that night.

He'd arrogantly demanded Jillian as a reward for his many years on earth, his many battles, as his sinecure against the despair of the loss of so many lives before. Perhaps, in his arrogance, he'd missed the most vital gift of all: Knowing Jillian truly was a reward. Not his, maybe, but the ultimate of all rewards. Knowing her loving, her trust, her innocence, feeling these gifts, these were the greatest of all the things a man could hope to discover in a lifetime of lifetimes.

And to a man not wholly of one life or another, this gift transcended all other possibilities.

And, by his own selfishness, his need for her, his craving for her life force, he'd forsaken her. Allowed her to mistrust him, to expel him—however briefly—from her home.

But this physical expulsion wasn't what troubled him. That was already written in his loss of blood. What troubled him was the emotional separation, the severing of that fragile bond of trust. He'd bound her home to him by force, but nothing could coerce her love. Nothing could forge her trust.

She had given that to him freely. She had welcomed him, *trusted* him. Loved him.

It might not have been the love she'd offered her husband Dave, but it had been love from the deepest part of her nonetheless.

And once having discovered that slender, fragile bond, he'd thoroughly destroyed it in his sudden and arrogant determination to bend the rules, to destroy the portals. And, worse, by telling her bits and pieces of the truth, in his panic, and in his conviction that what had transpired between them would *force* her to believe him, he'd pushed the bonds of loving too far... and had abandoned her.

To Beleale. To *Lyle* who lived within her home. Who lived to destroy her and her kind.

If this was a lesson, a test of sorts, he didn't seem to be able to learn it. He didn't understand the nuances of the lesson. He'd lived as a man for ten thousand earth years, and now that he'd acted as one, he was forced to forsake the one mortal who could claim his heart? Where was the lesson in that?

Was this a test of his basic need to be as he had once been? Was it that even such as he couldn't fully love, couldn't fully enter into a mortal's domain?

But he could. He loved her. Apart from her now, locked in this cell of bars and noxious smells, he wanted her. It wasn't the steel that held him inside this terrible place, it was confusion, uncertainty, the knowledge that his heart beat for her now, not for mere existence.

For the first time in his too-long life, Steven was scared. Terrified. For the first time he had that razor-blade fear of knowing that what he loved most in the universe could be stolen away from him.

The man-made bars weren't what was keeping him from immediately walking away, it was a crippling awareness that Jillian felt betrayed, that she had totally lost the trust she'd shown him only that afternoon. Yesterday afternoon, now.

And what bound him even tighter was the realization that he'd thrown that trust away by not telling her the truth, by not letting her know who and what he really was, by not showing her sooner, letting her really see. By playing that damnable waiting game, by wanting her to see him as a mortal, as a man, he'd forsworn her love.

He cast his mind back over the past few hours, the past few days, searching for a way out of this fear, this mind-numbing awareness of love and loss.

He closed his eyes in agony. He *loved* her. Nothing had ever prepared him for the shuddering intensity of this emotion. Nothing he'd ever felt—not sorrow, not rage, not even grief—had clued him in to the pain of such loving, of loving and losing.

If he were to be granted one perfect moment, as he would have once forced her to take from him, he would choose that afternoon...yesterday. He would take that moment of holding her in his arms, feeling her fingers digging into his shoulders, her lips upon his. He would live and relive that moment of hearing her cry his name, passion clouding her voice.

For in that one moment, lost to passion, lost to loving, she'd opened an entire world of possibilities for him. She had made him a man. A mortal man, in spirit if not wholly in body. And she had opened a doorway of possibilities and futures such as he'd never dreamed could exist. She'd made him long for a tomorrow, and a day after that. And she'd made him able to fear the future, rue the past.

That would be his perfect moment.

And she couldn't grant that to him. She didn't have to. He'd have it forever.

Steven slowly raised his head, leaned forward.

She *had* granted it to him. She'd given it to him freely. Openly. Without guile, without need. She'd simply and oh, so very honestly, granted him what he'd always craved most.

God, how blind he'd been all these long years. He hadn't been giving those poor mortals anything they didn't already know. He'd been granting them only a memory, a refreshed, refurbished element of that which they'd already encountered.

He, on the other hand, had never known such perfection.

Was this the lesson of loving Jillian? Was this the lesson that all mortals understood? That loving someone was such a fragile, wonderful gift? That a moment's twist could rip it all away? Did they crave love, need love, because they knew that like living—and dying—it could be torn from them at a moment's hesitation? Was the secret to loving its contrast . . . losing?

She'd refused to prosecute. Had sent his jacket to keep him warm.

Steven slowly stood up, new resolve filling his veins. He might have lost her in that reality of loving, but he hadn't lost her to Lyle's machinations yet. He still had the slim chance of saving her life.

And for the first time, Steven recognized hope, another of Jillian's gifts.

He reached behind him for his ever-present longknife and realized he was, of course, weaponless.

He calmly, deliberately, rolled up his sleeve and held out his bared forearm. A narrow, bitter smile twisted his lips. His fingernail dug deeply into the arm that she'd so recently tended, so gently healed. The police might discover his absence within the hour, perhaps within minutes, and when they did, they would surely seek him at Jillian's home. But he couldn't worry about mortal caretakers now. They couldn't battle what they couldn't even see. And they didn't feel for Jillian what he now knew he did.

He held his cut arm through the bars of his narrow cell and watched as the blood dripped onto the floor outside.

A moment later, he pushed the metal bars aside and stepped through the doorway.

CHAPTER TWELVE

"So what are you going to do?" Elise asked. She carried two mugs of heavily spiked coffee from the kitchen to the dining table.

Jillian had called her almost as soon as the police cars pulled out of her driveway. Elise had arrived not fifteen minutes after that.

The curtains blocked out the early-morning darkness, but instead of making the room cozier, friendlier, they somehow lent an impression of gloom to the usually warm center of Jillian's home.

"I'm not going to do anything," Jillian said.

"Oh, come on, Jill, you have to go downtown tomorrow and make a statement."

"You sound like somebody on television," Jillian said.

"Okay, but art imitates life. Isn't that the phrase?" Elise asked, setting the mugs on the table with sloppy *thunk*s. Creamy foam spilled over the wood grain.

Jillian pushed a napkin over the spill and watched as the mocha stain leaked into the white paper. She had the strong feeling that Steven had melted into her life in the same way, an accident that permanently stained.

"Okay, Jill, here's how I see it," Elise said as she sat down at the opposite end of the table, jarring it enough to send more mocha onto the napkin. "This Steven Sayers character is the person that wakes you up. Like Sleeping Beauty. You know, a kiss and bingo, you're back in the world of the living. He's not *the* one, the *right* one, but something about him made you take a look over that fence." She held her hands up like a child climbing over a high wall, her eyes wide, her eyebrows raising and lowering in mock awe.

Jillian looked at Elise with something akin to dislike. Steven Sayers hadn't done anything of the sort. Elise's statement was like the police officers saying Steven had threatened her life.

"Allie asked me about the equinox," she said.

"We all need a pick-up-the-pieces romance, Jill," Elise said, ignoring her.

"Allie also said Lyle was planning on inviting his friends over at that time."

"So, what are you saying?"

"Steven said Lyle would use the portals to bring his minions through."

"Lyle, who is really Beleale. Milton's Beleale."

"Exactly."

"You can't be serious," Elise said. "You can't really be contemplating—"

"You're the one who suggested that the Milton line might point to what's been happening around here," Jillian said, leaning forward, her eyes locked on Elise. "And the names are the same. And Allie said once—remember?—that Steven wasn't 'real,' either."

"This is not good, Jill," Elise said warningly.

"And Steven's arm... it healed immediately. I mean, it was completely healed by the next day."

"So what are you suggesting, that he's... an angel?"

Put like that, the notion did seem utterly ridiculous. Insane. Precisely the reason she'd called the police. But still, Jillian couldn't help but wonder. He hadn't known about the fifth painting, but he knew there were to be five. He'd *known*.

"What if he was what he claimed?" she asked.

The look Elise gave her would have filled a library full of books. "Listen to yourself, Jill. You're actually swallowing what this crackpot told you? That he's an angel? That he's lived for two thousand years—"

"Ten thousand."

"Oh, that makes it so much better. Some guy waltzes into your life, messes with your daughter's head—because you know it had to be him that fed her all that stuff about Lyle being an angel, and that business about inviting his demon pals over for dinner—and then he has the chutzpah to make love to you, even the gall to tell *you* how vulnerable you are, makes you feel good about your artwork...and then what? Tries to destroy your paintings, threatens you, tells you you're going to die without his precious help. I'm sorry, Jill, but this is all too much. You did the right thing. You had to call the police. He's certifiable. And ten to one, when they finish checking up on him, they'll find that he's escaped from one of those places with white coats and tissue-paper shoes."

"But, Elise...what if he was telling the truth?"

Elise's face could have won the million dollars some magazine might pay in a contest for a photo epitomizing extreme disbelief.

"No, really, Elise. I think he's here to do something important. I don't understand it. But think about it. In a weird, eerie way, it makes a bizarre sense."

"Bizarre is right, honey. Get a grip, Jill. The guy might be the sexiest thing this side of the Pecos, but he's about sixteen sandwiches shy of a school picnic. That's why you—"

"That's why I called the police. Yeah." Jillian paused and took a deep breath. "But now I think I was wrong. I felt it at the time." She still felt it. And that sensation of dark, impending doom was stronger, swamping her with grim and terrible foreboding. She had the feeling she could almost hear whatever it was coming for her, like heavy footsteps speeding up, coming closer and closer, louder and louder.

"When they were taking him away, he was saying something about searching inside myself, searching my heart. About the portals. About my doorway paintings. That I knew. And he told me I shouldn't paint the fifth one, whatever I did."

Elise leaned forward, her brow furrowed with concentration, her hands flat upon the wooden table. "Jillian Stewart, now you listen to me. I talk a great story about all sorts of strange things, but I'm telling you right here and now that I have never once really seen a paranormal or supernatural thing in my entire life. Okay?

"So, I want you to think about what all this guy is telling you. One, he's an angel—or something like that. Two, your daughter's invisible, *imaginary* friend is an angel too. Three, your paintings aren't really paintings, they're doorways or portals, to what? Other worlds? Hell?"

Jillian had to look away.

Elise reached across and took her hand. "Jill, you were lonely. He's different. *Very* different. And you fell for the guy. And he said enough good stuff to make you want to believe even the crazy stuff, because you don't want it to end. Doesn't that make a lot more sense than him being some immortal-type creature, one of Milton's dark beings?"

Jillian knew her friend was probably right. Was more than likely right. But...what if she wasn't? What if Steven had been telling the truth?

"Think about it, Jill—an *angel?* I mean, I thought I'd been with a strange one or two, but I can't imagine what I'd say to a guy who told me he was a bona fide angel."

"He didn't say he was bona fide," Jillian said, and gave a slight, less-than-ironic smile.

Elise choked. "Oh, now that makes all the difference. See? An angel without those credentials . . . can you trust them, hubba-hubba? Get serious, Jill. Listen to yourself. I'm nuts, but you're not. An angel? Like in wings and bells and *stuff?*"

"I thought you were the white witch," Jillian said.

"Hitting below the proverbial belt, Jill," Elise said. "Just for that, I'm going to drink about a half a dozen more of these and go home."

"You know what convinces me the most?" Jillian asked slowly, having gone over and over everything Steven had told her that night. "More even than the amazing way his arm healed?"

"I told you before, there's a perfectly rational explanation for that. Some people have extraordinary recuperative capabilities. I read about this man in South America—"

Jillian interrupted her. "His talk about the fifth painting. The fifth doorway."

"What about it?"

"He didn't know I've already painted it. I finished it yesterday."

"What? Where is it?"

"It was just so dark, so filled with turmoil, that I didn't set it out. I just turned it against the wall. Steven didn't know about it. But he knew there was supposed to be a fifth. He *knew*, Elise. If nothing about the story is true, how could he have known I would paint a fifth?"

Elise shuddered elaborately. "So there is a fifth painting."

"Yes."

Elise's face lost that determined I-don't-believe-any-of-this expression it had carried through the dark hours of early morning.

"You know, there's all sorts of mystical significance to the number five," she said.

Jillian quoted, "'Benjamin's mess was five times so much as any of theirs.'"

"Genesis?"

"Chapter forty-three, verse thirty-four."

"And Shakespeare's *The Tempest*..."

"'Full fathom five thy father lies...'" Jillian finished.

"Five points of a pentagram," Elise said. "Five seats of an altar, five mystic paths on the tree of life, five suits in a tarot deck, five—"

"Portals."

"Five portals."

They looked at each other for several long and stunned moments.

"Oh, Jill, I gotta tell you," Elise said, "this, I really don't like."

"Neither do I," Jillian agreed.

Elise pushed to her feet and shook out her permanently wrinkled skirt. "Okay. So show me this damned painting."

Jillian led the way to her studio. It seemed days since she'd been there, instead of a mere hour. She could so easily picture the knife in Steven's hand, the tortured expression on his face, in his eyes.

She crossed to the shadowed corner of the studio and pulled out the last canvas. The fifth portal.

Elise helped her place it on an easel, and both of them stood back to view the five displayed paintings.

A definite progression could be seen. Each darker than the one before, each more terrifying in its way than the one before it. The darkest, most frightening, of them all was the fifth and final painting. And somehow, when viewed together, there was a completeness, a unity. A magic.

"He was telling the truth," Jillian said. "I can see it now. I can feel it."

Elise didn't say anything, but Jillian knew her friend was feeling it, too.

"What do I do now?" Jillian asked softly, more to herself than to Elise.

Elise answered anyway. "I'll tell you what we're going to do. Here's the plan. We're getting out of here right now. You get Allie, I'm getting the cat." She turned away from the portal paintings, facing Jillian directly, her face grim.

"I don't have a cat," Jillian said.

"The car, then. I'll get the car. Same number of letters, same—"

Elise broke off suddenly, her inanities halted in midstream. Her eyes strayed to something just beyond Jillian's shoulder and lower. The four-foot level. Her face had turned an ashen gray, and her lips were slack with shock.

Jillian didn't want to turn around. She had to, but didn't want to nonetheless. She'd never *not* wanted to do anything so much in her whole life. Maybe two or three lifetimes.

Slowly, achingly slowly, she swiveled her head until she could see whatever held Elise in thrall.

Allie stood in the doorway of the dimly lit studio. Like Elise's, her face was slack, her eyes vacant. She appeared to be sleepwalking.

But it wasn't Allie that had shocked Elise into utter silence. It was the awesome electrical-rainbow creature standing beside her.

Lyle.

Allie had described him as something beautiful. And he was. Beautiful, awe-inspiring, grotesque, frightening. And horrifyingly, terrifyingly, *real*.

CHAPTER THIRTEEN

Jillian was too stunned to say anything, do anything. She could only stare at the awesome, magnificent and utterly terrifying proof of Steven's tale, the evidence that his story had been true. All true.

"It's not the equinox," Elise croaked. "It's not the right time."

The rainbow creature in the doorway inched forward, as if attracted by the rasped voice. Or perhaps it was drawn to the five paintings behind them.

"Stop!" another voice called out, making the creature freeze in place, making the room echo with a mellifluous thunder.

Jillian knew that voice. Knew it with every fiber of her being. She dragged her eyes from the creature in her studio to see Steven standing just behind Allie in the darkened doorway.

"Steven," she breathed aloud, and started forward, only to halt, realizing that the creature blocked her way, stood between her and Steven. Between her and her sleepy-eyed daughter.

The creature seemed to swell, gathering brightness, sending out rays of sharply defined colors, as if spewing forth pure color, the essence of color. It hurt Jillian's eyes, made her want to run and hide.

"You thought you could bend the rules?" Steven said. Again his voice seemed to ring throughout the studio, a deep bell, a rich sound. Hard. Metal on metal.

You did.

The creature didn't speak, but Jillian felt the unnatural voice sweep through her, sending waves of icy chills across her body. She heard Elise gasp and give a whimper of pain or fear.

"This isn't your time," Steven said.

All time will be my time now.

"You have lost already," Steven intoned.

The child is mine. The woman will be mine as well.

Jillian felt as if the creature had struck her. The child was his?

"No!" she cried out. "You can't have her!"

All mortals will be mine. A ripple of light radiated out from him, as if he were laughing at them, mocking them.

Jillian again cried out a negation, but Lyle took no notice of her or her sob of fear. He advanced a few more inches toward her, toward the paintings.

"It isn't the equinox," Elise said again, like a prayer, like a litany against what she was seeing.

The portals are open.

"For you to pass through," Steven said. He, too, had stepped around Allie's still form, and was steadily walking into the center of the room.

Never.

Jillian saw that Steven's arm was bleeding. Not the wound from days before, a new one. A ragged, raw tear. She didn't understand what it meant, but knew instinctively it related to his escape from the police, his presence in her home now. And before.

"Now, if you wish," Steven said. But he wasn't looking at the creature, he was sending an urgent message to Jillian.

She felt the shock of meeting his eyes. Her heart swelled in relief, in joy. He'd come back for her. He hadn't lied to her, he'd meant everything he said. Everything would be all right now. She felt it to her core.

But in his eyes, she could read some measure of the torture she'd seen earlier that night, that she'd suspected when they spent hours in each other's arms. And she could read the dark, dark foreboding. The time had come. The darkness was here.

Then she understood. Everything wouldn't be all right now. The rules had been changed, and the battle was about to begin. The final battle, he'd said. Incredibly, unbelievably, and all too obviously, the last stand of the fallen angels was beginning.

The beginning and the end.

One would win, the other lose. And the carrier of the portals would be lost, as well. She would be lost.

And she'd been the one to begin it, by creating the final portal, by finishing it. By arranging them in a curved row.

"What of Allie?" she asked of Steven then. "You didn't tell me about Allie."

"You believe now."

"I believed before," she said. "I believed." Somehow it was more important that he understand this than it was to know that she would survive this bizarre, cosmic battle.

"Take your friend. Take Allie. Leave now. I can hold him back for a time."

The woman will be mine.

"Go on, Jillian," Steven said. He stood as if he were a human barrier against the radiant light, keeping the creature from moving toward Allie, closer to her and Elise.

"Jill?" Elise whispered.

Jillian took hold of Elise's arm and inched away from Lyle, away from Steven. She didn't think she so much as drew a breath until she reached her daughter's side. She swept Allie up and into her arms and held her pressed tightly against her shoulder, swinging the thin legs around her waist.

"Mommy?" Allie asked sleepily.

"Shh...sweetie," Jillian said automatically. "I've got you now."

A cry of primal rage exploded from Lyle. Neither vocal nor carried with that ringing note of thunder marked by Steven's voice now, it nonetheless echoed in the studio, hurting all of them, rippling through them in waves of shuddering horror.

Mine! Mine! I'll kill you all, I'll rend your flesh, give it to dogs to feed!

Allie stirred and twisted, turning around to see what her mother was staring at. Her face shifted from stunned, sleepy and mildly curious to something akin to deepest dread.

"You said you wouldn't hurt my mommy!" she cried out. "You promised! That's why I let you be my friend. You promised me!"

Horrified, Jillian realized that all this time Lyle had been using some kind of coercion on Allie, had been holding her prisoner with lies and promises.

"Shh, sweetie," she said again. Empty comfort.

Steven didn't turn around, didn't so much as look their way. "Get out now, Jillian. Leave the house. Don't come back."

"Steven—"

"Damn it, Jillian. I can't hold him back for very long. Do as I say!"

He was holding the creature back. The creature who was what he had once been. She didn't think Steven insane any longer, but she was fairly certain she was heading in that direction.

"I can't just leave you here," she cried. "There must be something I can do!"

"There's nothing! Now, Jillian! Now! You have to go!" he ground out. She could hear the strain in his voice, wondered what power he was using to keep Lyle at bay.

With a cry of pure anguish, Jillian turned and raced down the long hallway, carrying Allie, feeling Elise at her heels. She'd felt she was betraying him when she let the police lead him away from her. But that was nothing compared to what she felt now.

When they reached the front door and burst through it into the faint rays of predawn gray, she stumbled on the threshold, and shoved her daughter into Elise's arms.

"I have to go back," she said urgently. "Take Allie out of here!"

"You can't, Jill!" Elise cried, hugging Allie tightly to her chest. "You heard him. We have to get out now!"

"I can't leave him in there to fight him alone."

"You can't fight him! You don't even know what he's capable of!" Elise cried out. "It's not your fight, Jill!"

"It's every bit my fight. I made the paintings. I created the portals. I don't know why, or even how. And I don't care. The only thing I know for sure is that I love Steven," Jillian said. "If I leave now, if I don't do something to help, anything, I can never forgive myself."

"What about Allie?" Elise asked, her arms tightening, her face raw with undisguised anguish.

"Allie knows why I have to go back, don't you, sweetie? You know I love you. And you know that people who love each other have to help each other. That's how it works. That's how it has to be. If we don't help...we might as well be like Lyle, something that doesn't have a place here. So now you have to go with Aunt Elise, and I have to stay. I have to try."

Please understand, she begged her daughter. She kissed that sweet, sleep-warmed face. Please understand.

"Jill . . ." Elise pleaded.

"It's okay, Mommy," Allie said suddenly. "That's how it works."

Jillian wrapped the two of them in her arms for a brief, shattering hug, then pushed them toward Elise's battered car. "Now get out of here. I'll . . . be there—" She broke off. She couldn't make any promises. "I'll be there if I can."

Elise tried to argue once more, but Jillian pushed her more firmly away from the front entrance.

"Get going," she said, and added on a broken sob, "I have to know Allie's safe!"

With an agonized moan, Elise turned and jogged to her car, thrust Allie inside, and hesitated before closing the door.

"Please, Elise—?" Jillian called.

Elise slammed the car door shut, and the moment Jillian heard the engine turn over, she raced back through the house, calling Steven's name.

Steven felt his hold on Lyle ebbing, felt Lyle's strength growing. At least Jillian was safe. Out of the house. Gone.

Part of him struggled to understand how Lyle had bent the rules so thoroughly as to wage this battle now, and then realized it had been through his own efforts. He had changed. Jillian had changed him.

Jillian, the last of the portal carriers, had not only created the fifth portal days before the equinox, she had wrapped loving arms around him, gazed at him with trust, with need, and he'd embraced that novel experience with profound joy.

He hadn't given her the perfect moment, the one magic he might have offered her, but she'd given it to him. Now he could enter this final battle with the knowledge of what it really was like to be mortal, to be a man.

He felt himself shifting, expanding, flowing into what he had once been. He expected all human emotion to slip away from him, lose itself in the transition. But it didn't leave him, it stayed, lingered in the light like melody to a harmony, like the sun to the moon. It burned brightly in him.

"Steven!"

Even now he seemed to hear her voice, seemed to hear her calling his name in desperation, in love.

"Steven! I can't leave you!" she cried. "I love you, Steven. I love you!"

She was here. She hadn't gone. A mortal, doomed to death if she stayed—she knew this, and yet she had come back. Out of love.

Beyond Lyle now, he could see the portals, feel them. No longer paintings, no longer abstract realities. He could feel the cold winds, hear the voices clamoring on the other side of the five doors.

He heard Jillian scream, felt it ripple through him, sound waves on a rainbow body. He ached for her. Longed for her. And had lost her forever.

But at least he wouldn't allow Lyle to take her.

He wrapped tendrilous bands of light around his enemy, his brother, his nemesis.

Mine! the other raged.

Never! the part of him that was still Steven vowed.

With a war cry felt—if not heard—throughout worlds, Steven lunged at Lyle, holding him, enveloping him, drawing the other into his own light, feeling the evil seeping through him, burning him.

And as he wrestled Lyle toward one of the portals, he heard a scream of defiance, an inarticulate cry of abject rage. But not from Lyle.

And at that moment, one of the portals abruptly ceased to exist.

"Which one is earth?" he heard Jillian cry. "Which one?"

Jillian screamed her question a third time, trembling with fear, reeling with horror. She looked down in shock at the X-Acto blade in her hands, at the ruined painting on the floor.

She didn't, couldn't, stare at it for long, for the lightning ball in the center of the room glittered and danced, parried and thrust. Two forms, melding, blending.

"No!" she cried out again, and turned with renewed strength on the second of the paintings. She slashed it to ribbons. Part of her died with each jagged slash of the blade, and part of her screamed in defiant rebellion.

She had created the portals. She would be the one to take them away!

No, Jillian. Run...run...

She felt Steven's voice rippling inside her, a human voice no longer, but his just the same. It seemed to lap through her like gentle waves on a summer beach.

"I love you!" she cried out instead, destroying her painting with almost superhuman desperation. Within seconds, only strips of color lay in ribbons on the floor. Shaking, feeling as if her entire body was an earthquake, she whirled toward the third of the paintings.

"Which one is earth?" she cried again, knowing instinctively, desperately, that she had found some solution, a solution. "Which, Steven? Which?"

As the second portal vanished amid cries of fury, wails of anguish, Steven understood what Jillian was doing. One by one, she was closing the portals, sealing them off, destroying them.

And her question—which was earth—let him know even more. Incredibly, she was trying to destroy all but one, one painting for him and Lyle to battle over, one portal to pass through.

And for Steven to come back to her through.

Was it possible? Could it work?

The last, he tried telling her. Would she understand? Would she see it?

The third portal evaporated, swirling away into nothingness, carrying with it a thousand angry screams. And within seconds, the fourth followed in its wake.

Steven could only imagine what Jillian must be feeling. Even in this state, he could see the tears streaming down her face, feel the anguish in her. These were her creations, her work. And, systematically, she was ripping every one to shreds. It must be like ripping her soul apart.

And she was doing it for him.

Lyle ceased struggling for a second, and Steven shuddered, shimmered in a swift feeling of conquest, of strength. But he'd underestimated Lyle. Underestimated his old enemy. Lyle was only employing the oldest human trick in the book, that of feigning weakness.

With a dazzling array of light, he broke free of Steven's grasp and hurled himself directly at Jillian... and the final portal.

No! Steven focused. *No!* But even as he cried out, sent his full force in chase, Lyle surrounded Jillian, washing her with terrible light, coloring her, enveloping her with streams of evil.

The X-Acto blade clattered to the floor. Jillian stood wrapped in bands of light, frozen, paralyzed by Lyle, by fear, by her destiny.

It wasn't her destiny, Steven raged. She had changed him. She had changed the course of events. The rules were rules no longer.

He hurled himself at Lyle, raking fingers of light through bands of color. For a terrifying, dazzling moment, he was certain he would fail.

Then he heard Jillian whisper. "Now. Push him through...now."

Ten thousand years he'd battled for this one moment, this final closure. And until he met Jillian, he'd never once understood what it was all for.

But he knew now. He understood everything.

And with a superhuman strength, a supernatural power, unleashed at last, Steven did as Jillian asked, and expelled the last of the cast-out angels through the last portal.

His many years on earth had led him to expect thunder, fire, earthquakes, and the gates of hell yawning beneath his feet. But all that happened was that Lyle gave one final scream of rage and disappeared through the last portal.

Shuddering, feeling as if she'd been locked in the coldest of freezers, Jillian numbly sank to the floor, gazing in horror at the destruction around her, the single rainbow ball of light before her.

"Steven—?" she gasped.

I'm here.

He was there. She'd been right. It was him and not Lyle who had pushed the other through that horrific portal.

But it wasn't the Steven she'd known. This was Steven as he used to be all that time ago.

The war was over. Time for all good soldiers to go home.

She couldn't ask him to stay. He'd given too many years already. But neither could she watch him go.

She buried her face in her cold, cold hands.

I love you, Jillian. I wish...I wish I could be with you forever.

She felt his words, his love, ripple through her, touch her, caress her skin with strange light.

She couldn't just let him leave without telling him more. Loving him was one thing, probably the most important thing, but without the rest it was empty, meaningless.

"I've never loved anyone the way I love you," she said. "You told me once that you didn't know what love could be like. I didn't, either. I didn't have a clue. Much as it kills me to lose you now, at least I've known what real love was all about. Oh, Steven, thank you for showing me. Thank you for letting me know."

"Jillian," he said.

"It's all right. I know you're going. The war's over."

"Jillian..."

She dragged her hands from her face and turned.

And saw Steven. The man. The man she loved.

He slowly knelt beside her and touched her face with wonder, with stunned, joyous tenderness.

Then he drew her into his arms. A muffled sound behind them made her turn in swift fear.

The last portal, dark and terrifying, began to smoke, curling inward on itself.

Safely wrapped in Steven's arms, Jillian watched as the last of her five paintings shriveled into ashes. It was one of the most beautiful sights she'd ever witnessed.

"I think . . ." he said unsteadily. "I think I'm being allowed to stay."

EPILOGUE

Elise and Jillian sat at the dining table, watching Allie and Steven romping in the late spring snow.

"He's really a big kid, isn't he?" Elise said.

"He says he lived ten thousand years without joy, he's not letting a single day pass without it now."

Jillian smiled, but couldn't help feeling that wrenching deep inside whenever she remembered that dark, dark day six months earlier.

"Has he decided what he wants to be when he grows up?"

Jillian didn't take her eyes from the golden man laughing with her daughter. "Aside from having saved the known universe, you mean?"

Elise choked. "Okay, aside from that. And, of course, when he's finished all those hours of community service he's paying for his blood-curdling escape from prison."

"We've decided to coast, just coast. Steven's never had a chance to experience all those little things that make up love, family. Marriage. Even things like colds or the flu. Anything. He says he wants to do it all. I'm still going to paint, of course, and I've got an opening next month in Dallas. And Steven says he'll probably try his hand at writing, or maybe baby-sitting. We don't know. I don't care, really. I just want to be with him every second I can. Beside, I've got enough money to last three lifetimes. We're going to enjoy every blessed cent of it."

With a whoosh of cold wind, Steven and Allie tumbled into the dining room, stamping the snow off their feet, onto the floor, where Steven's blood had once dropped.

Jillian's smile broadened. About two weeks after the last portal had burned, after he'd told her everything, she'd pressed a set of keys into his hand.

"What's this?" he'd asked.

"I could be corny and say the keys to my heart," she'd said with a laugh, and then grown deadly serious. "But, in reality, it's just the keys to the house. They're yours. It'll save on doctor bills."

He looked up from his stomping now and, as if reading her mind, smiled mischievously.

"Okay, okay," Elise said, standing up and shaking out her permanently wrinkled skirt. "We can take a hint, can't we, sweetie? They've got wedding plans to talk about."

Allie looked from Steven to Jillian, her face open and unshadowed. Whatever hold Lyle had held over her was long gone, and she'd accepted Steven with almost astonishing alacrity.

"All right," Allie said. "But are you sure I can't tell anybody that my new daddy is really an angel?"

Elise laughed, but said, "From the look on that angelic face, I'd hazard there was a bit of the opposite in him, also." She thrust her arms in her baggy coat and hustled Allie from the room.

As the front door opened, Jillian heard Allie ask Elise, "What did you mean, the opposite?"

"We can only hope Elise doesn't tell her," Steven said, slipping behind her and drawing her into his arms. He was cold from the outdoors, and wholly, utterly, alive.

"But you're going to show me, aren't you?" Jillian asked, leaning against him.

"I don't know about opposites...but I sure intend proving I'm only human."

Jillian turned in his arms, relishing the feel of him, sighing when she felt his arms encircle her waist to draw her closer still. She locked her hands around his neck and smiled up at him. "I love it when you feel the need to prove a point."

"As we've discovered...some things never change."

MILLION DOLLAR SWEEPSTAKES (III)

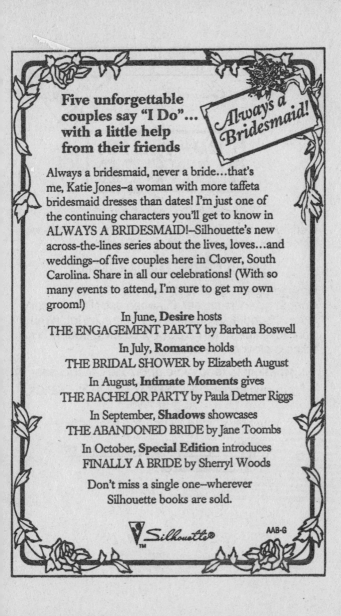

Five unforgettable couples say "I Do"… with a little help from their friends

Always a Bridesmaid!

Always a bridesmaid, never a bride…that's me, Katie Jones–a woman with more taffeta bridesmaid dresses than dates! I'm just one of the continuing characters you'll get to know in ALWAYS A BRIDESMAID!–Silhouette's new across-the-lines series about the lives, loves…and weddings–of five couples here in Clover, South Carolina. Share in all our celebrations! (With so many events to attend, I'm sure to get my own groom!)

In June, **Desire** hosts
THE ENGAGEMENT PARTY by Barbara Boswell

In July, **Romance** holds
THE BRIDAL SHOWER by Elizabeth August

In August, **Intimate Moments** gives
THE BACHELOR PARTY by Paula Detmer Riggs

In September, **Shadows** showcases
THE ABANDONED BRIDE by Jane Toombs

In October, **Special Edition** introduces
FINALLY A BRIDE by Sherryl Woods

Don't miss a single one–wherever
Silhouette books are sold.

Silhouette®

AAB-G

CODE NAME: DANGER

Because love is a risky business...

Merline Lovelace's "Code Name: Danger" miniseries gets an explosive start in May 1995 with

NIGHT OF THE JAGUAR, IM #637

Omega agent Jake MacKenzie had flirted with danger his entire career. But when unbelievably sexy Sarah Chandler became enmeshed in his latest mission, Jake knew that his days of courting trouble had taken a provocative twist....

Your mission: To read more about the Omega agency.

Your next target: THE COWBOY AND THE COSSACK, August 1995

Your only choice for nonstop excitement—

MAGGIE-1

And now for something completely different...

In April, look for
ERRANT ANGEL (D #924)
by Justine Davis

Man in Crisis: Dalton MacKay knew all about grief. It consumed him...until a troubled teen and a well-intentioned teacher barged into Dalton's very private life.

Wayward Angel: Evangeline Law was no ordinary woman—or educator. She was a messenger of hope in a seemingly hopeless case. And her penchant for getting too involved reached the boiling point with sexy Dalton....

**Get touched by an angel
in Justine Davis's ERRANT ANGEL,
available this April,
only from**

SILHOUETTE... Where Passion Lives

Don't miss these Silhouette favorites by some of our most distinguished authors! And now, you can receive a discount by ordering two or more titles!

SD#05844	THE HAND OF AN ANGEL by BJ James	$2.99 ☐
SD#05873	WHAT ARE FRIENDS FOR?	$2.99 U.S. ☐
	by Naomi Horton	$3.50 CAN. ☐
SD#05880	MEGAN'S MIRACLE	$2.99 U.S. ☐
	by Karen Leabo	$3.50 CAN. ☐
IM#07524	ONCE UPON A WEDDING	
	by Paula Detmer Riggs	$3.50 ☐
IM#07542	FINALLY A FATHER by Marilyn Pappano	$3.50 ☐
IM#07556	BANISHED by Lee Magner	$3.50 ☐
SSE#09805	TRUE BLUE HEARTS	
	by Curtiss Ann Matlock	$3.39 ☐
SSE#09825	WORTH WAITING FOR by Bay Matthews	$3.50 ☐
SSE#09866	HE'S MY SOLDIER BOY by Lisa Jackson	$3.50 ☐
SR#08948	MORE THAN YOU KNOW	
	by Phyllis Halldorson	$2.75 ☐
SR#08949	MARRIAGE IN A SUITCASE	
	by Kasey Michaels	$2.75 ☐
SR#19003	THE BACHELOR CURE by Pepper Adams	$2.75 ☐

(limited quantities available on certain titles)

AMOUNT	$_____
DEDUCT: 10% DISCOUNT FOR 2+ BOOKS	$_____
POSTAGE & HANDLING	$_____
($1.00 for one book, 50¢ for each additional)	
APPLICABLE TAXES*	$_____
TOTAL PAYABLE	$_____
(check or money order—please do not send cash)	

To order, complete this form and send it, along with a check or money order for the total above, payable to Silhouette Books, to: **In the U.S.:** 3010 Walden Avenue, P.O. Box 9077, Buffalo, NY 14269-9077; **In Canada:** P.O. Box 636, Fort Erie, Ontario, L2A 5X3.

Name:_____

Address:_____ City:_____

State/Prov.:_____ Zip/Postal Code:_____

*New York residents remit applicable sales taxes.
Canadian residents remit applicable GST and provincial taxes.　　SBACK-MM

Silhouette®